About the Author

Kevin Bailey was born in Newtown, Wales in 1975 and grew up with his 3 younger siblings in and around the town of Ludlow, Shropshire, (which the fictional town of Chelmesbury is based on). He has been married twice and has 3 wonderful children.

He has been writing fiction for over 30 years and ideas come to him in the strangest of places; for example, when he is delivering bathroom equipment around the country he has to pull up and write them down on scraps of paper, much to his wife's annoyance at finding them in his clothes in the washing basket.

This is his first novel, which he hopes will be the first in a series of books based on Simon Eliote. His ambition is to be a success and maybe one day write a James Bond novel.

He lives at present in his little house in the city of Worcester, where he balances writing, being a husband and a dad and driving around the midlands delivering bathrooms.

THE DEATHLY ANGEL

To Louise

Hope you enjoy

By
Kevin Bailey

Cover Photo © Richard Gadd
Used by kind permission

Cover designed and © ShipRex Designs

First published as an eBook on Amazon
May 6th 2014

This book is dedicated to the memory of my Grandad
who is greatly missed.

THE DEATHLY ANGEL

By

Kevin Bailey

PROLOGUE

That dark evening, the sleepy market town of Chelmesbury shivered in winter's icy grip.

Across from the centre of town, the bitter cold wind howled like a dog through the gaping windows and doorways of the ruined medieval castle, its impressive stone keep seeming to peer over the fortified walls to see what the people of the town were doing.

It was on this monument of the past that a dark figure stood, his arms outstretched. The full moon cast a dark shadow onto the market traders packing up their goods, oblivious to him.

They would be witnesses to the birth of a killing spree not seen in the town since the Civil War; the Shropshire earth would again be soaked in blood.

The darkened figure looked from the market over to the tower of the fifteenth-century stone church of St Bartholomew, the religious centre of the town; but to the figure and the witnesses in the market below him, not even God would be able to prevent what he must do.

One of the traders looked over at the castle and did a double take at the dark image, which to his astonishment, quickly vanished into the night. The trader shook his head and rubbed his eyes, then after looking back at the empty space continued packing away his stall.

Next to the church was the three-hundred-year-old drinking establishment The Dog and Duck, and leaving the pub after a drinking session were two friends, laughing tipsily as they walked towards the churchyard.

They looked back at the black and white timber building: according to local history, it was the first drinking establishment to be built outside of the castle defences, but they didn't care about that, to them it was their local, a place to get drunk on a Friday and Saturday night.

James Gaston stood next to a moist lamp-post and took out a cigarette and lit it. He breathed in the smoke and relaxed, then exhaled over the head of his shorter, non-smoking friend Paul.

The pair moved on again, James shoving his hands into the pockets of his brown fleece jacket as he walked, he looked down at his friend, Paul Tomlinson, who was wearing black trousers, a navy blue shirt and a smart casual jacket.

Oblivious to the terror coming their way, the two joked together, discussing a beautiful woman they had spotted in the bar that night.

"So," Paul said "what about that Michelle Dalton?" James smiled wistfully.

"Michelle Dalton always was a looker at school. Shame she didn't look at me the way she used to look at Wayne, though."

Paul nodded in agreement. "Dead right," he said. "Would you give her one?"

James inhaled more smoke from his cigarette and nodded madly. "Would I give her one?" He grabbed his groin, and replied with a big grin, "You bet I would." "Did you see the way she bent over the pool table with that short skirt on?"

"I sure did, mate," Paul answered, almost drooling at the memory.

James made a sound that was half sigh and half grunt. "I wanted to come up behind her and…" He paused, thinking of what he would do to her if she had been his girlfriend. "I would have given her one, there and then, and I wouldn't have cared who had been watching."

"I bet you would have as well, you dirty git," Paul said, laughing, and the two friends continued home.

Behind them, they heard a car door open and they turned around to see the aforementioned Michelle Dalton getting into a blue Ford Fiesta.

They watched lustfully as the short blonde-haired woman got into the back, and a tall black-haired man dropped the passenger seat down and he too got in.

The driver then drove towards them, making the two friends quickly step out of the way.

"Fucking wanker," James shouted as he returned to the road and watched the car speed off.

Paul noticed Michelle turn and wave at them; he put up his hand and waved back.

James looked angrily at his friend. "What are you waving at that wanker for?"

Paul stuttered his reply. "I-I wasn't, I was waving at Michelle."

James turned and started to walk away. "Well don't."

Paul caught up and placed his hand on James's shoulder. "Sorry, I –" but James stopped him.

"That Sam Dalton," he said through gritted teeth, "he's gonna push the wrong button one day with someone and he's gonna wish he hadn't."

"Come on; forget about Sam, he ain't worth it." Paul looked around. "I've heard things about him."

James looked curiously at his friend. "Like what?"

"Well, it is only rumour, but I heard our friend likes to bat for both sides, if ya know what I mean." He winked and said, "Ducky," letting his hand go limp, and making James laugh.

"The mighty Sam Dalton a poof?"

Paul stopped and looked at his friend. "It is only a rumour, mind, but think of the stick we can give him, the next time we see him."

James rubbed his hands together and grinned evilly. "Oh I will, Paul, you bet I will." He took out another cigarette, lit it and continued walking.

Paul saw his reflection in the window of a house and then quickly looked at James.

"How can a man like Sam be such a lucky bastard and get beauties like Michelle and I can't even pull an ugly bird?"

James laughed. "You know what it is, Paul? you're a nice bloke and women like Michelle don't go for nice ones."

Paul looked deflated, so James put his hand on his shoulder. "Don't be down, buddy, there is a woman out there for you, you've just gotta find her. And as for Sam," he looked into the darkness, "according to Wayne, when Michelle's had a few, she's a bit of a goer, so I think tonight he will be the lucky one, but only for tonight."

"Why, what you gonna do?"

James pushed his hand through his greasy hair. "I may accidentally let it slip to Michelle that he likes cock and maybe Photoshop some fake evidence for her."

"But what happens if he comes after you?" Paul said, worried.

"Then I get some mates and take him on, mates like you." James looked solemnly at Paul, who as always just nodded in agreement and then they continued to walk further into the darkness.

A bit further on from the pub, the two friends heard James's name being shouted loudly from the darkness. They stopped in their tracks, and James looked around, squinting into the darkness, trying to see who was calling him.

"Who's that?" he shouted back, his voice echoing around the churchyard.

"James, James, James, have you forgotten an old victim so quickly?" The voice was blunt, cold and angry. "For I have not forgotten you." James and Paul stood squinting around at the dark, trying to detect any movement down the shadowy backstreets, but nothing moved.

James looked at Paul and then shouted, "Come out and show yourself, you… you coward."

"Me, I was never a coward, James."

"So show yourself," he snapped back sarcastically.

The voice that came back was calm. "Why, so you can bully me again?" The words hung in the air. "No, but I warn you, watch your back, James!" Then the two friends heard laughter, which seemed to disperse into the howling of the wind; then there was silence.

James and Paul decided to get home quickly, so crossing a street, they headed through what was called Dark Lane; it had for many years had a different name, the locals called it Lovers Lane. The lane ran around the town and out into a housing estate one mile from Chelmesbury and this was where James and Paul lived.

As they walked along the lane, past couples up against trees embracing each other, and others in steamed-up cars that rocked to the passion inside, James sighed, cursing that he faced another night on his own. Still, as he had said to Paul, there would be plenty of time for romancing women.

But as they continued past the old churchyard, James saw a man walking towards him, wearing a black pair of trousers, a white shirt and a baggy black hoody, his face hidden behind the hood. All you could see was a goatee beard on the lad's chin, but James recognized the stranger straight away.

"Well, well, well, look who we have here." He looked over at his friend. "I think a bit of a beating is in order, don't you?"

Paul looked over at the lad and then back at James. "Who is he, then?"

James smiled. "He is like Sam, a nobody and as we couldn't pull anyone tonight, I need to release some energy and he will feel the force."

Paul was still no wiser, but agreed with his friend, as he had always done.

The lad walked slowly towards the two friends and in doing so spoke softly and calmly.

"What? Two against one? That's a little unfair on you, isn't it?"

James and Paul started to laugh, but the laugh ended when the hooded figure raised his eyebrow and said with venom, "James!"

The way this stranger said his name made him feel fear, and the mighty James Gaston didn't fear anyone. This made him angry.

"You!" he said with anger and hate. "You were the one near the Dog and Duck, weren't you?" James demanded.

The stranger spoke from beneath the hood. "I may have been," the stranger looked from beneath the hood at James who stood laughing at him. The stranger's anger was rising – even Paul, who had kept his eyes fixed on him, could see this, and it scared him.

James looked over at his friend. "Did you hear that, Paul?" He pointed at the stranger and looked evilly at him, hatred in his eyes. "The little wretch, who I used to beat to a pulp when we were younger, is now threatening me." He started to laugh, but the stranger then started to walk slowly towards him, still not showing his face.

Then he stopped abruptly a couple of metres in front of James and the two men squared up to each other like gunslingers in a scene from a western.

They looked deep into each other's eyes, taking no notice of Paul, who could do nothing but watch the confrontation unfold.

James broke the silence. "Am I supposed to be frightened by you?" he said sarcastically.

The stranger stared deep into James's icy blue eyes and for the first time, they had fear in them and this gave him a sense of delight.

Paul noticed that James wasn't afraid of this stranger. Who was he and what did he want? Paul was about to find out as the stranger looked at James.

"You want an answer to your question, James?" James nodded. "Are you supposed to be frightened by little old me?" He pretended to shake. James nodded once more.

"Yes, but I already know the answer," he said, looking over at Paul and winking. "You see, I ain't afraid of anyone."

The stranger kept his eyes fixed on James as he replied angrily, "You and your gang will be." James stopped sniggering as the stranger continued. "But for you, it's payback time," and from beneath his jacket, he pulled out a butcher's knife and aimed it straight at James, who on seeing the knife just started to laugh once more.

"You haven't got the guts to use that. That's why we always picked on you – no guts."

A smile appeared on the stranger's face. "Shall we see who has guts?" he said, staring deep into James's eyes. "You see, when we were younger, James, I would never have hurt a fly, but that was a long time ago."

All this was having no effect on James, who continued to laugh, even louder now.

"You hear that, Paul, this gippo is taking on me. Ha, pathetic!" He looked at the hooded stranger. "Put that knife down and run back home to Mummy."

Paul could see twitching from the stranger and was about to warn James, when the stranger spoke again.

"Why, what are you going to do if I don't?"

James smiled, paying no attention to Paul who was trying to attract his attention.

"I'll come over there and beat the shit out of you, like I used to."

Paul noticed a small grin appear again on the stranger's face.

"Come on then, if you think you can," the stranger said, outstretching his arms and then quickly dropping them. He looked menacingly at James and Paul, and said, "Time's up, you had your chance." Then the stranger made his move, thrusting the butcher's knife towards James's neck.

James tried to block the knife, but the blade was extremely sharp and it sliced into his hand, like a hot knife in butter. James winced in pain and blood squirted quickly from the deep wound.

This seemed to give the attacker a burst of energy and again the knife was thrust towards James, slicing this time into his neck and severing the main artery. More blood squirted on to the assailant and Paul, who seemed to be glued to the spot.

The spray of blood brought Paul out of his frozen state and he turned on the stranger, trying to defend his best friend, but for his heroism, he was kicked brutally in the groin and then in the head.

Paul had never felt rage like this before; the assailant was like some crazed wild animal setting upon its prey, but even though the knife was still in the stranger's hand, for some reason he didn't use it on Paul.

With his eyes almost closed, Paul looked over at James, who was rolling around the floor in severe agony. Blood gushed from the wound, turning his replica England shirt red. The attacker had known exactly where to inflict the severest injury. But as the stranger smashed blow after blow at the helpless Paul, he just laughed.

After a while, the stranger stopped attacking and looked at Paul who was writhing in pain; a cut above his eye leaked blood, which mixed with his tears.

Even though he could hardly see through his puffy eyes, Paul could make out the outline of the face, still unrecognizable, and the eyes seemed to be almost red with hatred.

With his last ounce of strength, Paul asked, "Who are you? And why are you doing this to us?"

The stranger knelt down beside Paul and calmly said, "I could have killed you, you know." Paul nodded. "But unlike him," the stranger pointed at James, "you didn't hurt me and for that reason I have spared you your life. You will become my messenger to the others of his group. I want you to tell them," he said, walking towards the fallen James, the butcher's knife still in his hand, "that the clock has stopped ticking and their time is up." He looked back at Paul, who saw all the rage appear in his face once more.

"Who are you?" Paul asked again.

The stranger smiled coldly at him. "I am the Deathly Angel and I have come to terminate their time on this earth," he said, standing up straight and stretching out his arms, casting a shadow onto Paul in the shape of an angel.

Then with a wicked laugh, he turned back to James and what he saw made him snigger. It filled him with so much power and confidence that he took several seconds to absorb the scene, then he knelt back down and whispered into James's bloodied ear.

"I just want to say thanks, you see, you were the one I was always most afraid of – you, the leader of the pack." He looked at the night sky. "When you were around, I would cower. But not anymore, the rest will be easy compared to you."

A small strangled sound issued from James's bloodied mouth, and the stranger noticed tears trickled down his victim's chin, mixing with blood.

"I'm so sorry for what we did to you," James whispered, "We were only doing what was asked of us."

"But you did do it and that is why I must punish you and the others." He grasped the handle of the knife with both hands, and lifted it high above his head. "I think it is time I put you out of your misery," he said, and then like an Aztec priest sacrificing a lamb to his god, he brought it down, piercing the heart.

James twitched for a while and then as the life drained from his body, the stranger pulled the knife from James's chest and wiped the bloodied blade on his victim's shirt.

"I'm glad you got the point," he said jokingly amused by his pun, then he looked at James and without thought, he wiped his blood stained shoes clean on the deceased's trousers

Standing up straight, he approached the nearest streetlamp and with his back to the lamp, he outstretched his arms once again, causing the baggy sleeves from his hoody to fall, and the light projected the shadow of an angel, a bloody red angel on to the deceased.

This new entity, now known to Paul as 'the Deathly Angel', was happy and as the blood started to trickle towards him from James's remains, like iron fillings being attracted to a magnet, he knew now that his reign of terror had begun, and he couldn't wait for more.

He was disturbed from his pleasurable thoughts by Paul's whimpers and the sound of rapidly approaching footsteps.

He quickly stepped over the pain-ridden Paul, the only living witness to the birth of the revenge and terror that this

Deathly Angel was going to inflict on the quiet town of Chelmesbury.

As he walked away, he stopped to look back and admire his handiwork one last time. What he saw was indeed a work of art, and he wished he'd brought a camera to photograph the scene; he cursed himself for that mistake.

His eyes then fixed on the whimpering Paul and with a hushed voice, he reminded him, "Heed my warning, my friend." Then he laughed and disappeared deep into the dark undergrowth.

THE DEATHLY ANGEL

By
Kevin Bailey

CHAPTER ONE

On the outskirts of the town, a woman awoke with a scream. Charlotte Steel sat up in bed, feeling as if her blood was boiling. Something bad had happened and she had felt it.

Tangled in the duvet, she tried to get up, and struggled for several seconds, before she was able to toss it back on to the bed. Sweat made her silk nightdress cling to her slim body, and her reflection in the large mirror below her bed told her she had to go and tidy herself up.

She turned on the bathroom light and glanced at the small mirror above the basin, clasped a hand to her mouth to muffle a shriek of fright at what she saw.

Staring back at her was the bruised and battered face of a young man, and she could see that he was mouthing to her, “Help me, please.”

Instinctively, she jabbed at the switch and turned off the light. Her breathing, was erratic and coarse, her heart beating twenty to the dozen, she felt like she had awoken from a nightmare.

Slowly, but still shaking with fright, she turned on the light again, and dared to look in the mirror. This time, all she could see was her face, and she breathed a sigh of relief.

Had she imagined it? Her blue eyes looked back at her, as if they were the real eyes and she was the reflection. She touched her raven black hair, which due to the sweating was tied in knots.

"Dam," she cursed, knowing that it was going to take ages to get the knots out and walked back into the bedroom attacking her hair with a brush. She sat down on the side of the bed and turned on the radio.

"Breaking news, police have been called to Lovers Lane, where a young man has been found beaten to death and another seriously injured. Locals who found the body said it was like an abattoir."

Charlotte felt sick and quickly ran into the bathroom. After throwing up several times, she returned to the bedroom to get dressed, all her thoughts were for the victim. The images in her head were sickening; she could hear the pleas from the victims, the sense of anger and hatred from the killer. Those creeps at the station would have to take her seriously now.

She got into her car and drove to Lovers Lane.

CHELMESBURY POLICE STATION

In the stone Victorian wing of the station, which once housed the old CID department, Detective Inspector William Frashier sat in one of the offices, drinking a cup of coffee and going through several files on the desk.

Frashier was of a strong build, a little over six foot, with short raven black hair and a Mediterranean complexion. He wore a smart casual blue suit, white shirt and a striped green tie. His bright blue eyes looked over the rim of his glasses out of the window to the large new round building, which was being transformed into a state-of-the-art CID department.

Frashier looked around the bare office; he had taken down pictures and pin-boards that had hung on the now blank walls, boxes had been stacked up in a corner and a taped-up filing cabinet was ready to move to its new home.

The phone on the desk rang and he looked at it; he wasn't really bothered with answering, but it rang and rang and eventually he grabbed the receiver.

"Frashier!" he said, sighing.

The female officer responded calmly. "Sorry to disturb you, sir, but there has been an attack in Lovers Lane."

Frashier smiled. "Isn't there always?" He paused. "Okay, thanks, I'm on my way." He replaced the receiver and stood up, walked to the office door and entered the very heart of the old department. Wires were hanging down from the ceiling as computer terminals were being taken away to the new part of the station, whole sections and offices were empty, filing cabinets were open and emptied as plain-clothed officers were busy placing the files into cardboard boxes marked attic.

"Day?" he shouted. "Day!" He approached some officers packing boxes and asked calmly, "Have any of you seen DS Miranda Day?"

One of the officers looked up. "Think she went out for some, uh…fresh air," he said, miming the act of dragging on a cigarette. Frashier gave him the thumbs-up and went to what was the smoking area, a small room, just off the main staff canteen. It had five huge extractor fans in the ceiling to take away the smoke. The room was painted yellow to pre-empt the inevitable nicotine discolouration.

"Day, there you are!"

Detective Sergeant Miranda Day was a bright and attractive twenty-two-year-old, fancied by most of the male officers, including Frashier.

"What's up, guv?" she asked, as Frashier helped himself to one of her cigarettes.

"We have to take a trip to Lovers Lane."

"Is that a proposition?" she said, flirting with him. He winked at her and then took a couple of drags on the cigarette.

"Looks like we've got a murder; you and I have to go and investigate the incident."

DS Day drove the grey Vauxhall Insignia and when they arrived they were greeted by the usual scene-of-crime tape and a little white tent. She parked next to a squad car and she and Frashier crossed to a van where a Forensics officer issued them with protective attire. After slipping into his overalls, Frashier said, "Let's go and see what the doctor has for us," and they headed for the tent.

The chief pathologist emerged from the tent, removing his mask as they approached, and stood before them in a blue overall and blue wellington boots.

Doctor Richard Edward Strong was an old-fashioned doctor with old-fashioned values. He also dressed as if it were still the 'fifties, with snazzy waistcoats and tweed suits; a watch dangled from a silver chain on his waistcoat. Although a little under six foot, the high heels on his polished black leather shoes made him seem taller. He had a curly ginger moustache and the surgical hat he was wearing covered his flaming red hair.

"Morning," Strong said, his voice sounding a little odd to Frashier.

"Morning," Frashier replied. "So what have we got, Doc?"

Strong turned and looked back into the tent. "I hope you haven't eaten?" Day shook her head and so did Frashier. "OK then, two young men, one beaten up badly, the other stabbed, although stabbed isn't the word I should use to describe this murder. The poor fellow was mutilated, no, butchered to death." He lifted the cloth over the murder victim. Day felt sick and so did Frashier. Strong continued, "Stabbed twenty-three times in the heart, neck, hands and abdomen." His finger pointed, tracing the wounds. "The first would probably have paralysed the victim; the last would have killed him immediately, straight into the heart. The weapon was probably some sort of butcher's knife and the attacker knew how to use it fatally."

Frashier looked at his friend. "OK, anything else?"

Strong nodded. "This." He showed Frashier and Day a photo, it was of a school football team, and a red circle had been drawn around one of the faces. "That's the stabbed man," Strong said.

"Anything else?"

Strong shook his head. "There's no point doing footprint analysis or even DNA swabs from the scene, this road is too well used."

Frashier looked around; condoms littered the road. "You can see why they call it Lovers Lane," he said.

"They say they have nowhere else to go," Strong said sarcastically.

"Do it anyway. I don't want to run the risk of missing something," Frashier said, thinking of his meeting with Brightly next week.

"OK, Inspector I will do my best," Strong said with a wry smile.

Frashier patted him on the back, knowing that what he had asked for was going to be a tough job for Strong and his team to undertake, but he had a lot of faith in the doctor and his work. He smiled at his friend and as he walked out of the tent, looked back and said, "Thank you, Doctor. I'll need the report as soon as possible."

Strong sighed, grunted in the affirmative, and then went back to examining the body.

Outside the tent, Frashier turned and said to DS Day, "Get in touch with the station and ask Brightly if she can get some officers down here at once. I'll want them doing house to house; there had to have been witnesses, people using this place." He started to walk up the lane towards the housing estate, saying, "I'll go and interview the other witness."

"Okay, guv!" said Day. She took out her phone and called the station.

Frashier walked towards the ambulance where Paul was being looked after by two paramedics. The young man was severely bruised around both eyes, and had cuts and bruises all over his face and neck. Blood stained his shirt and trousers, which were ripped and dirty from the mud on the road. He looked like someone who had faced twelve rounds with Mike Tyson, Frashier thought. He smiled at Paul, took out his warrant card and showed it to the shaking man.

"Hi, I'm DI William Frashier, Chelmesbury CID." Paul tried to turn and look at him through puffy eyes and it clearly hurt when he tried to talk.

"I'm Paul Tomlinson," he said quietly.

"Paul, I know you're probably in a lot of pain, but I need to know what happened," Frashier said.

Paul nodded and when Day returned from her phone call with the station, she took out her notebook and then in as much detail as he could remember, he started to recount the incident.

As Paul spoke, Frashier watched Day writing down all the information he was giving them, he could see that she would wince at horrific parts.

After recounting the attack, Paul looked at Frashier and then at Day. "Please find this monster," he said. "He killed the greatest friend I had."

Frashier nodded. "I will, Paul, this killer has to be stopped."

Day asked, "Did you get a look at the attacker, Paul?"

Paul shook his head gingerly, trying to avoid more pain, and said, "Not really. He was wearing a hoody, so I couldn't see much of his face, but his eyes... God, his eyes... they seemed to be burning with hatred and anger, like bright red flames." Frashier frowned and said, as reassuringly as he could.

"Okay, son, you get better soon." Then he and DS Day left the ambulance and headed back to a group of Forensic officers who were scouring the scene for clues.

***

Charlotte had parked her green Mini Cooper in the church car park and walked slowly up towards the police tape. She was watching the scene unfold, when she spotted Frashier looking at her. She smiled at him, warmly.

Instead of returning her smile, the DI scowled and marched off in the opposite direction, muttering something to a uniformed officer, who finally approached her.

"I take it Mr Frashier's not keen on talking to me this morning, eh, Constable?" Charlotte said cheekily.

The male officer shook his head. "Sorry, Miss Steel, but you aren't allowed to be near a crime scene, you know what the judge said. If you don't move along, I'll have to arrest you."

Charlotte looked coldly at the man. "I do respect you, Constable, but I have evidence about this case, which I think the Inspector needs to hear."

The constable sighed. "Yeah, yeah, we all remember the last time you said that. We searched that house where you said we'd find two bodies, didn't we? Nearly two weeks we spent there, ripping it apart. And do you know what we found – sod all, that's what we found."

"You were looking in the wrong house," Charlotte said primly.

The constable started to get angry. "Are you going to move along, or what?"

Charlotte tried to beckon Frashier over, but he was talking with some Forensics officers.

"Damn you," she said and walked away.

***

Frashier watched her strut back to her car. Day joined him and said, "I see Loopy Lottie was here?"

Frashier nodded. "Yeah, she told the constable she had information on this case."

Day sniggered, and muttered, "I bet she had." Holding a hand to her forehead, she intoned dramatically, like some ham actor, "Oh, I see the future, ooh."

Frashier laughed, and then after telling her to stop, continued to investigate the scene.

***

Nearly a hundred miles away in southwest London, another man was unaware of what his future would hold, but unlike the killer, whom he would eventually hunt, this man was not evil. He was a good guy, a good copper, who had simply made a fatal error in judgement, an error for which he would be punished.

NEXT DAY

The A4 was one of the main trunk roads in and out of London, and since its transformation from a single into a dual carriageway, there had been many serious and fatal accidents.

One of the thousands of vehicles trying to use the A4 to get into the city this dreary morning was a red Ford Escort.

The female driver was listening to the Fearne Cotton show on Radio one, tapping the steering wheel as her favourite band was performing. The only hassle she had were her two children, who were, as always, arguing in the back seat. She glanced in the mirror and ordered them to stop; after blaming each other, they soon fell quiet, especially when she gave them an evil look.

The road ahead was busy but not too busy, so she minded her own business and thought of the clothes she was going to buy for the family holiday in a few weeks' time.

Something drew her eye to a white Vauxhall Cavalier in her rear-view mirror; maybe it was the way the car pulled out suddenly from a junction, almost hitting another car.

The other driver sounded his horn and flashed his lights, but the Cavalier took no notice and continued heading towards the Escort. It then overtook the two cars behind the Escort and when it was nearly bumper-to-bumper, the driver started to flash his lights.

She thought about turning the car into a junction, so the Cavalier would pass, maybe he was in a hurry, but in the distance, she spotted a long clear straight part of the road and sped up a little, hoping to get there sooner.

When she reached the clear straight, she eased off a little on the accelerator, expecting the Cavalier to pass, but it stayed behind her, flashing its lights.

Now she was scared, so she locked all the doors and looked in the mirror at her children; they too were scared. She faced front again and put her foot down, changing to fourth gear to get a bit more speed. As she went over the one hundred miles an hour mark, the Vauxhall started to back off; she looked in the mirror and smiled, taking her attention off the vehicles in front of her.

"Mummy, watch out!" her daughter screamed loudly. She turned her attention back to see a stationary Toyota TR2 in front of her, waiting for a lorry to reverse into a yard. She braked, but to no avail, and hit the car, flying straight over the top, and straight into the path of the reversing lorry.

The mother and her two children died on impact, the car split in two, one half on one side of the road, the other embedded in to the back of the lorry.

Traffic came to a complete stop. The driver of the Vauxhall got out and helped to pull the lorry driver from his cab, then he tried to get close to the Escort, but when he saw the blood pool on the floor, he stopped in his tracks, grabbed his mobile and called the emergency services.

Minutes later, the police cordoned off the area, and the local council removed the central reservation, so that the cars stuck in the crash could turn around and find different routes, off the A4.

Whilst this was going on, the paramedics, with help from the fire service, lifted the casualties out of the Toyota, then they examined the Escort. One of the paramedics checked the children first, then shook his head. "They're both dead," he said. The front part of the car contained the woman's body, her head and chest mashed and tangled into the steering wheel, her eyes open wide and blank.

Whilst the paramedics and fire brigade gently freed the three family members and lay them covered in blankets on the side of the road, one of the police officers typed the registration plate number in his handheld computer and pressed enter.

When he got back the owner's name and address, he felt sick.

He crouched down and lifted the blanket for a quick look, and his stomach churned as he recognised the victims.

"My God, I know these people, her husband is a detective in the Met," he said.

"You're sure?" his colleague asked.

The officer nodded. "Yes, this woman is Rose Eliote; I've been to many Christmas parties and events with her and her husband," he paused and looked over at the other covered bodies "and those are her children." He stood up and walked towards his squad car, where he was violently sick, then after composing himself, he grabbed his phone and dialled the station.

"Detective Sergeant Robertson, please."

"I'm afraid the sergeant is busy investigating a case," a female voice told him. Can anyone else help you?"

"Irene, its PC John Lock. It's very, very important that I speak with Sergeant Robinson."

"OK, John, don't worry, I'll try and find him," Irene said.

DS Richard Robertson or Dick to his friends and colleagues was a tall slender man in his mid-fifties; he wore a smart black suit, navy blue tie and white shirt. He had flowing greyish black hair and a small moustache, which he was playing with as he walked past a desk.

The phone on the desk rang, making him jump, but he picked it up, and sat on the edge of the desk.

"CID, DS Robertson."

"Sir, its PC Lock. I think you should get to the accident on the A4."

"I have a hell of a lot of stuff to do, what with our enquiries and other bits," Robertson answered, looking through some files on his desk. He sighed heavily, "And you want me to go to a serious accident on the A4?"

"Yes, guv it concerns your friend Superintendent Simon Eliote… it's his family."

Robertson had seen the information come on to the police computer, the vehicles involved, and then it hit him like a hammer through a pane of glass.

"Oh my God," he said softly. "I'll be there ASAP." He put the phone down and grabbed his coat, "Officer Hatfield, can you get me to the incident on the A4, as quickly as is possible," he asked a nearby constable.

The man turned and looked warmly at Robertson. "No problems, guv, we were just heading there." Robertson jumped into the back of the patrol car and Hatfield asked, "Is everything OK, guv?"

Robertson shook his head. "I know the people killed, so step on it."

Hatfield nodded. “No probs,” he said, placing the car in gear, “we‘ll get you there in a flash.” The officer in the passenger seat turned on the blue lights and they drove quickly out of the station and headed towards the crash, overtaking everything in sight.

Robertson didn’t know what to expect when he got there, but he knew it wasn’t going to be a pretty sight.

THE DEATHLY ANGEL

By

Kevin Bailey

CHAPTER TWO

When he arrived at the crash scene some minutes later, he got out of the squad car and was greeted solemnly by another officer.

"This way please sir." He followed him past the covered smashed cars towards two ambulances, the other two officers from the squad car followed in a sombre manner, their head bowed.

Robertson walked past other officers to the back ambulance where three stretchers had been laid out on the ground, blankets covering their horrific injuries.

The Sergeant crouched down and lifted one of the blankets. Though the body was badly mutilated, he could make out the features of Rose.

"Oh my," he said. "Sweet Rose." He replaced the blanket and walked towards the other officers, turned and looked back at the mangled wreckage that had been the Eliote family's red Escort.

Since Robertson and his wife Evelyn had come to London with their five children, they had been welcomed by the Eliote's into their family.

They had introduced them all to the neighbourhood. Now Robertson looked at the bodies, remembering times they had spent there, happy times.

Whilst he remembered the victims, the press had gathered at the police tape, asking if they could have a statement from Robertson, but were told to move on, there would be no statement except that there had been a fatal accident, involving three vehicles.

Robertson knew nothing of this; he had a predicament of his own. How the hell was he going to tell Simon Eliote? He took out his mobile, phoned the station and asked to speak to the chief superintendent.

"Harrison," the chief super answered.

"Guv, this is Sergeant Robertson. How can I get hold of DS Eliote?" There was a pause.

"Sorry, Sergeant, unfortunately he is unavoidably detained." Robertson heard papers being rummaged through and then remembered.

"Oh yes, today is the tribunal for the shooting."

"Yes." There was another pause as more papers were shuffled "Why?" Robertson froze; he wanted to be the one to tell Eliote, not anyone else.

"It's nothing Guv. Sorry to have bothered you." He hung up. "Poor Simon," he muttered. "His job is on the line and now his family is dead. He has had terrible bad luck."

Robertson straightened himself up and walked back towards Lock, who looked up at him.

"Are you all right, sir?"

Robertson shook his head. "No, not really," he looked at his colleague "probably the same as you, my friend." Lock nodded. Robertson paused to look back at the stretchers. "John, were there any witnesses?"

"There was a couple sir. This gentleman was right behind the Escort." Lock led Robertson to the Vauxhall driver.

"I didn't mean for this to happen," the man said, shaking.

"What do you mean?" Robertson snapped. "Explain."

"You see, that car is mine." He paused, seeing that Robertson was confused. "The red one, I mean."

Robertson's anger boiled up inside of him. "What do you mean it's yours? You must be mistaken, I know the deceased very well, I also remember her buying it."

"It's mine, I tell you. The ragged area on the back is where my other half reversed it into a lamp post." The Vauxhall driver showed Robertson the rough area. "I tried to patch it up and then had it re-sprayed."

Robertson walked away, and the Vauxhall driver walked behind him.

"Tell me how it was stolen."

"Well, me and the wife were visiting friends in Ashford. Before leaving, I went to fill it up with petrol."

"This car is diesel," Robertson said, looking at the driver, "but please continue." The driver nodded.

"Well, I had left my other half at our friends. I went into the service station shop to pay, there was a huge queue, but when I came out, my car had gone. I even had the keys." He paused to look at the wreckage. "It was my pride and joy, my other half thought I loved it more than her." He sort of smiled. "I bought this Vauxhall with the insurance money."

"So what happened today?" Robertson asked.

"Well, I was on my way to work, running late, rushing a little, so there I am sat at a junction, being a little impatient, when I see a red Escort. I had almost given up in finding it, but that was when I noticed the ragged area." He started to shake a little.

"It's OK sir; just tell me how it happened."

"So I chased after it. Yeah, sure, it had a different number plate, but it was my car."

"So what happened then, sir?"

"Well, I followed, trying to make her stop, so I could identify that it was my car, but she wouldn't stop. She put her foot down and I couldn't catch her, and that's when I saw her drive straight over the Toyota TR2, which had stopped in front of her, and into the path of that articulated lorry." A small sob escaped his chest.

"Go on."

"The worst part was when I approached the car and saw that it had split in two. I stopped and got out. I helped the lorry driver out of his cab and then I approached the one half of the car, but a pool of blood stopped me in my tracks. That's when I phoned the emergency services. I just stood there, looking at what I had done." "By trying to stop her, I caused a fatal car crash." He broke down and cried, "How can I live with myself?" Robertson looked at the man; he could tell the tears were real, not fake ones.

"I am sorry, Mr…?"

"Cartwheel, Richard Cartwheel."

"Richard, I am going to have to arrest you, for dangerous driving and possible manslaughter." Robertson looked at Lock. "Read him his rights then take him to the station." Lock nodded.

"Yes Sir." He turned and led Richard Cartwheel away to a squad car, which took him to Hounslow Police Station.

Robertson looked at the two halves of the Escort. He knew that Simon would want answers and boy was he gonna get them. He turned quickly and walked back to some other officers who were at the tape, stopping traffic.

"Colin, I need to get back to the station, is anyone going that way?"

A tall blond-haired officer nodded. "I am sir." Robertson jumped into the passenger seat and the blond-haired officer drove the car back towards the police station. All the way back, Robertson was thinking of how he was going to tell Eliote.

When he got back to the station, he swapped cars and jumping into his navy blue Ford Focus, he started the car and drove to where Eliote had bought the Escort.

Honest Harry's car auction was on the outskirts, just off the M25 and based on an old garage site.

Robertson parked his Focus on the old forecourt and walked towards the main entrance; it was locked, so he went around the back, where he saw a man examining a black Honda Civic.

The man looked up. "Can I help you?" he said.

Robertson showed him his card. "Detective Sergeant Robertson," he said and shook hands with the man.

"I'm Harry Roberts, the owner of Honest Harry's car auction."

"Mr Roberts, I'm investigating a serious crash, and I was wondering if you keep a record of cars sold here and where they came from."

"Yes I do Sergeant it's all on the computer in the office." Robertson followed Harry towards a de-mountable block. Harry unlocked the door and they both entered.

Harry sat down and turned on the computer, after several seconds Robertson was ready to type in the details of the Escort's registration, which he did quickly.

The screen went black and for a second he thought it had crashed, but then the form came back with loads of information.

Robertson scanned the information, looked at the previous owner and recognised the name Vince Turner as the alias of a local crook, Peter Watson, who was wanted by the police in several counties for a number of incidents dealing with stolen motors.

"Got ya," Robertson said. He looked over at Harry. "Can I have a printed copy of this, please?" Harry nodded.

Robertson thanked Harry and then walked out of the unit and back to his car. He dialled the station's CID number and was put through to one of his officers.

"Dempsey, I want all the information on Peter Watson or his alias Vince Turner," he paused, "and I want his whereabouts." Dempsey acknowledged him and the line went dead.

Harry watched him go, and grabbed his phone from his coat. He dialled a number and then waited for a reply.

"It's me," he said, looking out of the window to make sure that Robertson wasn't coming back. "The fuzz are investigating an accident involving one of our funny cars."

The voice on the other end was angry. "You said they would be safe." Harry gulped and then the voice spoke again, this time calmer. "So you're ringing to warn me that I may get a call from them."

Harry shook his head. "No, no," he stuttered, "I set the computer to say the cars came from our 'supplier'."

He heard the caller ask, 'Who?'

Harry replied, "You know, the one the fuzz have been after for ages, he's the one I pay to have the cars done." Harry was starting to sweat. "His work has been a bit sloppy of late."

The voice on the phone spoke calmingly. "What do you need, Harry?"

Harry grabbed his laptop and answered, "I need to get out of here before they investigate that twerp and find that I had something to do with these cars."

"Don't worry," the voice replied. "We'll send someone around to help you leave."

Harry smiled. "Cheers."

"Can the police link you to our organization?"

Harry shook his head once again. "No, all the information linking us has been burnt, as ordered."

"OK then, we will talk after we sort you a way out."

Harry smiled greedily. "I'll be on it as soon as you hang up." The line went dead and he replaced the phone and started to get ready to leave.

***

Back in Chelmesbury, the investigation into the death of James wasn't going very well. Detective Inspector William Frashier had begun the day, many hours ago, investigating the murder and was now at the spot where James Gaston had been savagely murdered by the killer known to Paul as the Deathly Angel.

Frashier stood looking at the spot in the road, and he could still make out several bloodstains. Next to them were members of Strong's pathology team, wearing protective clothing and crouched on trays, examining each spot.

Several were searching the hedgerows for any new piece of information and evidence.

Strong approached and Frashier asked him, "Anything else to report, Doctor?"

Strong nodded. "Yes we have found several footprints with blood around them, all heading off in that direction." He pointed up the road towards several farm buildings and open fields. "I would say the shoes were approximately a size ten."

Frashier looked back at the doctor. "We may have to widen our search then," he said, indicating the buildings with a nod of his head. "Send some of your team to have a look around up there."

The doctor left and Frashier decided to walk down the lane. After a few minutes, he came to a crossroads, and spotted a hooded figure watching him. Frashier turned in that direction, but as he got closer the figure vanished.

He continued on, up a slight incline, and when he reached the top, he saw an unmarked path disappear down an old stream bed. Fighting back the brambles and nettles, he pushed his way along the path.

He came to an old churchyard, which looked like it had been abandoned for many years. The church itself was a burnt-out shell, its windows had been covered up and the gravestones were covered in graffiti.

As he looked around, something caught Frashier's attention: it was a marble angel, pointing at the town of Chelmesbury. Nearby, a young man was sitting, staring at the sky.

When Frashier called out to him, the youth jumped up guiltily.

"I ain't done anything wrong, I didn't do anything," he said.

Frashier put up his hand. "It's okay, I'm Detective Inspector William Frashier and I'm investigating the murder of James Gaston."

The lad looked sombrely at him. "He was a mate, went to school with him," he said.

"Can you think of anyone who would want to kill him?" Frashier asked.

The lad shook his head. "He was well liked at school and was captain of many things, so unfortunately I can't." The young man turned his head more towards Frashier, who could now see what he had been hiding.

"What happened to you?" he said, pointing at the scarring around the lad's left eye.

The young man touched the top of his face and answered, "I was knocked down by a car several years ago, severe trauma to the face and hands." He pulled back the hood to show Frashier the scars "Does it bother you?"

Frashier shook his head. "In my profession, I see a lot worse."

The lad smiled. "Bothers a lot of people, even my parents, but they tolerate me." He looked glum, then he heard his phone ringing. "That's my mum telling me its dinner time."

Frashier looked at his watch. "Blimey, so it is," he said. "You'd better get going, Mr…?"

"Daniel Trent."

Frashier gave the lad a warm smile. “Well, Daniel, if you hear anything, give me a call.” He handed Daniel a card, which he placed in the pocket of his jacket.

As Daniel was about to leave the graveyard, Frashier stopped him. “Before you go, Daniel, what size shoe do you wear?”

The lad turned and replied politely, “Size nine, Inspector Frashier. Why?”

Frashier shrugged his shoulders. “I’m just curious.” Daniel smiled and left through the main entrance.

Frashier scouted around for a few more minutes, but there was nothing to keep him there, so he reported back to Strong.

Deep in the undergrowth, the lad known to Frashier as Daniel watched the detective leave the graveyard. He put up his hood and followed him silently; a few times, he thought he had been spotted, but Frashier never came back to investigate.

He watched as the detective returned to the crossroads, where he walked to one of the police cars and spoke to the driver, who looked back in the direction of the graveyard and himself.

He turned and headed for his home, and as he left the police area, he laughed loudly. His deception seemed to have worked, but only time would tell.

THE DEATHLY ANGEL

By

Kevin Bailey

CHAPTER THREE

NEW SCOTLAND YARD
LONDON
THAT SAME DAY

Along a magnolia-coloured corridor, deep within the towering and imposing building that houses New Scotland Yard, the lonely figure of Detective Superintendent Simon Eliote sat waiting for fate to come knocking.

He and the rest of New Scotland Yard were blissfully unaware of both the accident and the police investigation.

Except for the hushed voices from behind the many closed doors, the only sound he could hear was his strong heart beating faster.

He looked up the corridor with his green emerald eyes and apart from a few pot plants and benches which had been logically placed along the walls, it was empty.

Next to him was a large oak door, which was marked 'Do Not Disturb, Meeting in Session', and beyond that door he knew was fate, a fate that would determine his future.

He was distracted from his thoughts by the door opening and an older bearded officer looking straight at him.

"Detective Superintendent Eliote?" The man paused and smiled warmly at him. "Will you come in please?" the officer said in a deep commanding voice, which echoed along the corridor.

Eliote stood up and approached the door. Simon was thirty-eight, six foot three, with mousy blond hair, neatly parted on the side and his fringe had been flicked up at the front.

His muscular body was covered in a smart black suit, ironed white shirt and a grey tie; he always looked good in a suit, especially as this one was tailor made.

When he entered he saw the panel of two officers in front of him; he gulped and sat down. The officer who had shown him in sat to the right of a female officer who was sitting in the middle of the two male officers.

She looked up at him from behind her specs, reminding Simon of a school teacher he'd once had.

"Detective Superintendent Eliote," she said with a slight Yorkshire accent, "I am Assistant Commissioner Rachel Young, to my left is Detective Chief Superintendent Michael Watkins, to my right is Chief Constable Donald Yates," after they had acknowledged him, she continued, " this tribunal was arranged because of an incident where you shot dead an innocent man." Eliote bowed his head and nodded. "We have had other testimonies from officers who were there with you on the night in question, but as always in these tribunals we wanted to hear your side of the story, before passing judgment."

"I understand," he said sombrely.

"Good." She looked at the paperwork in front of her and then spoke still looking at the file. "According to your report, Superintendent, you were in a group of armed officers who were searching an abandoned shopping centre for a terrorist bomb, which Special Branch had got intelligence was hidden there."

Eliote nodded and replied, "That is correct. I was one of a few officers seconded from Special Branch to help in the search."

The female officer nodded in agreement; her files had already told her that. "Go on," she said commandingly.

"I was at my desk, when the call came through from higher up to report to the old Franklin-fort Shopping Centre." He thought back. "I was given protective equipment and a regulation rifle," he looked at the officers, "then we were split into teams and I took control of team Alpha Three."

***

The abandoned shopping centre used to bustle with tourists and shoppers wanting bargains from its many retailers and outlets.

But after Woolworths shut, the centre suffered badly from the recession especially when other shops closed and eventually customers stopped coming.

Simon Eliote led the way through the empty centre, it was like a ghost town, and he half expected someone to come out and ask him the way to the shops.

But like the rest of his team, he kept a lookout for anything that seemed out of place.

Behind him a female officer said, "What are we doing here in this urine and shit-smelling place, Superintendent?" She scrunched up her nose at the smell. "Should this not be an army job?"

Eliote turned and looked at her. "That it may be, Sergeant Clunes," he said almost snapping at her, "but if our intelligence is right, then there is the possibility that somewhere in here there may be a bomb or a terrorist cell." He continued to walk, keeping his eyes fixed on the empty shops and corridors. "The army has been called, but because we are near a housing area, those higher up wanted action and we were scrambled quickly. Imagine the death toll if that bomb goes off." He raised a small smile and looked back at Sergeant Clunes. “Anyway, it beats sitting at a desk, writing reports.”

Suddenly he heard what he thought was the sound of a door opening and closing. His reactions were quick and he pointed his rifle at the location of the noise.

His team did the same and a silent hush revolved around the group, all fixated on the same location.

The group slowly, silently, walked towards an old escalator, all the time aware of the distant noises overhead.

The escalator rose into the darkened area above. Eliote stopped the group and then pointed at one of the officers. “DI Baines, check it out,” he said, and a black female officer nodded and headed towards the escalator, her rifle aimed always at the darkness above as she started to climb the rusty metal steps. “DC Murray, follow Baines, back her up if she needs it,” Eliote ordered and Murray followed the DI up the stairs.

Eliote heard his team mentioned on his radio and pressed the button on his CB.

“This is Alpha Three go ahead” he heard crackle and then he heard the distinct voice of his superior.

“Report you progress?” Eliote replied calmly.

“We are investigating level 1, next level basement, will keep you informed.”

“Okay, Alpha Three.” Eliote let go of the microphone and looked up at the top of the escalator and waited until his two officers came back into view at the top of the escalators.

“Think it was rats, Gov,” DI Clunes reported. “We found several piles of droppings.”

Eliote acknowledged her report and ordered the two officers to re-join the group, which they did quickly and then they moved to the next target which is a twin glass sliding door, similar to the ones outside supermarkets.

He approaches the doors and after placing his rifle over his shoulder, he gets a crowbar from one of the other officers in the group and wedges the bar between the two doors and using all his strength he opens the door enough for another officer to get his hand in and open it fully.

***

"So," Detective Chief Superintendent Watkins spoke in a strong London accent and looks straight at Eliote, "everything was going to plan, a routine search?"

"Yes sir," Eliote nodded, "as routine as it could be under the circumstances. We had six teams searching different parts of the centre. My group, Alpha Three, was searching upper level one and the basement levels, the other teams were searching upper and lower levels two, three and four." Chief Constable Yates asked.

"Why were you leading the team?" "And why was such a small team sent into the lower basement area, where common sense would say is probably the place a bomber would hide a device?" Eliote agreed with him, but only on the inside, outside he was a good copper and he followed orders.

"I suppose it was my experience in the field, so to speak sir," he said quickly, then paused "Most of the team I had were CID officers, I am not saying they were bad officers sir, but as the operation was rushed, they had to grab whoever was available, especially due to the area the shopping centre was located in," Somewhere outside the room, Simon heard a trolley being pushed down the corridor, this distracted his thoughts, but DCS Watkins soon brought his attention back into the room.

"Who authorised the operation?" he asked.

"Acting Chief Constable Rawlings, sir, with full backing from Special Branch and I believe MI5."

"I see." The female officer studied the file in front of her that contained his statement. "So, Superintendent, when you opened the door, what happened?"

Eliote sat up in his chair and started to recall the incident. "I opened the door and found a set of stairs going down to the basement levels, we proceeded with caution until we reached the bottom, then we split up."

Assistant Commissioner Young raised her eyebrows. "You split up?" she said. "How many were there in each team?"

"Well, Alpha Three was comprised of ten officers, not including myself."

She did some calculations and then abruptly said, "So you had five officers with you?"

Eliote nodded. "Dawson, Singh, Halifax, Clunes and Johnston," "We slowly walked down a long corridor, checking each door and room carefully, I was about to call the whole search of the level off, when I saw a light escaping from a far of window. At first I thought it was sunlight coming in from a broken frame, but as we got closer, we saw that it was artificial and it was coming from a small boiler room."

***

Simon looked around the dark corridor and at the rest of his team of officers and then he grabbed his CB radio and pressed the button to transmit.

"All Alpha teams, this is Alpha Three, converge on lower level we have found something." He heard voices acknowledging his order and then he got his team to circle the entrance; they did what was instructed and aimed all their weapons at the door.

Eliote approached the door; he moved his hand towards the door knob and turned it. To his astonishment it was unlocked and he slowly and quietly opened the door.

When he entered he saw a man in overalls and a hat looking into a locker. Eliote could hear a ticking clock and he aimed his rifle at the man and shouted, "Freeze, police, hands on your head," he demanded "now!" The overall-wearing man stood still, then slowly turned. Eliote gave him the warning again, "Hands on your head," but the overall-wearing man didn't do as was instructed, instead he placed his right hand inside the overall and grabbed something.

"Don't be stupid," Eliote ordered the man and switched off the safety on his rifle. "Just put your hands above your head." The man just stared at Eliote, his hand firmly on something beneath his overalls.

Then in a split second utter chaos erupted in the room, for as the man started to pull something metal out of his overalls, Eliote's mind went into overdrive: was he pulling out a gun? Was his life in danger?

He searched the man's eyes, trying to get anything from them, but they gave nothing away. What was he doing? he thought, but then his thoughts were distracted by a new look in the man's eye, a look of hatred towards him, he knew what he was doing and quickly pulled out the metal object.

Eliote acted quickly and shot the man straight between the eyes, a clean kill.

The man fell backwards onto the metal locker, making it start to sway and collapse. Eliote watched it crash to the floor and shouted to all his team to get down.

***

Eliote stopped recalling the event and looked up at the panel with tears in his eyes. What he had done was wrong and he knew it.

The female officer said, "There was no bomb was there? It was a hoax."

Eliote shook his head and looked up at her with his red eyes. "It was a hoax, there was no bomb, the informant disappeared," "the ticking noise was an alarm clock and the gun was a circular cigarette case, with the picture of his wife and kids inside." "He was an immigrant, who had escaped persecution in his native country; the hatred in his eyes was probably because he thought we were going to send him back there."

The female officer nodded. "That it may have been, Superintendent, but that does not answer for why he died," she said.

"I acted in self-defence, I thought he had a gun and was going to kill me, but I was safe, if only I had waited."

She nodded in agreement. "I concur you acted in self-defence, Superintendent but," she paused and looked at her two colleagues who both nodded, "we are going to have to deliberate on the best course of action to take." She looked over at the bearded man. "Chief Constable Yates, Will you escort Superintendent Eliote to the door please?"

The bearded officer stood and beckoned Eliote to the door, but Young gave Eliote an instruction, "Superintendent please wait outside, we will get back to you in due course," Eliote got up and went and sat back on the bench outside the room.

After a while he heard shouting coming from inside the tribunal, looking back at the door, he wondered what were they discussing about his future?

"What?" he said angrily out loud, only time would tell.

THE DEATHLY ANGEL

By
Kevin Bailey

CHAPTER FOUR

Back in London, Dempsey and Robertson approached the garage, which was situated under a tower block. When the convoy of police vehicles came to a stop, Robertson could make out mechanical noises, drilling and compressors, coming from one of the garages.

He parked across the road from the garage and got out, Dempsey in a long black leather jacket followed and they waited for the vans to stop. About twenty officers in riot gear approached him.

"Right team, listen," Robertson said. "I want to surround the property, make sure that no one can escape, okay? So spread out."

"You're with me, Constable," Robertson told Dempsey, and the two officers walked to the main entrance, the noises from inside growing louder.

"Get ready, all units," Dempsey said into the walkie-talkie.

Robertson knocked on the steel door and he heard a loud cockney voice inside call, "Coming," then he heard footsteps approaching the door, which opened and a man wearing overalls stood cleaning a piece of an engine with an old rag. "Yeah?" Robertson showed him his card. "What you want, copper?"

"I have a warrant to search these buildings in connection with the deaths of three people killed in a cut-and-weld. According to Honest Harry's computer, the car came from you."

The overalled man threw the rag at Robertson and in a flash, quicker than the two officers could grab him, ran back into the garage, calling out, "Carlos, it's the fuzz, get out quick." The other mechanic tried to get out of a window at the bottom of the bay, but landed in the direct path of two officers, who arrested him and escorted him to a waiting police car.

Back inside the garage, Vince Turner was running around the workshop, throwing spanners and screwdrivers at Robertson and Dempsey.

Dempsey ran straight at Vince, spanners missing him by inches, then he pounced like a cat on to him, and the two men rolled on the floor, both trying to beat the other. Robertson got up from his position and ran to the two men, hearing a blood-curdling scream of pain from Dempsey as he drew near.

When Vince got off, blood covered his hand and Robertson could see what had made Dempsey scream: Vince had stabbed him through his heart with a flat-ended screwdriver. The officer lay there looking at the handle, blood soaked his white shirt, and he wasn't moving.

Vince sat on the floor shaking with shock, as five officers burst into the garage and Robertson ran to Dempsey as the other officers arrested Vince.

Robertson shouted at one of them, "Call an ambulance quickly, one officer down."

Robertson looked at his fallen colleague.

"OK, my friend, stay still, help is on the way."

"I always looked up to you and DSi Eliote, sir," Dempsey grunted. "I wanted to be just like you two, but now I never..." Blood poured from his mouth and his eyes glazed over.

Robertson confirmed he was dead, then took off his coat and placed it over his colleague's head.

As Dempsey was taken away in a private ambulance, Robertson kicked angrily at a spanner. A female officer walked towards him.

"Are you all right, sir?" she asked.

Robertson shook his head and then said, "Do you know what, McCall? It really pisses me off that four good people have died because of that bastard and I personally will see to it that he goes down for this."

Robertson and Sergeant McCall walked outside and went around the back to a compound. Inside was a number of cars, some in pieces, others intact, but with damage to wings, sills and mangled fronts, then Robertson saw something red, sticking out from beyond a lorry.

He walked to it and saw two halves of a red Escort; both parts were mangled beyond repair.

So, he thought, the car that killed Rosy was two cars welded together. Then he saw one of the wrecks had a mangled number plate; he untwisted what he could to reveal the registration number.

He turned to the female sergeant.

"Can you get an identification of this plate?" She nodded and Robertson looked at the mangled halves as Sergeant McCall turned and headed for her car. Robertson stopped her and asked what she was doing.

"I'm getting my phone, sir."

"Here use mine, Sergeant," he said and handed her his mobile.

"Hi, it's Sergeant McCall; can you do a check for me?" She read out the number of the plate. "Owner of the vehicle is one Richard Cartwheel, it was reported stolen one year ago," she relayed to Robertson.

"So it was his car, so to speak." They walked towards the front of the garage, where a police photographer was waiting for him.

"There are two halves of an Escort, round the back; take as many photographs of it as you can, also the number plate, then can you take photos of the place where Detective Constable Dempsey was murdered?" The photographer nodded and got to work.

Robertson walked into the garage and went to the office, where pictures of naked women hung on the walls, plus safety signs and calendars of more naked women, some pornographic. He also saw a filing cabinet, and opened the top drawer to find fake MOT certificates, fake car log books.

The second drawer contained quite a few sales notes, naming garages and car dealerships they had supplied to, including a number of cars which had gone to Honest Harry's car auction.

In the bottom drawer, he found a large black book containing all of Vince's records – pages and pages of cars, their registration numbers, the lists of suppliers who had stolen the vehicles, how much Vince had paid for them: a bible of information.

Robertson pulled out an evidence bag from his pocket and placed the book inside it, then all the sales notes.

He took out another bag and placed all the MOT and log books in to it, then sealed both bags and handed them to Sergeant McCall

"Take these back to the station and get Maxwell to check them on the database, see how many are stolen." She nodded and departed, leaving Robertson to look at more office files. He turned on the computer and printed off more information.

INTERVIEW OF VINCE TURNER
(Aka PETER WATSON)

"Interview commences sixteen-twenty, interviewing, Detective Sergeant Robertson and Detective Sergeant McCall," Robertson said into the microphone. Vince Turner's solicitor was an attractive brunette, who wore a suit, like someone wearing a tight fitting glove; she spotted him studying her and turned her radiant blue eyes in his direction.

"Sergeant Robertson, I must protest at the way my client was arrested. You burst into his garage, you arrest his workers, you rummage in his office without the proper care and now you charge him with murder. I want him released on bail right now," she ordered.

"I am afraid I can't do that, Miss…?"

"Wilson," she said abruptly.

Robertson continued, "Miss Wilson, your client left the door open, his friend tried to jump out of a window and he had every intention of killing either me or the deceased Detective Constable Dempsey." He paused, feeling guilt at the loss of a good colleague and friend. "Your client has broken the law, he has built a car from two vehicles that he joined together with weld and that car yesterday morning killed a mother and her two children."

"Where is your proof, Sergeant?"

Robertson looked at Sergeant McCall, who was sitting next to him, and nodded. She picked up off the floor a large brown envelope, opened it and handed Robertson the photos taken at the garage and at the crash. She also passed him the big black book, confiscated from Vince's office.

"Here is my proof, Miss Wilson." He said into the microphone, "I am showing the accused and his solicitor the evidence against Vince Turner."

Miss Wilson was shown the photos of the crash, and the weld on the sills that had joined the two halves of the Escort together. She was clearly shocked. Then Robertson showed her the images of the other halves of the Escort in the compound. She looked at her client with disbelief; he looked at her all sheepish.

Robertson hammered the last nail into the coffin; he showed her the book, the lists of cars, their vehicle makes, models, registration numbers and identification marks.

"Are these yours?" she asked Vince. He just grunted and then she turned back to Robertson. "I would like five minutes alone with my client please."

Robertson nodded. "Of course" he said. "I could do with a break. What about you, McCall?" She nodded. "Fine. We will take a break for ten minutes, and then I want your full co-operation." He ordered and then spoke into the microphone. "Recording stopped." He scanned his watch. "Seventeen-forty." The two officers walked out of the room, leaving Miss Wilson and Vince Turner to talk amongst themselves.

Robertson joined them again ten minutes later and restarted the tape.

"My client wishes to confess to building cars," said Wilson, 'but says the death of Detective Constable Dempsey was self-defence."

Robertson got angry. "Self-defence it was not. He had me in a corner, and that screwdriver that killed my late colleague was intended for me. Detective Constable Dempsey attacked him to protect me." Wilson spoke back sarcastically.

"Well, if that is not self-defence, then I don't know what is."

Robertson took a deep breath, counted to five and then continued, "Miss Wilson, Your client's actions caused the death of four people, and I want him to confess to it all. Yes, he has confessed to building that car, but by doing so, he killed the family members of a very respectable officer of this station. I am in one sense glad that that officer is not here." He glared at Vince. "Detective Superintendent Simon Eliote would have thrown him around the room, till he made him confess to a series of crimes, weather they were true or not, but that is not the worst part of all this, Miss Wilson. You see, DSi Eliote doesn't even know about it yet, he is at New Scotland Yard fighting to keep his job, so how do you think he will take the news?"

Vince took a gulp of tea and said, "OK, I confess, I did build that bloody car, but it was never supposed to be sent to Honest Harry's car auction." He paused and his tone of voice was of remorse. "It was built for a museum. They asked if I could build them one car from two, for a display of welding; they had asked for it to be done quick and cheap, so I got in touch with my contacts in the underworld and they found me two identical cars, both had been stolen and were involved in crashes. But then once I had finished, I lost a game of cards to a bloke, and to get the money I sold the thing. Yes, I knew what I was doing was wrong, but this bloke said he would kill me, if I didn't pay up."

"So you gave it to Honest Harry's car auctions."

Vince Nodded. "Yes, I can't remember how much I got for it, but it was enough to pay the debt."

"What about Constable Dempsey's death?"

Vince looked down at the table. "I didn't mean for that to happen, I was angry, he surprised me and in the struggle, I stabbed him, I didn't mean for him to die."

Robertson sat forward on his chair and looked at him.

"Four people died, Vince. Are you prepared to face the consequences of your actions? When you go to court, the judge could be in a good mood and class it as manslaughter," "or he could be in a foul mood and class it as something else."

"Is this you trying to frighten me, Sergeant?" Vince said.

Robertson banged his fist down on the table. "No, Vince, it isn't, I just want the bloody truth." "If you're trying to cover for someone, why do it? They have dropped you in the shit; no one is coming to rescue you." Vince just stared at him, his eyes cold as ice.

Robertson was getting nowhere, and Vince wouldn't answer any more questions.

"OK, we will take another break, about half an hour," Robertson said.

When they were outside the interview room, Robertson banged his head against the wall, several times; he needed to take his anger out on something.

McCall placed her hand on his shoulder and he looked at her.

"I'm okay, I just want to nail that son of a bitch," he said, calming down and rubbing his aching head. "Find out if this museum exists and if so, did they authorise this build?"

She nodded. "And you, guv?" He started to walk towards CID, but stopped and looked back at his colleague.

"Well, first I'm going for a fag, then I'll go and sort out what other information I can find from Honest Harry and I'll try and find this card player."

She nodded and left. Robertson decided to let Vince sweat in the cells for a night, and instructed a colleague to go to the interview room and tell Vince and his solicitor that he'd been called away, so the interview would have to reconvene tomorrow morning. The officer nodded and headed off, but Robertson stopped him. "Also, ask him the name of the card player, so that we can confirm his version of events." He nodded and Robertson walked away.

Constable Blake walked back into the interview room and looked at Vince and then at his solicitor.

"Miss Wilson, unfortunately Sergeant Robertson has been called away, so we will be keeping Vince in protective custody for the night." The solicitor clearly wasn't happy about this, but Constable Blake stood his ground. "The interview will reconvene tomorrow morning, at ten o' clock."

Reluctantly gathering her stuff together, Wilson said, "Fine, Constable."

"We would also like you to tell us the name of the card player please, Vince, to confirm your story."

"We are not in the interview now, Constable Blake," Miss Wilson said coldly. "My client doesn't have to..." but she was cut short by Vince touching her wrist.

"It's OK," he said. "If it proves I am innocent then what have I got to lose?" She smiled at him and nodded. Then he looked at the constable. "Mike Swinbourne, twenty-two Bishops Row, Ashford."

Blake wrote down the information and said, "Thank you. Another constable will take you to one of our holding cells.

Heading back toward CID, Blake went through his notes, making sure everything Vince had said to him was jotted down on his notepad. As he entered the large CID room, he spotted Robertson and approached him.

"Here is the information you asked for, Gov." He tore the page from his notebook and handed it to Robertson.

"Thank you, Constable." Blake nodded and left CID.

Robertson walked down the middle of the desks towards a member of his team and said, "Constable Connor, can you check an address for me?" Connor nodded and Robertson handed him the piece of paper with the address on it. "Go round and interview this Mike Swinbourne, and ask him if he has ever played cards with Vince. See if Vince owes him any money."

In his office, Robertson opened one of the drawers in his large filing cabinet and pulled out a two-litre bottle of cherry flavoured Coke.

"Got to give up this stuff," he said to himself, took a couple of swigs from the bottle, and replaced it in the drawer.

His eyes fixed on the photo of him and his family. *What would I do if I lost one of you*? he asked himself, lifting the photo and looking at his five children and his wife and blowing her a kiss. They were his life.

He replaced the photo on his desk and opened the brown file in front of him. The first image was the car in two pieces. He looked at them with a large magnifying glass and saw the small specks of blood, his friend's blood. He examined the edges of weld and bolts, trying to detect something amiss, but if there was anything there, he couldn't see it.

He cursed under his breath and thumbed through the other contents of the file, until he came to some more photos. He studied the images of the bodies.

After several seconds of looking at the twisted carcases that had once been his friend and her two beloved children, he sat back in the chair and stared at the ceiling.

Rubbing his tired eyes, which were sore due to the amount of crying he had done, he wondered if he should be the one looking into this case. He walked to a small window overlooking the car park, and glanced across at the dark grey building opposite.

Inside that building were the two halves of the Escort. The SOCOs were going through it with a fine-toothed comb, trying to find any evidence to link its construction with Vince.

He looked down at the Saab, which was parked in a visitor space. Simon had asked him if it was OK to park there, as he was catching the tube into the centre. Robertson's gaze drifted in the direction of the centre of London, wondering how things were going with his friend.

***

Simon was asked back into the room by the bearded officer; he sat down in front of the panel and waited for their verdict.

"Superintendent, we have discussed the matter in great detail."

"Thank you, ma'am," Simon said.

The woman inspected him from behind her glasses.

"We feel that the killing of Jacques Fermi was not an unlawful killing, you acted, from your own testimony and from those of your team, in self-defence, preserving not just your life but the lives of that team. However," she said sternly, "Jacques Fermi did die and someone has to be held responsible for his death." She paused and looked at the others, who were both nodding in agreement, then looked back at Eliote. "The general public, whom it is our duty to protect, and his family will want answers and they will want justice."

He nodded. "I agree, ma'am, and for that reason, I stand ready to take the blame." She seemed shocked at his decision but he just looked at her. "I was the team leader and I was the one who pulled the trigger, so therefore I must be punished."

The others on the board tried to protest, but she raised her hand, silencing them.

"Your file shows that you are a bloody good copper, Superintendent. Your colleagues next to me do not think you should be blamed, but as this is an independent enquiry, then I must act."

"I understand, ma'am."

She smiled warmly, the ice cold exterior that he had thought she had, had gone.

"Thank you for your cooperation Superintendent, but remember this: there is somebody out there who tipped us off about the bomb, and that somebody is the guilty party."

"Yes, ma'am," Simon said as she took off her glasses and placed them on top of the file in front of her.

"Your actions as a police officer must be to find this culprit and bring them to justice." He nodded. So, he wasn't being kicked out of the service he loved, he realised gratefully, and a big smile appeared on his face as he looked back at the head of the board.

"Above all else," she said, "we must show the general public that we are doing our jobs, and so I must punish you for your actions."

"Ma'am," he said, bowing his head.

"So you are hereby demoted to the rank of Detective Inspector. If there is not a vacancy for you at your station, then one will be found for you. Do you understand?"

"Yes I understand Ma'am."

She picked up her glasses and placed them into a case. "Okay then, you are dismissed, Inspector."

Eliote didn't like the sound of that, he had worked hard to get to the rank of Superintendent, and now he must work hard again. Still, at least he had his family to motivate him.

As he left the building, he grabbed his iPhone and dialled his home number. It rang and rang. They probably weren't back yet from shopping and he needed a drink, he decided. He knew one person who would never refuse a drink, so, scrolling down the list, he found the Hounslow CID number and rang.

***

In the room he had just left, the female officer was watching Eliote walk down the street. The bearded man came up to her and peeled off his beard.

"How long do you think it will be before he's a superintendent again?" she asked him.

"Our Simon Eliote is and always will be a good officer. He was a great agent and he didn't even realise."

She smiled. "Brainwashing?" she asked.

"Sort of," he said, waving his hands around.

"Well, Special Branch isn't gonna like you messing around with one of their officers."

The man took out some cleaning wipes from his briefcase and started to wipe away the glue from his face. "He was never one of theirs," he said, shocking her. "He is one of ours, codenamed The Falcon – one of our top agents."

"So do they know?"

The man placed the dirty wipes into a bin, shaking his head. He lit a cigarette. "Of course they don't. You think they would trust him so much if they did?" She shook her head in agreement, "besides, we gave him a bloody good cover story, which he has stuck to."

"So what now?" she asked.

He threw his cigarette butt out of the window and then answered. "We do what this enquiry set out to do; we find the truth, so therefore, Operation Black Swan must be given the green light, do you concur?

"I agree, but Simon must not know of this until the time is right," she paused, "We must get him away from London," she looked at the other officer, "John find him a post in the country, we'll leave you to deal with the arrangements!" the other officer called John nodded.

"Leave it with me," he paused and took off his uniform.

The female looked back to her clean faced colleague, "What of Simon's friend Magna and Special Branch?" the man wiped away some more glue from his face.

"John will deal with Special Branch." The man nodded and grabbed his phone and disappeared into one of the corners, speaking orders to someone on the phone, the other two looked on and then the clean-faced man smiled and then looked back at the female.

"Before then we must find the hole in our department, somebody is using us and MI5 does not like being used."

"Okay, Julius, let's get out of here," she paused, grabbing her files, "before they come looking for us."

"Then," he pointed at the door, "after you, Mari."

The two of them left leaving “John” to tidy up.

HOUNSLOW CID

DS McCall had just got off the phone to the museum that Vince had mentioned and was writing down the info to give to Robertson, when the phone rang again.

“Hounslow CID, this is DS McCall, how can I help you?” She heard Simon’s familiar voice and started to panic.

“Hi, Sergeant, is DS Robertson about?” She knew that she must lie, to a superior.

“Unfortunately, he’s in a meeting, I’ll get him to call you back.” Simon agreed and hung up.

DS McCall replaced the receiver and headed quickly for Robertson.

Robertson was in his office still going over the file, trying to find something he could use to wear down Vince’s armour, something to break him.

The knock at the door distracted him.

“Come in,” he ordered sharply. The door opened and in rushed Sergeant McCall. “What’s up Sergeant?”

“Two things Gov.” She paused. “The museum has just rung back, and they have never heard of Vince, or of even asking anyone to build a car.”

“Well, well, well, the lying bastard.” “Let’s see what Constable Connor comes up with, then I want very much to nail that lying, murderous bastard.”

McCall looked sombrely at him. “You have another problem, Gov.”

“What is it?”

“Simon Eliote is on his way home.”

Robertson's time had come and he knew it; the thing he had been dreading since the crash was now upon him. He picked up the phone and dialled Harrison.

"What's up, Sergeant?"

Robertson didn't know where to start, so he took a deep breath and began. "I have just had word that Simon Eliote is on his way home."

Harrison gasped. "Oh my God, what a hero's homecoming."

Robertson was confused. "Gov?"

Harrison explained. "Inspector Simon Eliote –"

Robertson butted in. "Inspector?"

Harrison continued, "Yes, Inspector – he has been reduced in rank," he paused allowing this information to sink into Robertson, "for the family of the deceased, he has taken the blame for the tragic death, till the real perpetrator, the one who tipped us off about the hoax bomb, is brought to justice."

Robertson was still in shock.

"How long is that going to take?"

"Knowing the system, it'll probably take years," he paused, "anyway you'd better get there quickly. I think it would be better coming from you."

Robertson agreed and when Harrison hung up, he sped to Eliote's home, hoping that he would get their first.

Eliote got out of the taxi, having decided to leave his car at the station. He would either get Robertson to bring it home, or he would go and collect it.

He paid the Asian driver and walked towards the Victorian maisonette's long drive.

As he turned in, he was shocked to see Robertson's car parked outside. He walked past it and up to the front door, which he found to be ajar.

As he opened the door, he had a bad feeling. Something was wrong.

"Hi, is anyone at home?" he called. "Hello, Rosy, Michael, Jane, anyone?" He walked upstairs and into the three bedrooms, which were all empty and quiet. Then he returned downstairs and into the kitchen: still nobody, and nobody in the study.

In the front sitting room, he found Robertson sitting waiting for him with a folder. He stood up when Simon entered the room.

"Dick?" Robertson sort of smiled at his friend. "What are you doing here and where is my family?"

Robertson looked solemnly at him. "Simon, I think you should sit down. Please." Eliote sank into his leather armchair and Robertson fixed him a double whisky, "here, you are going to need this."

Eliote took the glass and looked at his friend. "Dick, what is it, what's wrong?"

"I'm…" Robertson froze, not knowing where to start.

"Just tell me what the fuck is going on. Where's Rosy?"

Robertson sat down, took a couple of deep breaths and began.

"While you were in your disciplinary, there was a terrible accident."

Eliote interrupted, "Yeah, I heard about it on the radio in the taxi on the way home. The road is still semi-closed."

Robertson continued, "The accident involved two cars and a lorry. One of the cars was a red Escort." Eliote's body started to tighten up. "The car split into two parts, the front part was embedded into the lorry and the back had been thrown on to the opposite lane."

Eliote got up and approached the window. "No, don't tell me anymore, I don't want to hear it."

But Robertson continued, "I have to Simon, I am so, so sorry." "When I got there, I found three corpses; I personally identified them Simon, as Rosy, Jane and Michael,"

Eliote threw the glass at the wall. "No! Oh God, no!" He placed his head in his hands and sobbed, whispering, 'Please, God, no.'

Robertson approached him and touched his shoulder.

"I'm sorry, Simon, I thought it best coming from me. I did attempt to contact you, but was told I could not disturb your tribunal."

Eliote looked up at him, anger in his eyes.

"You could have interrupted it, of course you could – I would have," he shouted at his friend. "If this had been you, I would have entered that room, no matter how important it was." He approached Robertson, his face contorted in anger. "They are dead and you were told you couldn't contact me… Call yourself a friend? Get out of my house!"

Robertson stayed where he was, knowing this was the pain talking, not his friend.

"I'm not going anywhere; I have to tell you how they died."

Eliote turned and went and poured himself another glass of whisky.

"Okay, tell me," he snapped. "Tell me how they died." "You said the car was in pieces so what happened?"

"Seems the car had been welded and bolted together." Robertson took a deep breath. "A mechanic told us that if a car like yours had been involved in any sort of accident, serious or otherwise, fatalities were a high risk."

Eliote couldn't believe what he was hearing; he hoped it was a big surprise and that they would all spring around the corner welcoming him home.

"So what you're trying to tell me, Dick, is that I had bought a car that was a wreck to begin with, a car that shouldn't have gone on the road?"

Robertson nodded sombrely. "Yes, Simon, I am afraid so. I am so, so sorry."

looked back at him and coldly said, “Sorry won’t ack, Dick!” He swigged down more whisky and ured himself another one, while Robertson watched, wondering if he would feel the same if the tables had been turned and it was Simon telling him that his wife had been killed.

Eliote looked at Robertson, hatred and anger in his eyes.

“I want to be alone, please go.” Robertson tried to argue but Eliote stopped him. “Please, just go.”

Robertson placed the folder on the coffee table and grabbed his coat, turning before he left. “If it’s any consolation, I am close to bringing someone to justice for the deaths.”

Eliote grabbed the bottle of whisky and went and sat down on the leather sofa. “Just go,” he ordered.

Robertson nodded and said, “If you need me, you know my number, he then turned and left.

Eliote looked deeply into the glass in his hand and wept, wishing he had not gone to work that morning. If he hadn’t, maybe he would have been killed with them, the whole family together. He looked down at the whisky on the coffee table and poured himself another double. What had he got left?

As he drank the whisky something in his mind clicked. He felt like he was no longer in control; the pain was gone, replaced by nothing, his body and mind were calm, he was dead inside. Now he knew what he wanted, and that was to be with his loved ones, not alone.

Struggling to stand up, he grabbed hold of the sofa and used it to get to the wall. He then used the wall to hold himself up, his body wanted to collapse in a heap on the floor, but his mind was made up. He climbed the stairs and headed to the medicine cabinet.

He grabbed the three boxes of headache tablets and went into the master bedroom, opened every sachet and tipped the tablets onto the bed. Then with tears in his eyes and feeling at peace with himself, he popped all forty-eight tablets into his mouth and swallowed the lot, washing them down with the whisky.

After looking at a photo on the bedside table of the whole family, he whispered to them as if they were near, “I’m coming, my loves.” He then drank the rest of the whisky and lay down on the bed beside his old and beloved cuddly dog, closed his eyes and waited.

The tears stopped and as he cuddled up to the tatty old soft toy, he knew his wait was over as he felt his consciousness slipping away.

He whispered once again, “I am…” then the world was gone, the pain was gone, he was in total darkness, he felt nothing and he was no more.

THE DEATHLY ANGEL

By
Kevin Bailey

CHAPTER FIVE

Outside Robertson looked in to the back of the car and realised he had some of the family items from the crash, also a set of keys.

After grabbing the keys and the items he went back into the house.

"Simon," he shouted, "I have some personal effects from the crash. I know it's not the right time but I feel you should have them." He paused, waiting for a reply from his friend and colleague. "Simon, Simon," he called and looked into the sitting room, where he had left him alone, but the room was empty. "Simon," he shouted again.

The feelings he had now worried him. Had he done something stupid? He wondered as he checked the lower-floor rooms.

He started to climb the stairs and noticed wet spots, which he touched and smelt his fingers. It was whisky. "Shit," he cursed and ran up the stairs. He had never been up here before, so he would have to check one room after the other. "Simon, where the fuck are you?" he said as he entered room after room.

When he came to the last door, he saw more whisky stains on the cream carpets.

Through the gap at the side of the half-opened door, he saw the boxes of tablets and the empty bottle of whisky; he slowly opened the door and walked in.

"Simon?" he said anxiously, but his gaze turned to the large mirror at the bottom of the bed and there, he saw Simon in a heap cuddled up to a soft toy. "Oh shit," he said and ran to him to check his pulse; it was beating but very slowly.

He took out his phone from inside his jacket and phoned for an ambulance, he told them the address and that the patient had taken an overdose.

Then he grabbed him and tried to shake him.

"Simon," he shouted. "Stay with me, Simon, please."

A couple of minutes later the front door burst open and in came two paramedics, carrying a stretcher.

"This way, quick," Robertson told them, he's taken some drugs.

The paramedics examined Eliote and one asked, "Why did he want to end his own life?"

Robertson said, "Because I had just told him that, while he was in a meeting that would determine his future in the force, a fatal accident killed his wife and two children."

The paramedic shook his head forlornly. "Sorry, mate," he said and then they lifted Eliote on to the stretcher, and wheeled him quickly to the ambulance. Robertson locked the door and jumped in, and they drove off with their lights and sirens blazing.

Simon was alive, barely. At the hospital, Robertson dialled the station, and was put straight through to Harrison.

"Dick, what's up?" Robertson explained everything and his superior answered, "I am on my way, Sergeant,"

Robertson returned to the unit. Through the glass, he could see Eliote with pipes in his mouth and nose to help him breathe. He also had a heart monitor attached to his chest; he looked awful.

About ten minutes later, Harrison approached him.

"How is he?" Robertson looked at him.

"They haven't told me." He indicated Eliote's supine form. "Look at him."

"It was better coming from you, Dick. If he had come home and found no one or heard it on the radio, imagine what would have happened," Harrison said. "Anyway, you saved his life."

"I know, guv, but I still feel bad." Harrison didn't say any more and the two officers waited, but Dick was distracted by his phone vibrating in his pocket. He took it out and saw it was the station.

"Robertson…ah, Connor, what you got for me?" He listened intently. "Really, that lying bastard…" He looked at the resuscitation room door and replied, "I'm on my way, I want Vince in an interview room when I get there, with or without his solicitor, understand?"

"What's up?" Harrison asked.

"I just had Connor check on Vince's activities. The bastard's been lying to me."

Harrison could sense the anger in Robertson, and said, "Do you think it's wise for you to continue with this enquiry? I could get Cole to deal with it."

Robertson looked coldly at his boss.

"With all due respect, guv, I want to get this piece of scum off the streets, and I wouldn't trust Cole with trying to find an apple. Besides, I owe him," he pointed at the door, "that much." Harrison nodded. "Go get that son of bitch," he said.

Robertson left Harrison to wait for news on Simon Eliote.

***

Back in Chelmesbury night had now descended, groups of people who had been out drinking and partying were on their way home, and no one seemed bothered that a serial killer was on the loose.

Heading to a housing estate on the outskirts of the town and overlooking picturesque views of the countryside were five friends.

The group – three men and two women – were drunkenly horsing around on their way home from a night club. One of the men tripped over a dustbin bag and fell into a puddle, but he laughed as his girlfriend helped him up. "Bloody bag," he said kicking it, spewing its contents across the street.

They were approaching a wooden fence, behind which was an old hedge, marking the outer boundary of the estate

Crouching low, squeezed into the gap between the hedge and fence, a dark figure watched the progress of the five friends through a telescopic lens attached to a silenced rifle. Satisfied that he'd correctly lined up his target, he squeezed the trigger, feeling the recoil of the gun even as one of the women fell. The other woman screamed as a second shot took down her male companion.

Chaos erupted in the small cul-de-sac as people came out of their houses to find out what was wrong.

In all the confusion no one heard the sound of an engine start and a small car drive away.

THE DEATHLY ANGEL

By
Kevin Bailey

CHAPTER SIX

Frashier was just about to leave the station and head home when his phone went Off "Frashier."

It was Day again. "Sorry, Gov, but there's been a shooting in Aden Close, two people dead and Strong is on his way."

"Okay, Day, I'll be there in ten."

When he arrived, he was greeted by a detective constable.

"What happened?" Frashier ordered.

The officer started his report, "it happened about thirty minutes ago, sir. The two deceased," he looked down at his notebook, "Teresa Bennett, Richard Hatfield, Richard's friend Graham Thomas, Anita Bennett and her boyfriend Anthony Glastonbury were walking home from a local club. They had left the Lazy Fox hotel early and were approaching Teresa's house, but when approximately thirty feet from the front door, they were fired upon twice."

Frashier patted him on the back. "Good work Johnny."

William got into a protective overall, and walked towards the white tent where an annoyed Strong, wasting no time, began giving his briefing.

"The weapon was a rifle of some sort." He pointed quickly to the bullet holes on both victims. "The skull shattered on impact, so they would have died immediately." The doctor pointed to the fence. "According to our ballistics, the shot came from over there." He got up off the ground and beckoned Frashier. "So let us quickly go and investigate." He grabbed his bag and the two friends headed for the fence in the dark. Strong held a torch and they could see scorch marks and black dust. They had indeed found the killer's shooting point.

Frashier said, "Whoever the killer was knew about the fence, so it's probably someone familiar with the area and the family." He could see DS Day approaching so he apologized to Strong and he and Day headed for the house. A constable outside opened the door and they were shown to a large front room.

Before entering the room, they removed their protective overalls and handed them to the officer who had allowed them in.

Frashier opened the door and immediately noticed the family photos on the wall; they looked like a happy bunch, he thought, and couldn't understand why anyone would want to spoil that happiness.

The surviving friends were together on the settee clutching cups of tea.

Frashier felt like he was intruding so he went to the kitchen, beckoning Day to follow.

"Miranda, can you bring the friends in one at a time so I can interview them?"

"Yes, sir," she said.

They were all shocked at the shooting and asked him to bring the culprit to justice. At Anita's interview Frashier asked, "Was there anyone who would want her dead?"

"No, my auntie was well known and well-liked by everyone in Chelmesbury." Anita paused and wiped away tears on her sleeve. "She has lived here since she was born."

"What about boyfriends? Would any of them want her dead?"

"No, of course not, she was a loving person." A thought came into her mind. "Her last one, Steve Marston, was a bit freaky, they had been together for years, but after a terrible row they split up." Frashier stopped writing and looked over at the upset woman.

"Why do you say he was a bit freaky?"

"Cause he was."

"Explain."

"She got scared 'cause he would sit in his car and watch the house, ring her in the night, text her all the time and stalk her." She sighed. "But he has just recently met someone else and apologised to her for causing her so much pain. According to what she told me last night, she hasn't heard from him for months."

Frashier was intrigued by this information and asked, "Where does this Steve Marston live?"

She explained and he thanked her and said that they would probably be in contact with her again, then she headed back towards her boyfriend and they sat cuddling each other.

One of the constables asked Frashier if he wanted a drink, to which he nodded and he was given a cup of tea.

He walked outside with the cup and watched as a black van reversed to the tent and the two bodies were loaded into the van and it drove away.

Moments later, he heard a car speeding towards this end of the cul-de-sac. It came round the corner at the top of the road and pulled up sharply outside the police barricade. A tall man with black hair and a large face spoke to the officer on duty there and Frashier was called over.

Ted Rowlings, the children's father, identified himself and Frashier led him into the house. The children ran to him and he hugged them tightly.

***

Charlotte watched all this from her green Mini. She got out and approached a post-box and peered over, watching the house and the activity around it, but her thoughts were on catching Frashier before he left.

She ignored the feeling of anger, hatred and satisfaction that was emanating from an unknown person who also was watching from a dark location, nearby.

Looking down at her watch, she knew it would be late before Frashier left, so headed back to her Mini and grabbed the local paper and continued to read.

***

Next morning in a smart housing estate in the centre of Chelmesbury, an alarm clock started ringing on the bedside table of Steve Marston. His mother June banged on the stairwell wall and shouted at her son.

"Come on, Steve, time to get up; it's seven thirty!"

There was a groaning sound from one of the rooms upstairs and the floorboards creaked.

Steve was a lanky young man with brown hair, dark green eyes, and a pale complexion.

He opened his bedroom door and after yawning and stretching, he headed to the bathroom. He had a shower, dressed in green trousers and white shirt with a tie, then went downstairs and had a breakfast of toast and strawberry jam with a large cup of coffee.

As he went into the front room, he switched on the telly and watched the local news on BBC.

The familiar face of the newsreader began: "The top story this morning: two separate murders in the peaceful Shropshire town of Chelmesbury have surprised residents and alarmed the police." Steve watched intently when he heard Chelmesbury mentioned.

One of the clips on the television showed Lovers Lane, and Steve smiled remembering a past encounter in the lane. Another clip of a street in Chelmesbury surprised Steve and he almost choked on his toast, staring at the screen as if frozen. "At approximately ten o'clock last night, a couple were shot dead by an unknown assassin. A police spokesman at the scene of the shooting gave us this statement."

The screen changed to show another man who was captioned as Detective Inspector William Frashier, investigating from Chelmesbury CID.

"We have no answers to why these two were attacked and are describing the incidents as tragic wastes of life. Teresa Bennett and Richard Hatfield have been identified as the victims; we are asking anyone who has any information to come forward, thank you." He paused. "We also would like to take this opportunity for anyone who was in Lovers Lane the night before to step forward if they saw or heard anything concerning the stabbing."

Steve burst into tears. After grabbing his suit jacket, he ran out of the house, not listening to the rest of the broadcast or the following reports…

"And in other news, following a serious accident on the A4, police raided a premises in Hounslow, south west London and found several stolen vehicles that were being used to make cut n' shuts, they arrested two suspects and a police officer was killed in the raid."

His mum came into the front room to say something to her son, but found the telly on and the front door wide open.

"Bloody kids, as if we got money to burn," she said slamming the front door and turning the television off.

Steve hadn't heard his mum slamming the door, he didn't even hear the traffic on the busy A49, or the children playing in the park as he ran past them, he just ran down the road as fast as he could towards Aden Close.

As his heart pounded, he didn't know what was making him run – adrenalin, fear, a bit of both – no matter what it was, he had to see it for himself; he just couldn't believe what he had heard.

Aden Close was a housing association-run area and each house in the street was identical to the next.

When Steve approached the close, the police blockade was still in operation. He looked at the house, somewhere he had spent many happy times – birthdays, Christmas, his engagement party – it had been his home for so long, but he hadn't really looked at the other houses in the street.

As he quickly glanced over to a fence that had been cordoned off by tape, a police officer approached and asked him if he was all right.

"I didn't believe what I had seen on television, but it's true, isn't it?" The officer nodded and Steve turned and ran back home.

As he ran he cried and after grabbing what he needed from home he headed for the station.

He jumped onto the train as soon as it pulled into the station and as it left Chelmesbury, he stared out of the window and sobbed.

***

Detective Sergeant Miranda Day had come back to Aden Close early to try and get a head start on the case. She had seen Steve running back from the close but he could have been a person running to catch a train or a bus, so had paid no attention to him

She was met by Strong's assistant, Penny, who informed Day that Doctor Strong was back at Lover's Lane.

Penny was investigating behind the hedge, Day had her protective gear on and approached the hole in the wall which had been cut away and taken to the lab. They looked down at the floor and found two empty cartridges and some boot prints.

Penny got to work and collected the shells and started taking casts of the prints, whilst Day set off to follow the footprints.

They led her to an industrial business park. The footsteps stopped at some indistinct tyre tracks.

Day took off her coverall and looked across the road, to a garage with a camera facing the business park

She approached the garage entrance and entered. A young mousy-haired lad looked up and she took out her badge.

"I am Detective Sergeant Miranda Day from Chelmesbury CID. We are investigating the Murder of Teresa Bennett and Richard Hatfield." The cashier nodded. "I see you have a camera on the wall outside facing the pumps and industrial site?" "we would like to borrow the footage from last night, if we can, please." The young lad got up from his desk and headed out the back.

A few moments later, a stout gentleman approached and handed her a compact disc.

"You're very lucky, Sergeant. At ten o'clock, I record over the night's surveillance film." She thanked him and gave him a receipt for the CD, then walked out of the door.

"That was bad last night," the young lad said. "My brother will be devastated." the stout gentleman looked at him and replied.

"Of course Steve used to go out with Teresa, didn't he?" the cashier nodded and watched as the attractive detective walked back across the road.

"He did and I hope for his sake that they find the killer!"

***

Steve got off the train at Glayton, the busy market town some thirty miles from Chelmesbury.

He still had puffy eyes, but managed to make it into the town centre, where he managed a small book store and was very popular with his staff and customers.

He opened the front door in the shop and typed in the code to disarm the alarms, then after locking the door behind him he headed up to his office.

As he walked down the corridor to his office, he thought of the happier times with Teresa. She had been his everything, his life, and now she was gone.

He took out a key and opened his office door, walked in and placed his belongings on the sofa. At the sink, he splashed water onto his face, dried himself and walked over to his desk.

He heard the main door open and close and a couple of seconds later his assistant manager Patricia Crane came in and comforted him.

"I think you should go home, Steve," she said lovingly.

"What, and sit and mope all day? No, Pat I won't" he said commandingly, "we have a bookshop to run; anyway it'll take my mind off it." even though Steve knew his assistant manager was worried about him, he stayed the same and she eventually gave up and went and opened the store.

Steve sat at his desk and read through the memos from his headquarters, but the thought of his ex-loves death kept haunting him.

And Like Simon Eliote in London, Steve's mind kept going over the same thing: if only he had been there, maybe she wouldn't be dead.

***

Miranda Day returned to the station with the CD and whilst she sat at her desk, William Frashier walked into CID looking pleased with himself, especially considering he had just come from a meeting with his boss, Chief Superintendent Brightly.

"What's with you, guv?"

He touched his nose and smiled, grinning from ear to ear. "It's none of your business, Miranda." She gave him a stern look and he walked up to her desk and whispered in her ear, "Can you keep a secret?"

"Of course I can," she said almost annoyed at him.

"Well, I just spoke to Brightly about applying for the job of head of CID and she said that I had a great chance as no one else had applied for the post."

Miranda smiled. "Congratulations, guv," she said.

"I haven't got the job yet, Miranda, but thanks anyway." He paused, still beaming with pride. "I have wanted this job for years, but DCI John Webb," he said with venom, "didn't think I had it in me."

"He was a stuck up git," Day said. "Anyway, when will you know?"

"I have a meeting with the board on Monday and I'll find out a week later if I've been successful." He looked around the CID office. "So I want this lot working hard to solve the shooting in Aden Close and the stabbing in Lovers Lane. If I am head, then I'm going to need a bloody good Inspector." He winked.

"OK, guv, I'll help you get the post."

"Thanks. Call the team together in the new observation room; I want to see if we can get the investigations moving faster."

She nodded and picked up the phone.

***

THE DEATHLY ANGEL

By
Kevin Bailey

CHAPTER SEVEN

Back in London the newly demoted Detective Inspector Simon Eliote awoke and looked at the ceiling. This wasn't heaven, it was a hospital room.

His head hurt as he tried to sit up, making him curse under his breath.

A passing nurse happened to see that he was awake, walked in and looked at him with a big warm smile.

"Welcome back, Mr Eliote, you gave us all a nasty shock, going in and out of consciousness like you did."

"I don't want to be here."

"And where do you want to be, darling?"

"Dead," he said his voice bitter.

The nurse left, a worried expression on her face, and spoke to a doctor and another man who were standing outside the room.

Simon could not hear what they were saying, so instead leaned back against the pillow and tried to assimilate all that had happened to him and his family.

Sometime later, he was startled from his reverie by the silent arrival of a grey-suited man, whose features were at first difficult to make out in the darkness of the room. But when Simon could see who the man was, he sighed heavily.

"Magna McGuiness, what the hell do you want?"

"Hello, Simon, I heard the news, and I wanted to say that I am truly sorry."

"I don't want your sympathy," Simon snarled. "I don't want a job, I don't want anything from you, Magna."

"I know you don't think much of me anymore," Magna said, "but I want you as a friend again."

"You want me to be your friend again?" Magna nodded. "Forget it," Simon said.

"I know what I did was wrong. I should never have left you on your own, especially in a situation where you could have been killed," Magna said. "But since then I have protected you."

Simon turned and laughed at him. "Ha, you protected me? I just got demoted to DI – where were you then, Magna?"

"I tried to get the case dropped, but who am I to interfere?" Magna said.

"I heard you were the assistant head of Special Branch. I was supposed to be one of your agents."

Magna sighed heavily. "That you may be, Simon, but according to sources, there's more going on here than meets the eye. Somebody wants you out of London."

Simon sat up. "Why?"

Magna shrugged his shoulders. "I don't know yet, but I'm looking in to it"

***

Superintendent Dorothy Brightly's office phone rang.

"Hello," she answered,

"Good morning, Superintendent Brightly."

"Who is this?"

"I am known only as John and all I will say is I am part of MI5."

"Is this a bloody windup?" she snapped. "I will have this call traced and I'll have you arrested for wasting police time."

The voice was calm, clear. "Superintendent Brightly, I am afraid tracing my call will get you into serious trouble."

"What can I do for you then John?"

"I understand you have a vacancy at your station?"

She still wasn't sure whether this was a windup.

"A vacancy? Indeed we have one here. Why, are you thinking of applying, John?" she said sarcastically.

"Please do not patronize me," he said almost snapping at her. "I could have you demoted to a mere constable, or worse still have you removed from the force you love," he paused, "and to prove my credentials further, I will open a file we have on you." She heard papers being shuffled through. "When you were a seventeen-year-old student, you had trouble with –"

She stopped him. "You've made your point. I believe you, sir."

"Good. I have sent a request to the chief constable that the post you have at Chelmesbury has now been filled."

"May I ask by whom, sir?"

"You may ask, Superintendent, but I will not tell you that yet. Plans are in place." "I understand that one of your own officers, a..." again she could hear papers being shuffled "...Detective Inspector William Frashier, has taken an interest in the job."

"Yes, sir, he has applied," Brightly answered.

"Maybe he should be told that the chief constable wants someone with a little more experience to take the job," John suggested. "Leave it a few days and then inform him."

"Very well, I'll –"

"I will keep you informed of the situation, Superintendent." The phone went dead and Brightly sat and stared at the wall.

How was she going to tell Frashier? She stood up and looked out towards the new CID building and saw Frashier in the observation room, going over the cases. He was a good officer, and should be the new DCI. He had worked hard for it.

She headed over to the CID building and up to the observation room.

***

Simon sat in the hospital bed, studying his ex-friend; how much he hated him, this man had left him to die on a fact finding mission in Iraq, and if it hadn't been for a local who took pity on him and offered him a phone, he would surely not be here.

"What are you up to? No, forget it, I'm not interested; whatever it is, I don't want it so please go."

"Please believe me, Simon; I only want to talk to you

"What could you say to make me want to talk?"

Magna walked back towards the bed and looked at his friend. "I have heard of an opening at Chelmesbury CID for a Detective Chief Inspector." Simon sighed but Magna continued, "If you want it, I am sure I can pull some favours with a few of my contacts in the West Mercia Constabulary."

"Really? Well, don't bother because I have decided to leave the force," Simon said.

"Okay," Magna said, deflated, "but if you change your mind, this is the file." He placed a folder on the side table and started heading back towards the door and grabbed the handle.

"What's in this for you Magna?" Simon asked.

"Nothing, Simon, I was looking out for you, but obviously brotherly love is not good enough."

He opened the door and left, leaving Simon alone.

After a while Simon picked up the file with curiosity. Why on earth would he take a job in his old hometown, especially in that decrepit old station?

What he saw as he looked over the pages in the file shocked him. A new superintendent had arrived and had gained support from the chief constable to start a rebuilding programme of the station.

He looked at the photos of the old buildings and for the first time, he smiled, remembering his time as a constable in the dreary, humiliating old place. That was why he had asked for a transfer to London.

Then he saw the pictures and blueprints of the newly constructed station, and what he saw surprised him: a state-of-the-art CID building, and the old buildings still standing were to be refurbished to offer the community the support they needed.

In his mind he imagined himself working in that building, but he couldn't leave London, it was his and his family's home; all his memories were here.

A knock at the door brought Simon out of his thoughts, and he looked up expecting to see Magna in front of him again, but instead it was DS Robertson who had entered.

"Sorry, Simon, were you resting, I can go if you were..."

Simon shook his head and said, "No, please..." He beckoned his friend to sit on a chair beside him. "How are you, Dick?"

"I am not good," Robertson said, "but hey," he saw the file on Simon's chest, "what have you got there?"

"Just a job offer in Shropshire, an old friend dropped it off for me." Eliote handed the folder to Robertson who started to go through it.

"Blimey that's a great offer!" He paused to look at his friend. "You are thinking of taking the job, right?"

Simon shook his head. "I'm not going to take it, Dick."

"But why ever not?"

"Two things: first, the person who gave me that file will want something in return. And second, this is my home, Dick, I can't leave, it's all I have left of them."

Robertson stood up and came and sat on the side of the bed. “It’s your decision, buddy, but as you got stuff to sort out I’ll come back later, OK?” Simon nodded.

“When I get out of hospital, can I stay at yours for a bit, till I build the confidence to go home?”

Robertson got up and approached the door. “No problems, I’ll tell Evelyn to get the spare room sorted.”

“You’re a good friend Dick.”

Dick smiled warmly at him. “See you later,” he said and left.

Simon watched him go and looked at the file. Like his friend had said, it was a tempting offer, he would again be DCI Eliote, which wasn’t as good as Detective Superintendent Eliote, but hey it was something; his wife would love that, he couldn’t wait to tell her.

At that moment there was a cold wind in the room and this made him think of his loss.

***

As Simon had read in his file, the Observation Room was a state-of-the-art briefing room; it was like a small theatre auditorium and all the chairs had small table’s which could be extended to give the sitter something to put their papers on to write notes.

At the front of the room was a large plasma screen, which was attached to a huge computer housed underneath the small raised area, where the briefing was conducted from.

Just in front of the screen was a highly sophisticated lectern, it had a small touch screen terminal built in and if the person giving the briefing used a white pen, the image could be seen on the large screen.

Standing to one side of the lectern was Frashier, the pen in his hand, and he was looking at the whole team who were watching the recording that DS Day had taken from the garage.

They had been watching it for a while, when at about nine forty on the readout a small car appeared and turned into the car park of the units. The driver of the car got out and disappeared into the darkness.

A tall, bearded uniformed officer took out a remote control and fast forwarded. At about nine fifty, the driver returned, went to the boot of the car, took out a heavy carrier and returned to the darkness.

The officer fast forwarded again till about five past ten when the man came running back, chucked everything quickly into the car and drove off, almost hitting a fence as he did so.

Frashier looked at the officer who pressed play once more and they watched the tape again. Everyone in the room tried to concentrate on the driver and the number plate of the car.

After a few more viewings of the DVD, the officer took out the disc and handed it to Frashier.

"Right then, I want checks on this car, I couldn't make out the number plate, but there can't be that many of them in Chelmesbury." He was about to give more orders to his team when he heard a female voice shout his name.

"Inspector Frashier." William looked up and saw Superintendent Brightly standing at the back of the room.

"Ma'am?" She walked up to him and as she did she gave her orders, which shocked Frashier.

"I want you to concentrate on the shooting, use…" she looked around at the officers in the room and said their names, "Dawson, Pickington, Wright and Hagley." She paused looking at the officers and then at Frashier who was upset.

He knew something was wrong. Since the death of his previous DCI, she had left him alone to run CID, but now she was giving orders.

He was about to say something when she looked at him, sternly.

"I gave you an order Inspector. If you do not follow my orders, then Sergeant Day can take over and you will be suspended."

He was taken aback and quickly replied, "Right, ma'am," Brightly moved to one side, to allow Frashier to give the team his orders.

"Dawson, you and Hagley check the houses up and down the A49 check the businesses and see if any other cameras were aimed at the road, we might get another picture of the car." They nodded and then he looked at the rest. "Pickington, I want you to go round all the local gunsmiths and gun-enthusiast groups, see if anyone has bought a rifle in the last few days and then join the others and make door-to-door enquiries further afield; objective: see if anyone knows the car and if anyone wanted the two victims dead." The group started to talk amongst themselves as they got up and left.

Frashier nodded at DC Wright, a black haired skinny officer who wore jeans and a smart navy blue top. "DC Wright, you're with me."

He gave his superior an almost evil look and then the two officers left, watched by the others. When they left the briefing continued.

Frashier was angry, he had wanted to be involved with the stabbing, but instead he had been taken off that case; why, he did not know. He headed to his grey BMW that was parked in his spot. DC Wright got into the driver side and said, "Where do you want to go, sir?"

"I was going over the case notes before the meeting, and in an interview with one of the witnesses she mentioned a Steve Marston, so we will go and interview him, see if he knows anything."

DC Wright started the engine and looked at the address on the piece of paper that Frashier was carrying. "Twenty Rayon

Close, okay." She placed the car in gear and drove out of the station.

***

DI Simon Eliote walked into Hounslow CID, tapped his six-digit number into the key code machine, and entered the station.

A couple of officers greeted him as he passed, heading for the interview room.

Outside the room, he took a deep breath and opened the door.

In the interview room Robertson was getting angry; he was standing against the wall and listening to Vince babbling on about his innocence.

The room went quiet as Eliote walked in and sat down in front of Vince and his solicitor. Robertson looked worryingly at him, but Eliote just stared deep into Vince's eyes.

"Detective Inspector Simon Eliote has entered the room, time ten forty-eight," Robertson said.

"Simon Eliote?" Vince said.

"I wanted to come face to face with the man who killed my family."

"I didn't kill them," Vince protested.

Eliote glared at him and spat, "You may not have driven the car but you killed them." "I don't see horns or a fork attached to a tail, you ain't red, but in all ways you are the devil and I will always hate you."

Robertson walked over to Eliote and whispered in his ear. "Simon, you shouldn't be here."

Eliote let his anger be known. "*I shouldn't be here*?" he snapped. "That bastard," he pointed at Vince, "killed my wife and my two children, so don't tell me I shouldn't be here." Robertson backed away.

"Sorry," Vince said.

"I don't want your apologies, but you will be sorry."

Miss Wilson looked over at him. "Are you threatening my client, Inspector?"

"That's Detective Inspector, thank you, and yes, I am – got a problem with that?"

She nodded and was about to say something when he blanked her and looked at Vince. "Do you know how it feels to lose someone, Vince, someone you love?"

Vince shook his head. "No."

Eliote stood up and walked to the wall. "It's like a part of you has been ripped away," he said. "I wanted you to see me, see the man you destroyed and I hope for your sake, you never lose something important." He walked to the door and left, slamming it behind him, making Vince jump.

"Detective Inspector Eliote has left the room, followed by DS Robertson," McCall said to the recording machine.

Outside the interview room, Simon leant against the wall of the corridor, and said, "He ain't a monster, Dick, I was hoping he was."

Dick placed a reassuring hand on his shoulder. "He is a monster, Simon, just a monster in human form."

"How could he do something so evil, build a car that is a death trap and then let someone buy it – how?" He banged his hand against the wall. "How?"

"I cannot answer that yet, my friend, but I believe that Vince is just the tip of a very big iceberg and that the real perpetrator is getting away." Robertson spotted a familiar face walking down the corridor and he beckoned him over.

"Constable Connor, can you take DI Eliote to my home?" The constable nodded and then Dick looked at Eliote. "Evelyn knows you are coming, Simon."

Eliote nodded and followed Connor, but when they got to the end of the corridor, Eliote looked back at his friend.

"Dick, I want you to crucify that bastard and the others."

Dick smiled. “You have my word, old friend. I will not rest until they are behind bars.”

Eliote nodded. “Thanks, and I’m sorry for what I said to you, you are a good friend, I will never forget that.”

“Don’t mention it, Simon. I would have said the same if it had been me.”

Dick returned to the interview room, McCall timed him back in and he sat down in the vacated chair that had just been filled by Simon.

“Was that supposed to scare my client, Inspector?” Wilson asked. Robertson ignored her.

“Okay, Vince, why don’t we just cut to the crap?”

***

THE DEATHLY ANGEL

By
Kevin Bailey

CHAPTER EIGHT

Frashier and DC Wright arrived at the address in Chelmesbury some ten minutes later.

Number twenty was right at the bottom of the close next to a railway line and when they got there they knocked on the brown door and waited for a reply. Somewhere in a back room of the house they heard a dog barking, but nothing else.

A neighbour popped her head out of an upstairs window and looked down at the two officers

"They aren't in!" she said.

Frashier called up to her, "Do you know where we can get hold of Steve Marston? It is urgent we speak to him."

The neighbour nodded. "Steve will be at work in Glayton, he runs Books for You."

Frashier thanked her and the two officers headed back to the car.

***

Back in Hounslow, Dick was angry once again. He was getting to the point of grabbing Vince and smashing his head down on the table, like Gene Hunt from *Life on Mars*.

"You're nothing but a lying wimp." Robertson slammed his hand into the table making everyone jump. "You see, Sergeant McCall here checked out your story," he pointed to the paperwork in front of him, "and another detective tracked down this creditor, Mike Swinbourne. He has heard of you."

Vince smiled. "He has verified my story then?"

"No, turns out you have never paid that debt you owe."

Vince looked at Robertson and gulped. He could see the anger building up in the officer and his mind went into hyper drive. He was about to say something in his defence but Robertson butted in.

"Now, I want answers and by jove I am going to get them, even if it means me banging you up against a wall and beating the information out of you."

James's solicitor stood up and looked coldly at Robertson. "Detective Sergeant, I must protest at the way you are treating my client."

Robertson took a couple of deep breaths, counted to five, then said, "I'm sorry, but as you could see by my reaction to Simon Eliote's entrance into the room, the family that died was a family I loved very much."

"Then maybe, you should not be conducting this interview," she said looking down her nose at him.

"No, I am the person who will get to the bottom of this case, I made a promise to DI Eliote that I would." He looked at Vince. "Right, I want some answers, matey."

"Okay, Sergeant, I am ready, but I don't want to go back to jail. Please, I'll do anything for you, grass on a couple of people, whatever you like, but please don't send me to jail."

"There is nothing that can help you now, Vince; you have killed a police officer and three civilians, so even if you could help me there is nothing I want except the truth." Robertson paused and took a couple of deep breaths just to calm himself, then he continued, "You built the car; I know that because you've already told me, but I want to know why and for whom."

"For Harry," he burst out, "he pays me very well to build these bloody things; he calls them 'funny cars'."

"You build them for Honest Harry?"

"Yes, the very same, every now and then he'll bring two smashed motors to me and pays me to build them into one."

McCall asked, "When did it start?"

"About five years ago, just after I came out of prison. He knew my dad and promised he would look after me, so he set me up with the garage and I repay that kindness by doing him a few favours."

"How many have you built?" Robertson asked.

"I've built him a car every month and have done so for five years. Where he gets the motors from is his business."

"So, Robertson said, you've built him sixty cars. How much a car?"

"I don't know."

"I'll repeat the question," he snapped, "how much does he pay you for each of these 'funny cars'?" Robertson shouted.

"Three grand a car." McCall did a quick calculation.

"One hundred and eighty thousand pounds,"

Robertson continued "with that kind of money, you can't even afford to repay a debt?"

"I have a child to support and a wife, their home is paid for, you can check that out, but the house is in her name." He paused. "I didn't want to start, but three grand to weld two cars together was too much to resist."

Robertson looked at McCall and smiled, then looked at Vince and Miss Wilson.

"Thank you, I have all the information I need," he said.

"Right, Vince," McCall said. "I need you to sign this statement, you too, Miss Wilson, as a witness." They signed and she placed it in a folder.

Robertson ended the interview, stood up and walked to the door. He opened it and beckoned the constable outside into the room and then he looked at Vince.

"Vincent David Turner, I am arresting you for manslaughter. You will be taken into custody, until you are taken to a court of law to stand trial."

The constable placed handcuffs on Vince and led him away to a cell.

"Congratulations Sergeant," Miss Wilson said coolly, "but let me tell you that I will be taking your actions in the interview to your superior." She collected her things and left the interview room.

"Well done, Dick," McCall said to him as they were walking down the corridor.

"You too, McCall." He paused as they approached a set of stairs. "Drink tonight?"

"Maybe," she said smiling, "see how we get on."

"OK," he said, returning her smile, "get Connor and a group of spare officers and go and arrest Harry. I'll get you a warrant to search and take all the info you can against him."

She left and he headed to Harrison's office.

When he opened the door, the superintendent looked up and beckoned him to sit down at one of the chairs in front of him.

"Ah, Sergeant Robertson, how's it going?" Robertson sat down in front of him

"Fine, Gov; I need a warrant so that Connor and McCall can go and search to recover information from Honest Harry's car auction, can you make that possible?"

"I'll see what I can do."

Robertson got up and headed for the door; he then turned around and looked at his superior.

"You may get a complaint from Miss Wilson, the interview didn't go as was planned and she didn't take kindly to it," the superintendent nodded and then with a lot of pride said.

“Good work, Dick,” he paused to smile, “and good luck, we’ll miss you when you leave.” Robertson nodded.

“And I’ll miss this place Gov,” he said before leaving the office.

GLAYTON
SHROPSHIRE

DC Wright parked in the multi-storey car park and the two officers headed for Books for You! This was occupying the site of the old Woolworth’s store. Frashier and Wright headed for the main counter, where an attractive young women looked up at them as they approached.

“You’ll have to wait at the back of queue, guys,” she said in a strong Shropshire accent. Frashier and Wright flashed their warrant card and she turned to a small, black-haired middle-aged woman with cold blue eyes standing next to her.

“Excuse me, Pat; there are some police officers here.” The woman took her place and looked at Frashier and Wright.

“Can I help you, officers?”

“Hi, I am Detective Inspector William Frashier, and this is Detective Constable Beverly Wright.” He paused to look around and then continued, “Sorry to disturb what must be a busy time for you, but we are investigating a shooting. Is Steve Marston around?”

Pat walked out from behind the counter and started to walk to a back door. “This way please,” she said, and escorted the officers down a long corridor. When they reached Steve’s office she knocked on the door.

“Come in,” a man’s voice said. Pat opened the door and the two officers walked into the tidy office. Steve sat at a desk and was on the phone. He beckoned the two to some chairs in front of him and they sat down. Pat closed the door behind them and returned to the shop floor.

After finishing on the phone, Steve replaced the receiver and then looked at the two officers.

"Can I help you?"

Frashier explained who they were. "We are investigating the shooting of…"

"…Teresa and Richard," Steve said softly.

"Yes, sir, and we would like to ask you some questions if we may."

Steve nodded. "Of course." DC Wright took out her notebook.

"Where were you at about ten o'clock last night?"

Steve smiled. "I was leaving my girlfriend's house at that time, Emily Trent, she lives in Glayton West." He gave them the address and continued, "I feel so sorry for Ted and the kids, he didn't like me very much when we first met, but after a while he sort of got used to me." Steve's voice caught as he said, "You make sure you catch the person who did this, Inspector."

"We will, don't worry, sir," Frashier said. "Can you think of anyone who would want to kill either Teresa or Richard?"

"Teresa, no… Richard, I'm not so sure, he was a bit of a jack the lad in the town, stealing other blokes' girlfriends and then dumping them."

"Did he steal Teresa from you, Mr Marston?" Frashier asked.

Steve looked angrily at him. "What type of question is that?"

"Just answer the question please," Frashier snapped.

"No, he didn't, me and Teresa had been apart for about two months when they got together. I was pleased for the both of them, Richard had always had a soft spot for Teresa, but because me and him were mates, he waited." He stood up and walked to a window. "I think you should leave me now, I am very busy."

"We may come back to speak to you again, Mr Marston," said Frashier standing up. "Thanks for your time."

"Drop me off near Aden close, I want to check up on Pickington and his team," Frashier told his colleague when they returned to the car. "Then I want you to check this alibi, and if anything doesn't fit, I want Steve brought in for more questioning." She nodded and started the car.

DC Wright dropped Frashier off near to where the others were and headed back to Glayton West.

Glayton West had once been a tiny village on the outskirts of Glayton, which after nineteen ninety-nine had been incorporated into the town as its western part.

This was due to the expansion of the town's boundary and the excessive building work on new housing and business estates.

DC Wright approached the slip road and turned down it. After approximately two minutes she pulled into the housing estate address that Steve had given her and found the house.

She stopped outside and parked up, then she got out and headed for the front door, pressed the buzzer and waited.

She heard the sound of footsteps and then the door was opened by a tall blonde in a figure-hugging dressing gown.

"Hello," she said in a soft voice.

DC Wright took out her warrant card and said, "Can I come in? I need to ask you some questions regarding Steve Marston."

The woman allowed the officer in and they went into the kitchen.

"Why, what's he done?" she said. "Would you like a drink, Officer?"

"Tea please, white, one sugar."

"OK." She turned to a kettle and switched it on, then she got some cups ready. "Would you like to wait in there," she pointed to a door, "I'll go and get changed." Wright nodded.

When Trent returned, she was wearing a white blouse and black trousers.

"Right, where were we?" she said, bringing in the tea. "Steve – what has he done?"

"Miss Trent, when was the last time you saw Steve?"

She poured the tea from the teapot and answered, "Last night actually, he left earlier than usual, would have been about nine thirty. I had woken him from a sleep and he was startled, he kissed me quickly and left. He had given me the excuse that he was getting up early this morning."

"Are you positive about the time, Miss Trent, it is quite important?"

She nodded and answered almost angrily, "I am, Detective, very sure."

Wright put away her notebook. "Thank you; we may need you to answer some questions at a later date."

"Okay, if I am not here I'll be at the Elephant & Castle in the high street."

Wright stood up and headed towards the front door; she thanked Miss Trent once more and then went to the BMW. When she got there, she took out her phone and dialled Frashier's number.

"Hi, Gov. Alibi isn't very good, Miss Trent is adamant that he left at nine thirty, so that would have given him enough time to get back to Chelmesbury and kill both."

"Okay I'll get someone to go to the train station and check with the station staff, to see if anyone saw him. Go and bring Steve in for questioning."

"Right, Gov." DC Wright headed back to the town centre.

Frashier placed the mobile into his pocket and turned to a black-haired officer.

"Constable Hagley, can you get to Glayton Railway station and see if anyone saw Steve Marston on the night the two victims were killed."

“Yes, Gov.” He left and Frashier headed for Brightly’s office.

Chief Superintendent Brightly was at her desk when Frashier knocked on the door.

“Come in,” she ordered and in walked Will, carrying a folder, Brightly smiled up at him. “Yes Inspector?”

“Sorry to bother you, Ma’am, but I need a search warrant to enter a suspect’s house, one Steve Marston, an ex-boyfriend to Teresa Bennett.”

Brightly nodded. “I’ll see what I can do.”

“Thank you, ma’am.” She looked at him

“Inspector, sit down please, I have some bad news for you,” Brightly said.

Frashier did as he was told.

“It’s… well, there’s no easy way of saying this, so here I go. It’s about the head of CID position: unfortunately you have been unsuccessful.”

Frashier looked coldly at her. “Can I ask why?”

“The Chief Constable doesn’t believe you are experienced enough at the moment.”

“So what you’re saying is I am not good enough.”

Brightly looked at him like a mother to a son. “I didn’t say that, Will.”

Frashier got up and walked to the door, turning before he left. “I’ll be getting the experience in CID, if you need me,” he said with sarcasm in his voice.

“Will…” But Frashier left, slamming the door behind him.

***

When DC Wright entered the bookstore once more, Pat looked at her and then shouted at Steve who was helping a trainee on the till behind. He looked up and approached the officer.

"Mr Marston," DC Wright said, "I would like you to accompany me to the station."

"Whatever for?" Steve said abruptly.

"To answer some more questions Sir." Steve looked surprised at the request but said to Pat.

"Miss Crane, will you please continue to help these trainees? I'll be at Chelmesbury police station if you need me."

***

Frashier sat outside Chelmesbury police station in the smoking area. Since his meeting with Brightly, he had chain-smoked nearly a whole packet of cigarettes; his temper was flaring.

DS Day saw him when she got back from lunch and walked over.

"What's up?" she asked.

He explained about his meeting with Brightly and she looked shocked.

"Can they do that?"

He nodded and took another puff on the cigarette. "It's been done. Now I have to wait for my time in the big job."

"It'll come, Will."

Frashier smiled at her. "Will it?" He took another puff. "You'll be head before I am."

She stood up and smiled and walked back towards the CID unit, leaving Frashier to continue smoking.

But his peace was disturbed when an officer came over to him and handed him a brown envelope. Will thanked the officer, put out his cigarette and went back into the CID building. His team were waiting for him in the observation room, and he showed them the envelope.

"I want this house searched from top to bottom," he said, grabbing his coat. "No stone unturned."

All the officers headed out to an awaiting Mercedes police van, Frashier and the others from CID jumped into another minibus and they headed to the house in Rayon Close.

THE DEATHLY ANGEL

By
Kevin Bailey

CHAPTER NINE

RAYON CLOSE

They arrived at their destination, just as Mrs Marston was leaving for her night job.

"Mrs Marston, I am Detective Inspector William Frashier from Chelmesbury CID, I have a warrant to search your house."

"Oh, yes, and what do you expect to find, Inspector?" she said sarcastically.

"A gun, the one used to kill Teresa Bennett and Richard Hatfield."

She laughed at him. "You won't find a gun in here, I hate them."

Frashier walked into her house, saying, "We shall see…"

After half an hour, a constable approached him and said, "Sir, we've found a red Vauxhall Nova, matching the car leaving the scene of the crime, parked in the family garage."

"Who owns the car?" Frashier asked turning to look at Mrs Marston.

"Why Steve of course, why"

Frashier didn't answer but simply walked with the officer out to the parking lot, where he found Forensics going over the car with a fine tooth comb.

"Anything?" he asked but the response wasn't what he wanted.

"Nothing yet, I am afraid, sir."

"Keep trying." He heard his phone ringing and took it out of his pocket; it was DC Wright, informing him that Steve was in custody. Frashier smiled. At last something was going right! "I'll be there straight away." He replaced the phone and told one of the detective constables, "If anything comes up, phone me at the station."

As he drove away from the street, he saw the green Mini and pulled up alongside. Charlotte got out and approached him.

"Are you finally ready to talk to me?" she asked.

He got out and moved forward, invading her space.

"You made me look like a fool and now you want to talk to me?" she nodded, "forget it, I don't like feeling that way," she tried to reason with him, but he approached his car and sped off.

When he arrived back at the station he was still angry from his encounter with Charlotte, so instead of going to his office to calm down, he headed straight for the interview room.

He was met by DC Beverly Wright carrying a CD recorder and looking flustered and hot.

"The other one I'm afraid isn't working," she said puffing and panting.

"OK," Frashier said, "let's do this." The two officers walked into the interview room and Wright placed the device on the table and pressed record.

***

In the main office at Honest Harry's Car Auction, its proprietor was packing all his computers into boxes and burning loads of notes in the small wood burner, when there was a knock at the door.

"Ah, my lift." Harry said to himself and approached the door and opened it.

A smartly dressed man in a long navy coat stood looking at him. Harry didn't recognise him.

"Is everything packed up, Harry?" the man said in a strong London accent. Harry nodded and grabbed his coat.

"Yes, I have burnt a few incriminating invoices, so it ain't traceable."

The long-coated man, smiled. "Good, David will be so pleased."

"Isn't Dave here?" Harry asked.

The man shook his head. "He doesn't want to be seen with you, Harry. I was ordered to sort the mess out."

Harry smiled. "Of course, of course, the group Dave represents is a legitimate business; it would be stupid of me to think he would have come here to help me, so let's go."

The man stood still. "You ain't going anywhere Harry; orders from high above, you have become a burden to us."

"What?"

"So I am here to sort out the mess, your mess." He pulled out a silenced pistol and aimed it at Harry.

"Please, I'll pay you more than they are paying."

The man pulled the trigger and shot him between the eyes. "Loyalty is worth more than money," the man said as he placed the weapon into his inside coat pocket and then doused the room with petrol. He walked outside and, making sure no one was around to see him, he took out a box of matches and after lighting his cigar, he posted the bundle of lit matches through the letter box.

After hearing the sudden whoosh as the petrol ignited, he turned and headed towards a blue Jaguar XJS and jumped in.

He started the car, whilst dialling a number.

"Yes?"

"Hi it's me, the mess is tidy.

"Good, come back in."

"OK." Smiling at his handiwork in the rear-view mirror, he placed the car in gear and drove away.

***

INTERVIEW OF STEVE MARSTON

Frashier looked at the tape recorder and then said, "Right, Steve, let's begin, shall we?" He opened a folder in front of him and took out some papers. "When we interviewed you in your store you told us 'At ten-o-clock, I was leaving my girlfriend's house. Miss Emily Trent will vouch for me,'

"So?" Steve said.

"Well, when DC Wright did speak to Miss Trent, she says she woke you at nine-thirty and you left quickly."

"I bloody well did leave at ten, I caught the ten-o-two train back to Chelmesbury, had to leg it to the station."

"That is not what she says."

"Well, she's lying."

Frashier grabbed the photo and showed it to Steve, telling the tape what he had done.

"Is this your car, Steve?"

"It looks like it."

"This photo was taken from a closed-circuit television system, it shows the murderer's escape route from an industrial estate behind Aden Close."

Steve looked once more at the photo and then glared at Frashier.

"You think that I killed them, don't you, Inspector?"

"I'll tell you what I think, Steve." He paused to sit forward in his chair. "I think you weren't over them being together and because of your anger, you decided to kill them both." There was no reaction from Steve. "You spent the evening with Miss Trent as an alibi, she would vouch for you as you have said, you got home and grabbed a gun, then in your car you drove around to the business park, where you waited for them to come home."

Steve started to get aggravated, but Frashier continued, "You waited behind the fence and saw them coming up the road, then you fired, killing them both." He paused. "What I don't know is what you did with the gun. So come on, Steve, where's the gun? Eh, Steve, where's the gun?" He kept hounding him with the same question, and Steve's solicitor protested, but Frashier persisted till suddenly Steve lost it and stood up. He smashed his fist on the table with so much strength that he nearly cracked the surface.

"I DID NOT KILL THEM!" he shouted, tears coming down his face.

"Sit down," Frashier demanded.

"I loved her," the tears ran down his face more, "I wanted to marry her, even brought her a bloody ring." He collapsed on to the table and sobbed his heart out.

Just then there was a knock at the door and Detective Constable Hagley walked in.

"Interview paused…" Frashier stood up and walked to the constable and the two of them went out of the room.

"What you got, Hagley?"

He opened his notebook and read the notes he'd made. "Sir, I have just found the ticket collector who was working on the night of the killing. He says that the trains were about an hour late that night, there had been cows on the line, so even if he had left his alibi's house at nine thirty, he would not have got in till after the shooting," "he also remembered Steve because they had talked about life in general."

"Is he sure?"

Hagley nodded. "Yes sir. He had started the conversation by waking Steve up," "it means we have the wrong man."

"It would seem so." Frashier shook his head. "I thought we had the right man, how wrong was I?"

"What about the car?" DC Wright questioned.

"It can't have been his." He started to walk away and then turned. "Go and inform Steve that he is free to go, apologise for any inconvenience caused him, and I'll be in my office going over where I went wrong." Hagley nodded and entered the room, pressing record as he spoke.

"Interview of Steve Marston terminated; suspect is free to go."

Steve looked up at the constable, surprised at this change. "Are you speaking the truth?"

Hagley nodded and apologised and Steve got up and left the station.

Frashier sat in his office going over the case notes; there had to be something he was missing, but everything seemed to point to Steve. He had gone over every detail of the case, and now he rubbed the tiredness from his eyes and made himself a cup of coffee. He sat back down and went back over everything yet again, but he came to the same conclusion.

After a while he stood up and approached the window and looked out over Chelmesbury.

Maybe Brightly and the Chief Constable were right, he thought. Maybe he wasn't experienced enough for the top job?

He returned to his desk and again went back through the file.

***

Back in Hounslow, Dick too was annoyed, especially as Connor had rung him to say he should get to Honest Harry's as it was on fire. He had rushed there, as Harry was his next step in a hopefully long ladder, but when he arrived he cursed at the charred remains of Honest Harry's Car Auction.

The chief fire-fighter approached him as he got out of his car and gave him his report. "Looks like arson," he said. "We've found several petrol containers and a charred match. And, uh, there are human remains in the main office area."

Dick thought of Harry. "Bloody hell," he said. "Okay, has Pathology got to work yet?"

"Yeah, their over there." The fire-fighter pointed at several people in protective overalls examining the hut. Robertson nodded and walked towards them.

A young man saw him approach and stood up to greet him.

"Is there much to go on, Nick?" Robertson asked him.

The young doctor shook his head.

"Nothing really," he said in a Solihull accent, "shot through the head, point blank range." He showed the detective the bullet wound. "I think this was a hit."

"What makes you think that, Doctor?" Robertson asked.

"Just the way this looks: shot and then burnt to a crisp; sounds like a planned attack to me." Robertson cursed again and then thanked the doctor.

"Well, that's that sorted, I can't go any further." He walked back to his car and called over at Nick, "Report on my desk, when you can, Doctor."

"No problems."

Robertson smiled, jumped in his car and drove away.

***

The Deathly Angel

By
Kevin Bailey

CHAPTER TEN

A WEEK LATER

Simon sat at his wife's graveside, a rose in his hand; he was wearing a black suit, rosy red tie, white shirt and a yellowy brown long coat. Tears were trickling down his eyes.

As he sat there, he was touching the earth and speaking to his dead wife.

"Oh Rosy, I wanted to be with you so much, but I have failed you, I couldn't even kill myself." Aware of a presence, he looked up to see a tall man in a grey suit watching him from the edge of the graveyard. He recognised him as Magna.

"What the hell does he want?" he wondered out loud, then looked down at his wife's grave and blew her a kiss. "Good bye, my darling, I will always love you," and with one more smile and blowing her another kiss, he walked quickly following Magna out of the graveyard and into a car.

"It was a great service, Simon," Magna said as Eliote sat down beside him.

"What do you want, Magna?"

"I told you at your bedside, I want you to head this unit in Chelmesbury."

"And I told you I didn't want to," he paused and looked coldly at his friend, "Question; what the fuck is in it for you?"

"Nothing, just looking after you, that's all."

Eliote wasn't so sure. "Oh come on, I wasn't born yesterday."

Magna pulled out a folder and passed it to him. "Okay, this is a report from the Chief Commissioner; he wants Chelmesbury to be the model, which, if it succeeds, all other stations will hopefully follow." "Did you read the file I gave you?"

Eliote looked back out of the window at the grave. "Been a bit busy."

Magna didn't even bat an eye lid.

"The placement of Dorothy Brightly is beneficial to his cause; she was and still is, his golden girl. If she fails he fails."

Eliote nodded. "Of course, and if I help his cause, make it a success, it looks good on you." Magna sort of nodded. "And as you want the top job at Special Branch, he will help you get it."

"Something like that Simon," Magna said as he placed the file back into his briefcase, "you succeed and an opening comes available as assistant head of special branch, all past events, are flung out of the window."

Eliote looked coldly at him. "You fucking bastard!" he said with venom. "I do all the dirty work, you get the reward."

"It's not like that, Simon."

"So what is it like then?"

"I am helping you get the Superintendent rank back, all you have to do is take it."

"I'd rather work hard again at some small station in the middle of nowhere to get the rank back, than help you get promoted," Eliote said with gritted teeth. As he got out of the car, he couldn't resist adding, "And Chelmesbury – ha, not on your life." "I want no part in this affair, so good bye and good luck." Eliote continued to walk towards his wife once more.

Magna stepped out of the car and called after him.

"Okay then, Falcon."

Eliote stopped and looked back at his old friend, hatred in his eyes.

"Don't you dare, I have finished with you and bloody Special Branch."

"Under clause six, section thirty-three of the contract you signed in good faith, I re-awaken you from your sleep and order you to head this unit in Chelmesbury," Eliote walked back, anger and hatred in his eyes,

"That's blackmail, you have no right."

"You are re-awakened, that puts you under my direct control. I want all your issues dealt with, and then you must report to Dorothy Brightly in three weeks' time. If you are not there, then I put out an arrest warrant on you and you will spend the rest of your life in prison. Do I make myself clear, Falcon?"

Eliote reluctantly nodded. "I'll be there," he said gritting his teeth.

Magna smiled and then turned and got back into his car, the window opened and Magna looked out at Simon. "I did not want this, Simon, but you left me no choice, good luck." The window closed and the car drove away, spinning dirt and chippings at Simon.

In the back seat of the car, Magna picked up his phone and dialled a familiar number. He heard the ringing tone and then a husky voice answered.

"Hello Magna, are plans proceeding?"

Magna, replied, "I have sent one of my best agents to Chelmesbury, he is a good copper and will follow orders, so your organization can breathe again and can move there without hesitation."

"My clients will like that old friend, especially as your friends at the Met have been arresting a few of them and the others are getting scared. Moving the operation to the countryside may make them relax, especially as you have a puppet working there."

The man paused and Magna said, "Unfortunately for the organization, he isn't a puppet."

The husky man went quiet, then after a few seconds, which to Magna seemed like hours, he spoke once more.

"Can he be bought?"

Magna shook his head. "No," he said, knowing that the man was probably not impressed. "He is unique, but I am his controller and he will do as I say."

This seemed to please the husky man. "So he can be trusted then?"

Magna nodded. "Yes, I have known him for years; we were at police school together."

"Good," he sounded like the emperor in Star Wars, "your money will be transferred as soon as possible."

Magna smiled. "Goodbye, old friend." The phone went dead and Magna said to his driver, "Back to base, please." The driver nodded and Magna lay back, wondering how he was going to spend his money.

THE DEATHLY ANGEL

By

Kevin Bailey

CHAPTER ELEVEN

YERROKS FOODS LTD
ONE MONTH LATER

In another part of Shropshire, in the medieval riverside market town of Tenbury Wells, Yerroks Foods had been producing fruit sauce for yogurts, jam and pie fillings for many years.

In one of the large factory buildings, Wayne Warwick was stacking and arranging pallets of orange plastic trays with the help of his trusty electric-powered hand-truck. He was about to offload his latest batch of pallets next to some others, when he heard his name being shouted from the gantry above. Burt, better known as 'the Cook,' was waving down at him to get his attention.

"Hey Burt, what's up?" Wayne called.

"I'm just going to Quality Control for a couple of minutes to sort out this recipe," Burt yelled back. "Also, the girls should be back in a while, so keep your eyes on this batch until they get here, will you?"

Wayne nodded and gave him the thumbs-up. "Sure thing Burt."

Once the Cook had disappeared through a door and out to Quality Control, Wayne continued to move pallets around, until he heard the bottom door open and close. He was expecting to see the girls coming through the plastic door that split the bottom part of the factory to the top, but instead he saw a hooded figure in black approach the plastic door.

The figure pushed a button on a rail next to the door, and as it slowly opened Wayne felt all the hairs on the back of his neck stand on end. A gush of fresh air hit him, and he scrutinised the man in the hood and jacket who with eyes fixed on him continued to walk towards his location.

"Excuse me, you aren't allowed in here without protective clothing, so I am going to have to ask you to leave," Wayne said authoritatively, but the man continued to walk towards him.

"Well, well, well, if it isn't my dear friend Wayne Warwick, the forward and how forward you were, Wayne."

"D-do I know you?" Wayne asked, taken aback by this remark.

"It's me, you fool," the hooded stranger said in an almost feminine voice and removed the hood. Wayne sighed with relief at his friend.

"What're you doing here, Ade?" Ade was slightly smaller in height and build than Wayne, with brown hair and staring emerald green eyes. He smiled.

"Come to see if there are any jobs going."

Wayne wasn't buying this. "Pull the other one," he said giving his friend a smile. "Look, you gotta go before Burt comes back. If he catches us together, were both for the high jump."

"OK, calm down, I'm going," Ade said, "but we do need to talk."

Wayne stopped what he was doing and approached his friend. "I've told my wife I'm leaving her," he said.

"About time, you know you ain't happy with her."

"What makes you think I'd be happy with you?" Wayne said, flirting with him.

Ade looked up and down the factory. "If you can get out I'll show you," he said, winking at Wayne.

Suddenly they heard a door open and close and Wayne looked at Ade and pleaded for him to leave.

"OK, OK, I'm going," the lad said and after placing the hood back on his head, he turned and left.

After watching his friend leave, Wayne breathed a sigh of relief and climbed to the upper level of the plant, where something made him look at the top of Vat 1. Several photos were strewn across the surface, pictures taken of him and Ade in very compromising positions.

"What the…?" He looked around and saw a hooded figure staring at him. "I thought I told you to go," he said.

The stranger continued staring at Wayne, and then declared, "People like you deserve everything they get."

This remark unsettled Wayne and he knew that this wasn't his friend. "Who are you?" he asked.

This new stranger lifted his head and looked deep into Wayne's eyes and with terrible anger he bellowed, "You betrayed me."

"No, please listen…" But that was as far as he got, because the stranger stepped forward and pushed him from the upper level. Wayne hit the floor with a thud and groaned heavily as his assailant walked down towards him calmly and casually and approached the spot where Wayne had landed. He looked down at his prey and clenched his fist and then with all his strength, he brought his fist down, impacting it into the soft tissue of Wayne's nose. Blood spurted upwards towards the attacker, but this didn't stop the onslaught, and blow after blow hit Wayne, as the violence erupted in the hooded stranger.

Wayne was withering from the continued blows to his face, then the darkness took him and he felt his body go weak, but it wasn't until he lapsed into unconsciousness that the hooded figure smiled and stopped his attack. For a while he watched the blood streaming from his victim's wounds and made sure that Wayne wasn't moving. Then he took a couple of deep breaths and planned what to do next. But that was answered for him by something touching his back.

He turned, fists clenched, expecting to see someone standing behind him, but instead found that sticky toffee had spilt from the vat above. He smiled and looked down at his victim who was still fighting for his life.

"I think it's time for you to meet a sticky end," he said, and with little effort, especially considering the energy he had already used, he lifted the bloodied body of Wayne from the floor and carried him over his shoulder up to the plant level. Then he opened one of the huge vats, and threw him in.

Wayne let out a blood-curdling scream as he sank beneath the surface of the boiling hot toffee, and the hooded attacker watched as his victim's outstretched fingers, their flesh melting like butter on a hot day, slowly sank beneath the surface.

After shutting both the safety gate and the lid, he walked to the control board and looked for the button marked "Start Blade 1".

Hearing an upstairs door open and close, he looked back at the vat. "Good bye," he said, and before leaving, he turned on the blade and left.

As he ran through another large door, he heard the noise of something being crunched, and as he made his escape from the factory, he let out a laugh.

Burt came back on to the factory floor and heard the crunching noise.

"Oh no, not another bloody blade ruining another batch," he muttered and ran quickly to the control board, where he hit the emergency stop button. Then he checked the lower level, looking for Wayne who was supposed to be watching the plant. "Wayne," he called angrily, "Wayne, where the fucking hell are you?"

Just then he spotted red liquid on the floor. He followed the liquid up onto the plant, and saw what he now guessed was blood on top of the vat door. He walked slowly towards it, and when he reached the lid, he grabbed the handle and pulled it open.

What caught his attention first was the smell, a coppery, metallic, musky, sweet odour and he knew as an experienced "cook" that it wasn't coming from the toffee, which had been mixed nicely.

Burt cursed again and as he was about to close the lid, he saw the blood on the inside of the vat wall and the paddles visible above the toffee.

"What the hell..." he said, bending over to touch the blood, and as he did, something near the paddles made him glance at them, and he wished he hadn't.

Attached to the blade was a severed arm; it was steaming as if cooked by the toffee and from what Burt could see, had been violently severed from the rest of the body. He closed the lid quickly and was sick.

Mopping his brow, he grabbed the phone beside the small desk that he used for recipes and phoned 999 and waited.

At Tenbury Police station, a lonely detective sat looking through some notes he'd made whilst interviewing a robber who had stolen three cars and a van from the high street.

The Former DS now Detective Inspector Richard (Dick) Robertson had transferred from London to Tenbury to get away from the bustle of city life, on hearing of his new position, His ex-wife had run away with a builder and had left him to deal with their five children

He had longed for the quiet life so had put in for a transfer. And the quiet life was exactly what he had lived with for the past several weeks.

He picked up his ham sandwich and was about to take a bite from it when the phone rang.

"Robertson," he said, and listened to the caller. Minutes later, he was heading for his car.

Robertson arrived at the factory just as a number of squad cars entered the car park, so he asked a handy constable for an update.

"Seems a worker has been found in one of the vats of toffee, sir," he was told.

Dick headed towards the main entrance. "Has Forensics been called?" he asked.

"Yes, sir, they have. A Doctor Felicity Owen from Hereford has been called and is on her way."

"Thank you, Constable Teale."

Robertson and Teale walked under the police tape and then headed down the factory floor towards the plant.

They found Burt the Cook sitting on one of the pallets with a number of officers, who were consoling him.

"I believe you found the body," Robertson said, and Burt nodded.

"I did, terrible sight, I won't be able to work here again, I am going to have to quit."

"I'm guessing the body is up there in one of the vats?"

Burt nodded and pointed to the left vat. "Vat One," he said.

Dick walked up to it, pulled on two gloves and opened the lid to vat one.

The image that greeted him was shocking. He saw what once had been a face, the flesh melted off from the heat of the toffee, and the top of the skull smashed to pieces. The arm that Burt had seen had been mangled around one of the paddles and a foot had been ripped from the leg.

Dick closed the lid and returned to the lower level, where he saw the door at the bottom open. A red-haired woman wearing protective overalls entered accompanied by ten of her forensics team.

"Good afternoon, I am Doctor Felicity Owen, from Hereford Pathology Unit. I understand you have a body for me?"

Dick smiled at the doctor. "Hi, I'm DI Robertson, Tenbury police. I have a rather interesting one for you," he said and pointed at the plant. "Body in a vat of toffee; see what you can do."

"Okay, bit of a sticky situation then?" She giggled and got to work.

Dick sort of smiled and then escorted Burt away from the scene to allow the doctor and her team to get on with their work.

Over in the Canteen of Yerroks Foods, Dick asked Burt to sit down and then looked over at Constable Teale.

"Tea please Paul, two sugars for our Burt here and I'll have a tea with one sugar please." The constable smiled and went and fetched the order.

"Right, Burt," Dick said, "I realise this is going to be difficult, but I need to know what happened, how you found him."

"Well, I'd left Wayne to bring in the batches for Monday's Yogfruits and headed for QC."

"Quality Control, right?" Robertson asked.

Burt nodded. "Well, I must have only been away for about ten minutes, but when I got back I heard crunching sounds." He gulped and paled a little.

Robertson said, "I know it's hard but I need you to continue."

Burt nodded, feeling sick once more. "We've been having problems with some new paddles that we've been testing; two in the last month have smashed in the vats, losing the company thousands of pounds."

"So you thought, here's another one."

Burt nodded. "Yeah, and of course I was angry at Wayne, he was supposed to be watching the plant, so I shouted for him." He paused as PC Teale placed the cups on the table and sat down beside Robertson, then took a small amount of tea and continued, "He was nowhere to be seen. So I called him again, and that's when I spotted the blood trail."

"Continue," Robertson said.

"I followed the trail around and up on to the plant, where I spotted some blood on the lid to vat one and opened it. A rather disturbing smell caught my attention and looking down into the vat, I didn't see anything unusual at first. Then I spotted more blood and as I bent closer, I saw the arm." He turned and threw up on to the floor.

"OK, Burt, just one more thing?"

Burt sat back up on the chair and looked at Robertson. "Yes Inspector?"

"Is there anything else, Burt? anything strange or out of the ordinary, no matter how small or insignificant?"

Burt sat and thought for a few seconds. "Well, now you mention it, as I was heading towards the toilet to freshen up, in the corner of my eye, I thought I spotted a hooded figure up on the plant, a knife in his hand. But when I turned around, he had gone. Sorry I didn't mention it before."

"That's OK, you've helped us enough. You can go home now."

Burt finished his tea and then replied, "Thanks, I hope you nail the son of a bitch who killed Wayne. He was a nice kid. He's got a couple of children, and Laura his wife works here too, when he isn't. Poor girl... They both always wanted to work overtime. You catch him and bring him to justice, OK?" he said angrily.

"I will, don't worry Burt, you just get yourself home." Burt left the canteen and headed for his car.

"Terrible business, eh Gov," PC Teale said and Robertson nodded.

"Sometimes, Paul, I think I wasn't cut out for this job."

After putting on a fresh set of blue protective overalls, Robertson walked back into the factory and headed for Doctor Felicity

Owen, passing another member of her team who was emptying the pipes from the vat into large metal bins. The attached sieve captured the huge lumps of flesh and bone on top.

As he got near, he noticed she was wearing what looked like the large gloves vets used to wear to check pregnant cows.

She was scooping out clumps of human flesh and bone from another bin. "Parts of our Wayne?" he asked. Felicity nodded.

"I'll have to empty the vat before I can have a proper look at what's left of the body, and who knows what that will bring or what it will be like, but it won't be pretty."

Robertson nodded and walked up onto the plant and looked down at the half-filled vat of thick brown goo. Large parts of Wayne were attached to the paddles and two of the doctor's forensic team were preparing to examine the body.

One of them smiled at him and handed him an evidence bag; inside was the picture and calling card.

He looked at the red circles surrounding two of the players on the picture.

Just then he heard a commotion from down by the plastic door and headed in that direction.

When it opened he saw a tall man in a white Yerroks Foods uniform arguing with a police officer. The man spoke with a Irish accent.

"How long is this going to take? I have customers waiting."

The officer saw Robertson approach and pointed to him. "He's in charge, so he'll be able to fill you in."

"So, what's going on?" the tall man asked.

"Please calm down, Mr…?"

"Mr Johan Doherty, CEO of Yerroks Food." Robertson escorted him out of the factory.

"Mr Doherty, we have a human body in vat one, which was placed there deliberately. This is now a murder scene, so I suggest you contact your customers and say there will be a short or long delay."

"Well, how long a delay should I expect?"

"This could take weeks, Mr Doherty, so please let us do our job and stop trying to argue with my officers. All it will do is get you arrested for obstruction."

"Jesus Christ," the CEO said and stalked off towards his office.

***

THE DEATHLY ANGEL

By
Kevin Bailey

CHAPTER TWELVE

On the busy A4, which had claimed the lives of his small family, the newly appointed Detective Chief Inspector Simon Eliote sat in his metallic black Saab 9-5 turbo diesel, heading to a new life in Chelmesbury.
The Shropshire town had been his childhood home, a homecoming he did not want, but Magna calling him 'Falcon' was an order and until he could get out of it, he was going to do his job to the best of his ability.

But in a way he did feel a little brighter; the last month had been hell, and the sale of his home had been horrific for him, as had been the party that was supposed to have been his and DI Robertson's leaving do. It had turned out to be a little too emotional.

So had the court case, which had gone on for a little longer than expected, the case to him had been open and shut, but Miss Wilson had argued about police brutality, which had to be investigated and then the trial had continued.

But Vincent had still been found guilty of manslaughter and of the welding of cars, so finally, as he drove away from London, the last piece of his old life had gone and now he was alone to begin the next journey.

Simon came to a stop as the traffic took hold on this winter's evening; this was something he would not miss. In front of the queue on the hard shoulder a car had broken down and the drivers in front had slowed down to have a look.

It seemed to take ages to go anywhere when the traffic was bad and he still had a couple of hours until he arrived at his new home, a home he hadn't been to since his mother's death nearly ten years ago, a home which belonged to him.

When the traffic slowed once more, he passed a spot on the road, as he had often done, the spot that had destroyed his life.

The small bunch of dead flowers were still attached to the small cross which had been placed to mark the spot, and now next to the spot was a bunch of fresh roses, a flower perfectly fitting for the wonderful woman he loved and would never forget.

A small tear trickled down his cheek as he looked at the cross and the roses he had placed there to say goodbye. He hoped he would never pass this spot again.

Once again the traffic started to move, the sound of a horn from the car behind brought Simon out of his thoughts of the past and he drove quickly away.

The tears were still trickling down his cheeks when he passed the outer boundary of London and joined the M25.

He looked at the dull grey motorway in front; the traffic was starting to slow down as he turned off the M25 on to the M40 and headed for Birmingham.

It would still take another couple of hours before he reached his destination and he wondered what surprises lay in store for him there. Only time would tell, of course.

When he arrived some hours later in the town of Chelmesbury, night had fallen; he drove around the centre remembering times gone by.

After another trip around the centre he headed for his new home.

Simon turned the black Saab off the A49 and onto a back road, drove for several minutes and then signalled to turn left into a private drive. Two large stone pillars marked the entrance, and between them were two black steel reinforced gates.

He pressed the buzzer and heard a croaky voice.

"Can I help you?"

"Hi, Henry, it's Simon," he said. The gates opened and he drove his car up a long drive and emerged into the huge courtyard of what was once a priory.

Its conversion from a priory into a manor house had taken place sometime after the time of Henry VIII; three floors high, it was built in Cotswold stone, with large bay windows looking out over the picturesque countryside.

Above the door was a huge family crest, which Simon had never paid much attention to, thinking it must have belonged to the family who owned the place before his parents, who had bought it some forty years ago for a hefty price.

The first thing he noticed, was that the house hadn't changed much since he had left to go to London all those years ago, but now he had come to live in this decrepit former priory.

He removed his suitcase from the car, approached the front door, rang the bell and waited, looking up at the crest; its face was weathered, but you could still make out the outline of its design.

Now he was here, he wanted to find out all he could about the crest. Perhaps he could identify the family who had owned the place before his parents, maybe track them down and return the manor to them.

Even when his mother's will had been read out leaving the whole estate to him, he had never wanted the place; it held bad memories, ghosts from his past.

He was brought from his thoughts by the sound of footsteps, and then the oak door creaked opened.

"Welcome back to the Priory Master Simon." Simon looked at the tall bearded man standing on the door step, his grey eyes looked at his new master with pride and loving, his once black hair now streaked with grey, swayed in the evening breeze and in his black suit, he looked every inch the butler.

Simon shook his head and smiled. "Less of this 'master' stuff, please, Henry. Plain old 'Simon' is fine. And talking of old, what's happened to you, my friend?"

"Much the same as has happened to you, Simon, from the look of things. The years have regrettably taken their toll." The two men walked into the house and Henry closed the door.

Immediately, Simon spotted the big spiral staircase and remembered sliding down its banister, straight into the arms of the younger Henry.

"You've kept the place tidy, old chap."

The butler nodded and looked up at the large oil painting of Simon's mother. "She would be turning in her grave if she thought I wasn't taking care of the place." When Simon glanced at the painting, a chill went down his spine.

"Do you still live in the annex, Henry?"

"I do, indeed. Now, let me take you to your room." They walked up the stairs and came onto a huge landing; rooms went off in all directions.

Henry escorted Simon to a door, which he opened and Simon walked in. The room was huge, and had once been a large meeting room which his parents had turned it into an en suite master bedroom, a room they had never slept in, with a large king-size bed and built-in wardrobes. Simon walked up to the window and looked out. The lawn was freshly mowed, but there were no flower beds, just grass. Easier for Henry,' Simon supposed.

"Oh, before I forget, Simon," said Henry, "there are files from a Superintendent Dorothy Brightly, informing you of an incident in Dark Lane last month and a shooting in Aden Close. I've left them in your study."

"Um and where would that be?"

Henry chuckled and pointed at a door next to the bathroom. "Sorry," he replied. "Of course, you wouldn't know. It's through that door, down a spiral staircase and you will come to another door, go through and that is your study."

"Thank you, Henry. I suppose I'd better go and take a look." He followed the older man's directions and soon arrived at the study door. The room was simple in design, with an old oak desk, leather chair, a huge bookcase against the far wall, and next to the desk was a large corkboard on which clippings had been pinned.

Simon approached the board and looked at the clippings. They seemed to cover incidents in his career, arrests he made, criminals he'd put away.

A smile came to his face and he sat down in the leather chair. In front of him were two small brown folders. He opened one and read a letter addressed to him.

To Detective Chief Inspector Simon Eliote

I know you are not on duty till Friday, but I thought I would let you know of the activities from your department. At the moment there are two main cases being investigated by your team, these consist of:

1st) A man was stabbed to death and another beaten to a pulp about a month ago. As you can see from the pictures and all the notes included on the case, Doctor Strong has done an extensive autopsy on the body and the information will be readily available to you as soon as he has finished.

Simon looked at the two photos of the victims and the covering information that had been gathered.

"My God," he said looking up, shocked at the images.

When he had left London for this quiet life here in Chelmesbury, he really thought he had seen the last of these types of crimes, but now here he was, faced again with brutality and violence.

He looked back down at the note and continued to read the letter.

2nd) Two friends walking home from a night out were gunned down by an unknown attacker. DS Frashier (see notes below) has been in charge of this investigation, interviewing suspects and investigating different leads.

I hope the information provided helps you to fit in.
Hope to see you soon.

Yours sincerely
Dorothy Brightly

Simon replaced the letter and pictures in the first file and put it to one side, then he looked at the other file.

The title of the folder was written on a label on the front cover. It read:

FILES OF CID PERSONNEL

He opened it and began scanning the contents.

-DS WILLIAM FRASHIER-

Beneath a photograph, Simon found a brief, informal summary of the officer.

A highly regarded and confident detective, who always gets the job done and does it well, He will make a great head of

CID someday, but lacks that little bit of authority and experience at the moment, which you may want to help him with.

He works well with any one, but is not scared to tell you when you are making an arse of yourself or if he has an opinion different to yours.

He turned over the page and read the next officer's information. The photo showed a pleasant-looking female officer in uniform.

-DS MIRANDA DAY-

Another confident detective, an asset to the team, she is pleasant and hardworking; she transferred from uniform to CID a year ago, but is already proving her worth.
She and William share a special bond, nothing sexual; they work well together and, like her friend, she will work with anyone.

At that moment Henry walked in from another door, carrying a silver tray containing a pot of tea, some milk, sugar and a small plate of sandwiches.

He placed them next to Simon and poured him a tea.

"Thank you, Henry, but I would have come and made myself some."

Henry smiled. "That is my job…" he was about to say "Master", but Simon gave him a stern look, "Simon."

Eliote grabbed a sandwich and smiled. "I haven't had one of your sandwiches for years, Henry," he took a bite and then commented, "You always did make the best ham, cucumber and mayonnaise sandwich," he took another bite and then with his mouth full he said, "thank you." Henry nodded and then turned and left Simon to his business.

After taking another bite of the sandwich, he perused the details of several other detectives in the file, all with great written references.

Then he turned a page and the photo made him chuckle, reminding him of his uncle George whose portrait hung next to his mother's.

-DOCTOR RICHARD STRONG-

The Chief Pathologist is a well-respected part of your team. He can be a little eccentric from time to time but likes to know what you want and then he will work hard to get the information to you as quickly as he can.

Simon placed the file back in the folder and then closed it. Leaning back, he pondered his life. Had he done the right thing leaving London?

Not answering the question, he finished both of the sandwiches and the tea, and then decided to take a stroll in the garden.

As he ambled across the lawn, his thoughts were back in London and the life he had left behind.

He sat down on a garden bench and looked at the house, suddenly realising that he had never brought his family here. This upset him as he knew that his kids would have loved it. He closed his eyes and in his daydream he could see them riding their bikes around the acres of land that surrounded the house.

"Daddy, can you take me to the lake, please?"
"Coming, Jane," he answered and she held out her hand.

He awoke from his daydream to find his hand still outstretched; tears trickled down his cheek and he rubbed them away.

"You miss them dearly, don't you?" Simon turned quickly to see Henry looking at him; he hadn't heard him come out, Simon noted that Henry was no longer in his suit, but in some casual clothes, obviously only wearing his suit, because he knew that Simon was coming,.

"Yes, more and more every day." Henry came and sat next to him on the bench. "They were my life, Henry, I woke every morning and went to work for them, the thought of knowing that I would see them at night kept me going, they were everything to me."

"You have to make a new life now, Master Simon," Henry said, his tone fatherly.

"But I don't want a new life; I want my old one back."

"We all want things, Master Simon. I wish your mother was still alive, but she isn't and I have to move on, so do you."

"How do I move on, Henry?" Simon asked.

"I truly don't know," the old butler said, sighing and pushing himself gingerly to his feet. "But you're going to have to learn to cope, Master Simon, because it's likely to be with you for a very long time. How I wish I had a magic potion that would soothe your troubled mind and make you whole again."

"So do I. Oh, so do I, my friend," he said to Henry's retreating back as he walked towards the house, leaving Simon alone with his thoughts.

THE DEATHLY ANGEL

By
Kevin Bailey

CHAPTER THIRTEEN

Friday morning at last came and Eliote awoke to the sounds of Chris Evans and his breakfast team on Radio Two. He pressed cancel on the radio alarm clock, got out of bed and headed for the shower.

After taking out a freshly bought white shirt and red tie from the oak wardrobe, he put on the navy blue suit that Henry had hung up for him.

Taking a quick glance at the photo of his family which he had placed beside his bed, he blew them a kiss and went down for breakfast.

Henry was preparing scrambled eggs on toast and a large metal teapot similar to one he remembered as a child sat steaming away at the centre of the table.

"I hope you're hungry, Master Simon, I didn't know how much you would eat, so I think I have done way too much."

"I'm sure you'll help me eat it, Henry," Simon said with a smile.

"I've already had my breakfast, Master Simon, thank you. I had it at five this morning."

Simon shrugged his shoulders. "Oh well, I had better tuck in," he said, and after eating as much as he could, he tried to help Henry tidy up.

"Leave it, Master Simon."

Simon tried to complain but was told again to go.

Later as he got into his Saab 9-5 turbo, he spotted Henry waving goodbye through the kitchen window, and suffered a feeling of déjà-vu. It had been in this same spot in the courtyard that Simon had waved at Henry the last time he had left the Priory, all those years ago.

He started the car and drove towards Chelmesbury, for his first day and his meeting with Dorothy Brightly.

***

Chief Superintendent Dorothy Brightly was also nervous, waiting in her office in full uniform for the arrival of an officer she had not met or interviewed for the post of head of her CID. Even though she'd heard a lot about him from some of her friends in London – that he was a great officer, was brilliant undercover – she still didn't quite know what to expect.

What she did know was that Inspector Frashier wasn't happy with this new recruit; she had a file on her desk containing a request for a transfer from the station.

She had not done anything about it and had told Frashier that it was up to this DCI Eliote to deal with when he arrived and in the meantime he should just get on with the cases he was investigating. Since then Frashier had been avoiding her, even turning around in the corridor and going a different way when he saw her.

She stood up from her desk clutching her mug of coffee, and looked out of the window at the new CID wing. Frashier was once again giving a briefing, smartly dressed, waiting for his new boss.

Then on the road outside the station she saw the metallic black Saab 9-5 turn into the entrance. Her time for nerves was over and she went back to her desk and read some more of Eliote's file.

Simon drove the black Saab 9-5 to the entrance of the station, pressed the call button on the panel and announced himself.

"Show your warrant card to the small camera please," he was told.

He did as instructed and the gate opened.

Simon drove his car to a parking space, got out and followed the signs to reception. He walked through an automatic door into a round brightly painted area and approached a large glassed front.

"Simon Eliote. I'm here to see Superintendent Dorothy Brightly," he told one of the uniformed receptionists.

She wrote down the name, picked up a phone and dialled an internal number.

"Hi," she said. "I have a Simon Eliote in reception for Superintendent Brightly." He watched as she listened and nodded. "Superintendent Brightly will be down shortly. Can I get you anything?"

"A cup of tea would be nice, please," he said.

Whilst he was waiting for his meeting and his tea, a couple of youths came in; they approached the front and banged on the window.

"Where the fuck are they?" one grumbled.

Eliote tried to look away but one of the youths spotted him and said, "What you staring at?"

"Nothing, I'm just waiting to see someone."

The youth and his friend approached him.

"Well, watch it or I'll make sure you end up in hospital."

Eliote smiled and the other youth looked at his friend.

"Now he's laughing at us. No one's around – let's drag him outside and beat the fuck out of him."

The other youth nodded. "Yeah," he said and they grabbed hold of Simon and bundled him outside, where they threw him against a wall.

The bigger youth was about to hit Simon, when he grabbed the youth's arm and swivelled, throwing him to the ground. The other youth went to charge at him, but with lighting speed, Simon blocked that charge too and using a karate throw, had the second youth on the ground next to his friend.

He looked down at them and was about to say something when six officers came running out of the station. He took out his warrant card and waved it in the air.

"It's OK," he said, "I'm Detective Inspector Simon Eliote."

One of the youths swore. "Oh, bollocks, now we're fucked. What's mum going to say when she finds out we just tried to beat up a police officer?"

Eliote brushed down his suit and said, "Arrest them and charge them with violent conduct."

The officers nodded and walked the two youths inside.

When Eliote returned to the reception area, a woman he guessed was Dorothy Brightly came through a door marked 'Authorized Personnel Only', and stood smiling at him.

She was about forty-five years old and attractive for her age, with tanned skin and captivating brown eyes. Her auburn hair was perfectly coiffed and she looked more like an air hostess than a policewoman, her uniform failing to hide her curves.

Simon sensed she was also eying him up and he smiled.

"Do you know how long we've wanted to get those two pests for something?" she said, returning his smile. "They are the mayor's children, spoilt rotten, bad eggs, but they've been lucky until today, and we haven't been able to pin anything on them."

"Looks as though their luck has changed," Simon said, chuckling.

"Let's hope so. Anyway, welcome Inspector, to the Reception and CID wings of Chelmesbury's new three million pound redevelopment project, which will be fully operational in two to three months." They shook hands and while Brightly spoke to one of the officers who had arrested the youths, Simon looked around the foyer.

He had read that this station would command the others in the region, some of which would only be open at certain times of the week. And several of the older stations, the file had said, would be closed and the land sold for redevelopment.

The object of the transformation was to create a larger team to focus on crime prevention and detection in the surrounding areas, a mould for other big stations. Spending money to save money – he had never really seen the sense in that – but the proposal had been a sound plan.

Brightly walked toward the door to the right of the reception area and typed a six-digit code into a keypad and the door opened. She then beckoned him to follow.

They went through another door and out into a large area, which was also brightly lit and smelt of fresh paint. Several corridors ran off in different directions, and Simon could see a couple of interview rooms nearby. A large spiral staircase seemed to wrap itself around a lift, each floor's designation listed on a board to one side.

Brightly asked Simon to sign the visitors' book, which he did and she then gave him a visitor card attached to a strap which she placed around his neck.

"Until you get your official card, this will be your pass," she told him as they climbed the stairs to the next level.

Simon commented on how good the building looked from the outside; she smiled and thanked him. When they got to the next level, she turned left and opened another door and they walked along the corridor until they came to a door marked "Head of CID". She unlocked the door and opened it, the waft of fresh paint stinging his nose as he entered. He looked around his office and saw several brand new filing cabinets in the room, a seating area with a large red sofa, a drinks-making area with a kettle, some cups, a sink and a small fridge.

There was also a clean pine desk, with a computer terminal and two leather chairs.

"This will be your office and I can finally say Detective Chief Inspector Eliote..."

"Thank you, ma'am," he said, smiling warmly at her once again.

"If you require anything, it will be brought to you, all you have to do is ask."

"Thank you once again," she was just about to walk out of the room when he asked, "Ma'am. I would like to see Detective Inspector Frashier; if I can, you know to get to know him a little."

She came into the room and closed the door behind her. "I have to tell you something important about William Frashier," she said. He beckoned her to sit down on the red sofa and he rested himself on the edge of the desk, looking at her.

"Please feel free to tell me anything."

"Okay, I think you should know that he put his name down for this post and if your friend in high places hadn't ordered me to make you head, then he would be."

"Right, so I should expect a little tension from the Detective Inspector?"

She nodded. "Just a little, be patient with him as he is a bloody good copper."

After Brightly had gone, Simon filled the kettle and turned it on, then he went to the chair behind the desk and sat down. He was wondering what to do next, when there was a knock at the door.

"Come in," he shouted and the door opened.

"Good morning, sir, I'm Detective Inspector William Frashier," said the newcomer. The two men shook hands and Eliote beckoned him to sit in the chair in front of his desk.

"I thought I would get you up to speed on our two major enquiries," Frashier said, "before we go to the observation room and have the briefing."

Eliote nodded, pleased that he'd soon be getting to work.

Frashier opened a folder and pulled out the relevant information.

"First the stabbing in Lovers Lane. We still haven't managed to find anyone who was a witness – well, apart from Paul who was very vague with his statement."

"Okay," Eliote replied. "What of the shootings in Aden Close, have we had any leads?" Frashier seemed surprised that this new detective knew about the cases.

"Well, we have got a video of a car leaving the scene just after the shooting, forensics are still looking into it at the moment, but as soon as they get anything, they will contact us." Eliote stood up and walked over to the kettle which had just boiled; he turned and offered Frashier a drink.

"Coffee, please, a little milk and a spoonful of sugar."

"Inspector, I wanted to speak to you, not only so you could brief me and bring me up to date, but also so we could get to know each other a little before we venture down to the observation room."

"Right, thanks guv."

"I read your file and it says you're not scared to tell me your opinions, so what are your thoughts on the cases?"

Eliote looked over at Frashier and could see that Frashier was in a world of his own, he coughed which brought the detective out of his daydream.

"Sorry, sir, I was thinking about the case. Carry on, sir."

"As I was saying, you have had more time on them than me, so your opinion please?"

"Well, sir, the stabbing is likely to be a controlled attack, which I think will happen again. There is a photo of a school football team with a circle around the victim."

Eliote recalled the photo. "What about tracing them?"

Frashier shook his head. "It's ongoing, sir."

Eliote stirred Frashier's coffee and handed him the cup. "What of the shootings? What are your thoughts there?"

"I think we have another controlled killing, the attacker knew the victims, knew where they lived and definitely knew the perfect place to carry out the killing."

Eliote sat down and sipped at his tea, studying the Inspector as he mused.

"What is the likelihood of the players on the photo being recognised, Inspector?"

Frashier took a swig of his coffee and looked at Eliote. "Well, I'm keeping my fingers crossed. We've made enquiries at the local schools, but no one recognises the players or the team colours. As I said before, though, enquiries are continuing."

Eliote placed his cup into the sink. Frashier finished his coffee and did the same, then led the way to the new Observation room.

THE DEATHLY ANGEL

By
Kevin Bailey

CHAPTER FOURTEEN

Frashier had assembled all the CID officers in the large briefing room. Most had heard about their new chief's arrest of the two Mardon kids and were keen to meet him.

They were chatting to each other when the door opened and in came Frashier, followed closely by Eliote. The two officers walked to the front of the briefing room and turned and looked at the group of officers.

"Right, then," Eliote said warmly and the room went silent. He looked behind him at the large computer screen, which almost covered the back wall and joked, "Blimey, I'd love to watch a Liverpool game on that." The team laughed and then fell silent once more.

He grabbed a device that looked like a fat pen, moved to a nearby lectern and addressed the gathering. "Today is my first day here as head of CID," he said, sensing Frashier tense up. "I see a hellava lot of new faces," he continued, "and I will try and get to know you."

Feeling like a headmaster taking school assembly, he paused and applied the pen to the surface of the tablet on the lectern in front of him. "But now is not the time," he said, opening a file. The screen behind him changed to show what he had opened. "This is now, people!"

The screen had four pictures displayed, and he pointed the pen at the images. "James Gaston, Paul Tomlinson, Richard Hatfield," then he pointed at the last, "Teresa Bennett. These two enquiries are the major ones, the rest," he opened another file on screen and a list of cases appeared, "will need to be tackled as and when we can."

He briefly studied some documents, and then continued his address.

"Right, before we continue with the assignments, I want you to know that I'm a hands-on guy, and I will be out there with you, all the way to the end. If there are bodies to be moved, I will help, If families need to be told of loved ones being hurt or even killed, I will go and tell them." He looked around at the faces staring intensely at him. "If praise is earned for our actions in the field, I'll make sure you get it, but if condemnation is deserved, then I'll deal with it. The buck stops here, every time." He dug a thumb into his chest. "But if you cock things up, people, leave me alone or I will come down on you like a ton of bricks."

The room was silent as Eliote studied their shocked faces. "Right, now that's out of the way, let's get to it." He looked in the direction of Frashier and his small team. "As you have already reported on the progress of your enquiries, Inspector Frashier, I will allow you and your team to continue to investigate the shooting in Aden close." Frashier nodded and he and his team got up and left the room.

"Okay," Eliote said to those remaining; "now you can fill me in on your other cases."

Towards the end of the session, Eliote said, "This assailant with the knife …" he picked up the plastic evidence bag and looked at the contents "…this 'Deathly Angel', what can you tell me about him?"

“The problem is, guv,” said an officer who introduced herself to him as DS Miranda Day, “we haven’t been able to find many witnesses to the stabbing. All we have is a badly beaten lad in a hospital ward.”

“So a trip to the hospital is called for,” Eliote said, looking at the other remaining officers but not at Day.

“Right I know you’ve probably done it already but I want a new wave of door-to-door enquiries in the area around Lovers Lane, whilst this is going on, I want to set up road blocks on all routes in and out of the town, somebody somewhere must have seen something,” he said forcefully.

Day looked at him and smiled. “Might be a bit of a problem getting people to admit they were in Lovers Lane on the night in question, guv,” she said. “They’d be worried we’d arrest them for lewd conduct.”

Eliote returned her smile and grabbed the folders. “Do your best,” he said, and the officers started to leave. Eliote stopped Day. “You’re with me, Sergeant.”

They walked out to the Saab and Eliote jumped into the driver’s seat, then after the two had put on their belts, he started the car, reversed out and headed for the Princess of Wales Hospital.

The Princess of Wales was a huge, multi-functional hospital; Paul was in a room of his own, the curtains were drawn and he was sitting up in bed staring out of the window. Eliote knocked on the door and he and Day walked in.

“Mr. Tomlinson?” Paul nodded. Eliote introduced himself and his sergeant, and said, “I have taken over the investigation of your friend’s death. DS Day and I would like to ask you some more in-depth questions if we may.” Paul nodded again and Day took out a Dictaphone and placed the microphone near to Paul.

“I know you gave a statement before Mr Tomlinson,” Eliote began, “but as I wasn‘t there on the night in question I would like you to start at the beginning, and if you can remember anything else about what happened in Lovers Lane that you didn't tell DI Frashier, then let me know now."

Paul sat up and coughed. "All I can remember," he said, his voice croaky and slurred from drugs, "is we were walking back from the Dog and Duck, talking about some girl, when we both sensed we were being followed. Then this voice echoed in the street, shouting out James's name, so we both stopped and turned, trying to figure out where the voice was coming from. But whenever we thought we'd worked out its location, it seemed to change direction." He broke into another coughing fit and Day poured him some water. "James shouted out, 'Show yourself,' but the voice just answered, 'No,' and warned James to watch his back."

Eliote walked back from the window and sat on the chair next to Paul's bed.

"What happened then?"

"Well, as you'd expect, we upped our pace and headed for home a little faster," Paul said. Eliote could see that his breathing was becoming erratic and the poor chap was almost hyperventilating.

"Calm down, Paul," he said. "If you don't want to continue then we can come back another time…"

"No, I want to get this off my chest, it's just that James was a bloody good friend…" He paused and continued, "Well, we were in Lovers Lane, when we both saw a lad approaching. I didn't recognize him, but James did and he was ready to beat him up. When they got close to each other the lad stabbed James in the side and hit me repeatedly." Another cough. "Then he told me to warn the others in James's gang that he was coming to get them."

"Anything else?" Eliote asked. "Every single detail you can give us will help."

Paul nodded and continued, "I lay there watching as he attacked – no, slaughtered James with a knife, stabbing him repeatedly."

Eliote could see all this remembering was upsetting him. “If you want to stop, Paul, we will.”

“No, no, it’s OK,” Paul said. “The bastard stood up and walked off laughing, leaving me and James lying there on the ground. Blood was gushing from James’s side and I tried to get up and help, but I couldn’t because it hurt too much, so I grabbed my phone and dialled the police. At that point, people came running.”

Eliote took out the plastic pouch containing the photo and handed it to Paul and asked, “Do you recognize any of the other people in this picture?”

Paul shook his head and then smiled at his friend. “How young he looks. I met James when he was a lot older than this.” He held the photo and then he looked at the card showing the angel motif with the words ‘You have been killed by the Deathly Angel.’

“Can you think of anyone who would want James dead?” Day asked. “And what of this gang you talked about?”

“The James I knew was not a violent person – well, except for when he’d had a few beers, but then only when he was provoked.” He paused. “He always looked out for me… always.”

“You said he would only attack when provoked, but a minute ago, you said he was going to beat the lad up. Could there have been some rivalry between them?”

Paul shook his head. “No, this lad caused an impulse in James to bully him, but it was like he had done so before. You see, I heard the lad say that he was a ‘victim’, but he was a violent monster and I hope I never see him again, ’cause if I do…” Paul lay back on the bed and looked out of the window.

“Thank you, Mr Tomlinson,” Eliote said. “We may need to ask you some more questions.”

Paul nodded. “I’ll be at home. I’m sure you’ll know where to find me.”

“Tell me,” Eliote said, “this gang you were supposed to warn, do you know them?”

"I've known James for years; he wasn't part of any gang," Paul replied.

Eliote smiled. "OK, thanks." As he followed Day out of the room, he muttered, "The lad knows more than he's letting on, Sergeant, but he is too traumatized for me to push. I need to give him time."

"Do you believe him, guv?" Day asked.

Eliote nodded. "About the killer, unfortunately yes, I believe him. James knew his attacker. How, I don't know, but I need to find out fast."

They walked towards the Saab.

"What do we do next, guv?"

For the first time since he had come to Chelmesbury, Eliote didn't know what to do, but he was good at thinking on his feet.

"If he did tell the truth, then we had better nail this Deathly Angel, before he strikes again."

***

DI Robertson walked back into the taped-off area of Yerroks Foods and strode down the long factory floor, passing machines that were dormant. He found Flick and her team up on the plant. Flick was inside the vat of toffee, placing the large chunks of what was left of Wayne Warwick into plastic containers.

"Good morning, Doc," he said.

"Ah, DI Robertson, a pleasure as always," she said.

He looked down into the vat and it reminded him of the small dungeons in castles. "How's it going?"

"Its bloody hard work, Inspector. We've been here for two days and we're still finding parts of the deceased." He saw her place some toffee-coloured clothing into an evidence bag. "I may have to bring in some help from another area."

"Do what you must, Doc. I gotta find this killer, but the only evidence I have is a mangled body and a picture of a football team." He watched as a couple of teeth were placed into an evidence bag. "I'll leave you to get on. If anything crops up, I'm contactable at this number." He handed her a card, which she placed into her pocket.

"Okay, Inspector."

After a while, Flick looked at the clock and saw it was nearly time to quit, but as she was going home to no one, she grabbed her phone and scanned through the numbers. Friends, family... She spotted a number she had been meaning to contact for days, but was trying to put it off.

"Oh well, it's a shot in the dark," she muttered, and then rang the number and waited for it to connect.

> "*Hi, this is Richard Strong; sorry I can't take your call, please leave a message after the tone.*"

She heard the dull mechanical bleep.

"Hi, it's me, I really need to talk to you," she said then hung up and walked towards the factory's female shower block.

As she was showering, she heard her mobile ringing. Quickly turning off the tap, she grabbed her towel, wrapped it around her body and got out of the shower. But when she got to the phone in her handbag, it had stopped ringing. She cursed under her breath, dressed and then headed for her navy blue BMW Z3.

Once inside, she grabbed her car phone and located and dialled Strong's number

"Ah, good evening Felicity," Strong said when he answered. "Long time no hear. I am so glad you rang back."

"It hasn't been that long," she said, "has it?"

"No, only a couple of months, I suppose. So, what can I do for you?"

"You could start by buying me a drink, you old goat." She heard him laugh.

"Ha, of course; work or pleasure?"

"Unfortunately it's work, sorry." She heard him sigh.

"Isn't it always with you? And your mother thought it would be pleasure. Oh well, a father's work is never done, I suppose."

"Cheers, Dad." She started the car. "I'll meet you in the Crown at Leominster."

When she arrived at the pub, she saw her father's car parked in a space and pulled up alongside; she got out and headed for the front door.

Her dad already had a small glass of whisky in hand so she tapped him on the shoulder and said, "I'll have a Bacardi Breezer." He smiled and after ordering the drinks, they sat down at a quiet table.

"So how have you been?" he said almost nervously as if this was a first date.

"Yeah, I'm OK."

Strong smiled. "Your mother is worried about you."

She sighed and took a swig from her bottle. "She's always worried about me," she said. "But she hasn't been in touch for ages."

"That, I am afraid, is your mother, but you didn't ask me to meet you so we could talk about her, did you?"

She shook her head. "No, I must definitely didn't." Flick grabbed her briefcase, which was by her feet, pulled out a large brown folder and placed it on the table. She opened the file and passed it over to him. He turned the pages and saw the photos of the factory.

"Bloody hell," he said when he saw the pictures of human flesh being labelled and placed into plastic containers.

“The factory in question, Dad, is in Tenbury.” She took another a sip from the bottle. “According to the officer in charge, the deceased’s name is Wayne Warwick.”

Her father continued to look through the file, smiling in approval of her thoroughness. “What can I do to help?” he asked.

“It’s been three days since the attack and I’m still finding body parts. I could do with some help and resources from your department.”

“Couldn’t Howard help you?”

“Howard and I are no longer together, Dad, so he won’t help me.”

“Then as your father I will.” Then something in the file caught his attention, and he went as white as a sheet.

“What’s up, Dad? You look like you’ve seen a ghost,” Flick said, and looked down at the picture of the football team that he was staring at; two circles had been drawn around two players.

“Where was this found?” her father asked brusquely.

“Well, it was left on top of the vat where the body was found. Why do you ask?” she looked down at the faces in the photo. “Is there any significance to the photo, Dad?”

He nodded, still looking shaky. “Yes, there is. You’d better come with me to Chelmesbury; I think we need to talk to the head of CID immediately.”

***

THE DEATHLY ANGEL

By
Kevin Bailey

CHAPTER FIFTEEN

HOWDON MANOR
NEAR CHELMESBURY

The Manor on the Heath, built sometime before Henry VII's reign, was a beautiful sight when driving from Chelmesbury to Bridgenorth and it was also visible from the main sitting room at the priory.

On its walls hung huge paintings of past monarchs who had stayed in the residence, and the Mardon family, (who had lived in the house for nearly twelve generations,) were so proud of their home's historic heritage that they would tell anyone who would listen.

Godfrey Mardon, the present Lord of the Manor, was awoken by a noise from downstairs. The building was rumoured to be haunted, of course, but that didn't deter him from getting out of bed to check it out. He put on his dressing gown and walked quietly to his study, which was next to his bedroom, where he opened the gun cabinet, grabbed a 12-bore shotgun and some cartridges and made his way to the landing.

The lord was in his late fifties, with a podgy nose and receding black hair which had slight tinges of grey coming through. He was about six feet tall with blue eyes. He watched his weight and worked out most nights before he came to join his family for dinner.

In Chelmesbury, he was a well-established solicitor and most of the population knew of him. As a reward for all his work in bringing Chelmesbury into the spotlight, he was being appointed as their new mayor next month when the present mayor ended her term.

One of his sons opened his bedroom door and was told sharply to go back to sleep.

He approached the handrail to the large Victorian staircase that had replaced the old Tudor stairwell and shouted down the stairs.

"Who's there, Dorothy, is that you?" He waited for a reply. "Don't be silly, come out I'm not playing games, I have a loaded gun." Again, he listened but it was silent. He cocked back the hammer on the shotgun and aimed it in front of him, his finger tightening on the trigger; then he started down the stairs. To his annoyance, when he reached the third step it creaked; he cursed the step and vowed to repair it, then he descended the last three steps and looked around at the darkness that was the large hallway.

He heard a floorboard creak in front of him and in the light from the large hall window something moved. He aimed the gun at the noise then he heard purring.

He looked down at his feet and saw a black and white cat, moving around his legs.

"Sabetha, go on, go chase mice and stop giving me heart attacks." The cat meowed so Lord Godfrey bent down and picked her up and stroked her, then he turned and started back up the stairs. But he stopped as a thought came into his head.

"How did you get in?" he said to the beloved pet, for he knew that he himself had shut her out when he had gone to bed. Then he heard another noise which seemed to be coming from his downstairs study. He placed the cat on the steps and turned around.

The large grandfather clock struck two o'clock and then silence fell upon the house once more. Lord Godfrey headed for the downstairs study, the gun ready in his hand.

The silence was shattered by the sound of two gunshots going off from the doorway of the second study. Lord Godfrey screamed and fell backwards into a table, scattering its contents all over the hallway. Within seconds he was on to the floor in a puddle of his own blood, gunshot wounds to his head.

The sound of running footsteps and the front door opening and slamming shut woke the rest of the family. Charles, who was the eldest child, walked down the stairs and turned on the light.

When she heard his shout of horror, his mother called, "Charles, what is it?"

"You'd better call the police, Mother, someone has killed Papa!"

***

Back at the station, Strong parked his car in one of the visitor spots and both he and his daughter headed for the main reception.

The female uniformed receptionist smiled at him. "Doctor Strong, a pleasure as always."

"Hi, is the new DCI in?"

She shook her head. "You just missed him."

He was about to say something when he heard his bleeper go off. "Damn thing," he said. "Could I borrow a phone?" he asked the receptionist. She nodded and handed him a receiver. He dialled the number of the unit and was told of the shooting at Howdon Manor.

"Blast, going to have to love you and leave you, Flick. I'll speak to our new DCI and get back to you." He kissed her on the cheek and she smelt the alcohol on his breath.

"But, Dad, you've been drinking; let me go."

He held up his hand. "I'll be fine," he lied, "besides Detective Inspector Frashier will probably be there." As he spoke, Frashier walked quickly through reception and stopped when he saw Strong.

"Can you give my dad a lift, Will?" Flick asked, smiling at him warmly. "He's been drinking."

Frashier nodded and returned her smile. Then after kissing his daughter on the cheek, Strong left with Frashier, who said, "You didn't tell her that I had been drinking too, did you, Doctor?"

He shook his head. "No, what she doesn't know will never hurt her." They jumped into Frashier's car and headed for Howdon Manor.

***

Superintendent Brightly was asleep when her mobile phone went off. She grabbed the phone and saw that it was the Chief Constable.

"David, what's up?"

"Sorry to have woken you this early in the morning but what is that new DCI up to?" Brightly sat up and looked at the clock.

"He's investigating a case involving a vigilante. Why?" she said rubbing sleep from her eyes.

"I want him on another case as well. About twenty minutes ago, Lord Godfrey Mardon was killed in his home by an unknown assailant and as a close friend of the family, I want this crime solved and the killer brought to justice. Do I make myself understood?"

"Yes Sir," she said.

"Good," he seemed to pause, "keep me informed," then the line went dead.

After getting dressed she went downstairs, grabbed her telephone book and found Eliote's number.

***

At the Priory, Simon had left Henry, who had been giving him a brief tour of his new home. He had forgotten most of the place; his mother had redesigned rooms and moved things around in the garden and the grounds, so the place felt new to him.

He went up to his room and lay down on the bed, and his dreams drifted between his new and old life.

Eliote was awoken by the phone going off beside him. "Yep?" he said, yawning.

"There is a Superintendent Brightly on the line, sir," Henry said.

Eliote sat up and took the call.

"Sorry to wake you, but you are to get to Howdon Manor. It seems there's been a shooting." Eliote looked at the clock; it read two thirty. "The Chief Constable has instructed me to make you deal with this case, it is important to him."

"Who is the victim?"

"Lord Godfrey Mardon, the mayor elect."

Even though he had been in Chelmesbury for only a few days, Henry had been putting the local papers in his study, which he said he had always done for his parents. Lord Mardon had been on most of the front pages, smiling and dressed in what would be his new robes of office.

"I'll be up there as soon as possible, ma'am," he told Brightly.

"Okay, keep me informed," she said, and the line went dead.

Eliote got up and changed and then he headed for the black Saab parked in the garage and headed for Howdon Manor.

He was greeted by the usual suspects. Day had beaten him there and so had the pathology unit, the assistant pathologist Penny Hardcastle was busy looking at the body and writing down her findings.

When she saw Eliote approach, Penny got up and greeted the detective. "Ah, you must be Detective Chief Inspector Eliote," she said. "I am Dr Penny Hardcastle, assistant pathologist." She paused. "Doctor Strong has been called."

Eliote smiled at her and said, "Pleased to meet you." He looked at the body. "So, your verdict, please Doctor?"

She took out a pencil and pointed at the fatal wound. "It's Quite simple really, Chief Inspector. Shot twice through the head at close range, from about three metres, no further."

"Are there any similarities between this shooting and that of the others killed in Aden Close?"

"No, the Aden Close shootings, according to Doctor Strong's findings, were almost certainly done by a semi-professional, someone who had fired a rifle before." She looked down at the body on the floor. "This was down by an amateur, even I can see that."

"So we have three main cases to contend with," Eliote said to DS Day. She nodded. "Where do you think the shots were fired from, Doctor?"

Penny stood up and approached the study, pointing at powder burns on the door panels and side rails. "This would be where the shooter stood," she said.

Day nodded at the window as a grey BMW pulled up on the gravel. "Don't worry, Penny," she said. "The cavalry has arrived."

The cavalry, however, did not stay long. Eliote noticed immediately that the two newcomers had been drinking and beckoned Day over.

"Can you escort Doctor Strong and Detective Inspector Frashier back home, please?" he instructed her. "You two can come back in tomorrow when you aren't reeking of alcohol. The two men left with their tails between their legs.

Eliote had laid down the rules for all the officers and they now knew they couldn't mess with him.

"Sir," Penny said, "they are good workers, I think that was a little harsh."

"That may be so, Doctor, but this is not Inspector Morse, we do not drink whilst on duty, it's un-professional, especially in this day and age."

Penny sighed heavily. "There goes my day off," she said.

Eliote smiled at her and then said to DC Morecambe, "Get some officers and organize a search of the perimeter, see if we can find the murder weapon." Morecambe nodded and left.

"Okay, Penny, full report on my desk," Eliote said. "Oh, and I'm not putting any pressure on you but the Chief Constable is watching, so I need it ASAP."

She sighed again and then nodded. "Okay, you'll have it" she said.

***

Down at the bottom of the road, Charlotte watched Day drive past. She could see Frashier was cursing at her and Strong, and wondered where they were going. Still, at least she had a new contact to deal with and was this new detective going to give her the time of day?

She looked up at the house and could see police officers roaming the place like ants out foraging for food; a man in a coverall emerged from the main door and spoke to some officers.

This, she now deduced, was her target.

***

Back at the hall, Eliote took off his coverall and handed it to one of the officers who were guarding the building, then he re-entered the hall and headed for the drawing room.

He walked through the great hall, passing huge paintings of the Mardon family and headed for the oak door with a male officer positioned outside it. When he saw Eliote approaching, he opened the door and let him enter.

Two officers greeted him and he headed for the group of people surrounding an old lady seated in an armchair. He approached her and said, "Lady Mardon, I am the lead detective in this enquiry and I need to know if your husband had any enemies?"

"No," she said straight away, "not at all. Well, perhaps he'd upset a couple of people whilst defending them, or while out campaigning, but not someone who would want him dead." She paused to blow her nose, then started to cry again. "He was a good man and a good JP, why would anyone want him dead?" Eliote handed her another hanky and she wiped away the tears from her eyes.

"From what I've read in the papers, I believe you, but obviously someone didn't think like that." Mrs Mardon started to cry once more. Eliote hated women crying, as it always reminded him of the arguments between his parents when his mother ended up in tears. He looked at the elderly lady, pity in his heart for her.

"We'll come back later," he told her and handed her a business card. "If you think of anything, my number is on the card."

She took it from his hand and sort of smiled at him. "Thank you, Chief Inspector." Eliote went to find DC Morecambe, who was interviewing other members of the family. In the hallway, he came face to face with the two youths who had attacked him on his first day. They looked shocked at seeing him.

"Mummy, Mummy," one cried.

Lady Mardon came hurrying into the hall. “Arthur, Henry, whatever is wrong?”

They pointed at Simon. “This is the copper we told you about,” they said pretending to cry, “the one who attacked us, then arrested us.”

She turned and glared at Simon. “Is this true, Inspector?”

“I did arrest them, Lady Mardon, but only because they attacked me. We have CCTV footage of the attack; I can get it if you want me to?”

“No,” she said bitterly, “but I want your name. I will make damned sure you are back to being a constable.”

Eliote tried to say something, but she repeated, “Your name?” The two youths laughed.

“My name is Simon,” he said nervously, “Simon Eliote,” he sensed a change in her attitude towards him.

“From up at the Priory?” she asked.

He nodded. “Yes, but what’s that got to with anything?”

She turned and belted both of her children around the legs with her hand. “You little devils,” she exclaimed and continued to smack them in front of the shocked officers. “You picked on the man who could throw us out of our home.” Eliote didn’t know what the hell she was on about.

She turned to Simon. “I do apologise for my children, Detective Chief Inspector, my own fault, I have spoilt them rotten.”

He shrugged his shoulders and muttered, “No harm was done,” but he was still shocked at her outburst. “Tell me, what did you mean just then, about me throwing you out of your home?”

She started to make her way down the corridor. “Walk with me please.” Eliote obliged her and walked alongside her deep into the house. He had always loved historic buildings like this one, the long mysterious corridors, the elegant stately rooms, the beautiful dining room with its painted ceiling; he could almost hear the music of yesteryear and the sounds of the many servants running in and out with the food for the aristocrats seated at the oak table, drinking wine.

They arrived at a long corridor, much grander than the rest of the house, and as they proceeded, she pointed to the paintings of the Mardon dynasty on either side of the walls, and explained who was who. Finally, she came to a painting of a woman, whom Eliote recognized immediately.

"This was painted when your mother was twenty, before she met and married your father." She said the word "father" with such contempt that Eliote almost flinched.

He looked at the painting and saw the warm happy smile from his mother, which did not mirror the hated mother figure he had grown up with. Something must have happened to change her from this beautiful happy figure to the evil twisted woman he had known.

"But why is a painting of my mother on your walls, Lady Mardon?"

She ignored his question and beckoned him on. But the next painting, made him stop dead in his tracks; he recognized the parting in the middle, the green eyes staring down at him, the elegant clothes. It was a painting of himself as an infant. But why, when? He seemed to be eight or nine, but couldn't remember ever having a portrait painted. Much of his childhood had been spent going from one boarding school to the next, and the only happy memories he had were of the holidays spent with Henry and his father's parents.

"Look at the bottom of the painting, my boy," Mrs Mardon said.

His eyes moved to a plaque and on it was his name: Simon Nathanial David George Mardon Eliote. "But that's impossible," he said.

She smiled and put her elderly hand on his shoulder. "Your mother and father should have been the twenty-first Lord and Lady of Howdon, but your grandfather, my uncle, didn't want your father to have the title as he didn't like him, so instead her cousin, my husband, was appointed Lord Viscount of Howdon and your parents were given the estate that the Priory sits on."

"But I was told by both my father and mother that they had bought the Priory."

She shook her head. "No. Didn't you ever wonder about the crest?"

"I never really paid much attention to it. Why?"

"It is the Howdon Crest. Now that should have given the game away."

Eliote looked at his younger self then back at her. "I always thought it belonged to the family who owned the house before, and now you are saying it belongs to the Howden family."

"It does belong to the Howden estate, which, now my husband is dead, belongs to the heir."

Simon smiled. "I'm sure your son will want it back."

"You don't get it, do you, Simon? You are the heir, the land now belongs to you and that is why you can throw us out of our home." She was about to continue when his name was called by a female constable who had just come in.

"Excuse me, sir."

"Yes Constable?"

She apologized for disturbing him and then reported, "They have found what they think is the murder weapon in the garden."

He nodded. "Coming, Constable."

He turned to look again at the smile from his long lost relative. "We will continue this conversation another time, Lady Mardon," he said. "Right now I have to find the killer of your husband." He left the long gallery and followed the officer outside.

As he stepped outside, his phone went off; it was Miranda Day asking if he wanted anything from the station.

"Not at the moment, Sergeant," he answered tersely.

"Sir, are you OK?"

Eliote looked over at the house and then said, "No, not really, but I don't want to talk about it. I know you probably want to come back, but I can handle it here, so go home and get some sleep as we are all going to have a long day tomorrow. I want a briefing set for eleven o'clock Monday morning. Can you deal with that before you go home?"

"I certainly can Gov."

Eliote smiled. "Let's see if we can't solve a few of these minor cases and then use the resources of this new station to solve these other cases."

After she hung up, Eliote walked over to where Penny was examining an old army issue revolver in some bushes; she was using a brush to show up the fingerprints on the handle and trigger, then a photographer took a picture of the weapon and the prints and placed the weapon carefully in a protective container.

"Is it the murder weapon?" Eliote asked.

She looked up at him and nodded. "I think it is. Lord Mardon's head wound matches some of the wounds I've seen in pictures of soldiers killed with this weapon."

"I see you have fingerprints."

"The murderer was careless. Most clean the weapon to eradicate the prints, but our killer didn't, probably in a rush."

"Is there anything else to report, Doctor?"

"Yes, we've found tyre tracks that were left about the same time as the shooting; I am having them made into a cast and also some footprints heading for the tracks."

"Good work, Doctor, you'll be Chief Pathologist by morning." She laughed and he walked back to his car.

On the way, he spotted the green Mini, parked down the road from him; he walked to a constable who was blocking the main road up to the hall.

"Constable Cox, I'm guessing that is the press parked in that Mini?" The male constable looked down the road and saw the green Mini.

"No sir, that's Loopy Lotte."

"Loopy Lotte?"

"Real name: Charlotte Steel, local woman, says she has the gift of sight."

Eliote understood. "A psychic hey?"

The constable nodded. "Yes, sir, but she is not a good one."

Eliote watched the car and the woman inside who was obviously watching the encounter.

"Please elaborate, Cox."

"A couple of years ago, Inspector Frashier then a promising young Sergeant was asked by Brightly to re-investigate the cold case we all called 'the Christmas Day Murders.'" It was a case Simon had not heard of. "Well, Frashier got a phone call from Miss Steel saying that two bodies would be found in a house on the outskirts of Chelmesbury. We spent two weeks hunting that house but to no avail, so she was arrested for wasting police time, but Miss Steel would not give up. A few weeks later, she was again arrested after breaking in and searching the house again. She was sent to court and escaped a prison sentence; with a stipulation she was never to set foot near a crime scene again."

"Obviously she hasn't abided by that order." Simon left the constable and headed for the green car.

Charlotte watched him as he headed towards her; this was her chance to speak to him.

She got out of the car and met him. "Detective Chief Inspector Simon Eliote. I am…"

"Miss Charlotte Steel," he interrupted, and held out his hand, but she would not take it.

"Sorry, I learnt a valuable lesson years ago, not to touch anyone, I see lots of things, scary things, I think it's best if we just go and walk."

Eliote stood his ground. "I would rather not do that, Miss Steel," he said bluntly.

Her face fell. "I suppose they told you about the bodies." He nodded and she blushed, then she looked deep into his eyes. "Do they still call me Loopy Lotte?" Eliote did not answer, but she knew they did. "So you are here to tell me to go, just like Frashier does?" She did not give him time to answer and turned to head back to the car, but she stopped when he replied.

"I fancied a small walk, saw a strange car and thought I would see who it was." He paused and watched her turn around slowly. "So why did you want to see me? I know that's why you're here."

"I came to warn you."

"Warn me?"

"Yes, this new killer who attacks with so much rage and uses a knife, he will kill again and again, before you catch him."

"And you sensed this?"

She turned and walked back to her car, angry. "You got me there, Chief Inspector," she said with venom, "and I started to believe your friendliness." She got into her car and slammed the door, then opened the window and looked at him. "You're just like Frashier; he started friendly and then turned sour." She started the car and drove away, wheels spinning dirt at Simon.

Eliote watched her go.

"I wasn't acting," he said sadly and then turned and headed back to the scene of the crime.

THE DEATHLY ANGEL

By
Kevin Bailey

CHAPTER SIXTEEN

Sunday morning came quickly and the winter sun shone through the large bay windows of the priory, but Eliote was awake. He'd had a restless night, his mind constantly going over everything that had happened up at Howden Hall, especially with Charlotte accusing him of being like Frashier. But even that concern was surpassed by what he had learnt about his forgotten heritage.

He knew that there was only one place where he would discover the truth, so he got out of bed, threw on his dressing gown and headed for his mother's study. This was a part of the old house that he had never been allowed to enter, but it was somewhere he had to go. When he got there, however, he found to his surprise that the door was locked.

He cursed and crept down to the kitchen, where he sought out Henry's large bunch of keys. Once he'd returned to his mother's study, he found the right key and opened the door.

The room smelt of musty perfume, but it was still tidy and well looked after; he suspected that Henry would still come in and clean the room for his mistress. It was decorated in an elegant style, with royal blues and rich reds everywhere, even on the four-poster bed.

Beautifully woven gold cloth hung from the rails around the bed, held in place with elegant ties, and on the wall above the headrest, the coat of arms of the Mardon Family proclaimed ownership. It was so similar to the crest above the front door that he had to ask himself why he had never noticed it before.

As he looked around he felt like he was intruding. Of the two doors at the back of the room he knew that one led to the bathroom, so the other must give access to his mother's study.

He felt like a child with a wrapped-up present, as he opened the door and entered. He fumbled around the wall and found the switch that turned on the lights. The smell of dust burning prickled his nose.

He saw his mother's mahogany desk and sat down in her decrepit black leather chair. The top drawer on the left of the desk contained some old letters between his mother and father, going back to when they were courting, and bank statements for the estate. In the top right-hand drawer, he found more letters and bank statements, the second drawer contained the deeds to the house and grounds, but in the third drawer were two photo albums full of family photos and private letters. Some of the photos he had never seen before.

As he turned the pages, he saw his mother enjoying life, at parties, in the garden, in the house and with her son. But these latter pictures were hard to comprehend. He and his mother had always seemed to hate each other, and he could still remember the bitter feuds, torrid arguments and the heated discussions between them. These photos gave the lie to those memories though, and you would never have known…

Just then he heard a familiar voice.

"She really did love you, Master Simon." He turned and saw Henry in the doorway of the study, tears in his eyes.

"She never really showed it," Eliote said as Henry came and stood beside him, looking down at a group photo.

"How young I looked," the older man said.

Eliote smiled warmly at him. "After Dad left you were the only one I loved, Henry, you were like my uncle, you still are."

"And I treated you like the son I never had," Henry said, as Simon turned the page. "But tell me, why did you hate your mother, Simon?" He looked at the fun-loving woman, her hair flowing in the wind.

"I hated the way she treated my dad, to the point where one day he upped and left, never even said goodbye, and I never forgave her for that." Simon turned the page. The next picture was taken up at the Hall, and he saw his aunt and the murder victim, himself and his mother, who looked radiant and beautiful.

"That is what upset her the most after everything she put up with; the son she loved hated her." Henry sighed and raised an eyebrow, then continued, "You will never understand that, Master Simon, you were very young."

"I may have been, but she deserved the anger I showed her, Dad would still be here if it wasn't for her." Simon sensed anger and hatred towards him from Henry when he barked at him.

"No, she did not, Master Simon, and he wouldn't be here, he was a cruel and evil man, who I hope is dead."

"Don't say that, Henry!" it was Simon's turn to get angry. "It's my mother who I am glad is dead, she didn't even come to my passing-out ceremony. How I despised her for that." He paused. "To punish her, I stayed in London and raised a family, a family I would never bring here."

Henry looked at Simon with loving eyes as if he was going to tell him some great truth. "Turn the page." Simon didn't understand. "Turn the page," he said again.

Simon turned the page. There was a picture of him in his first police uniform shaking hands with the chief constable. Behind the chief constable was a smiling woman and Eliote could see it was his mother.

"That's…" He found it difficult to speak.

"Your mother. Yes she came, she was proud of you Master Simon, nothing would have stopped her from coming, but by then, you and her weren't talking," he paused looking at the photograph, "It took a lot of effort on my part to get that photo, but after it was taken, she vanished into the crowd."

Eliote was still confused and Henry turned and opened a cupboard. He pulled out another photo of the same image and his mother had her back to him and was unrecognizable.

"This was the photo that adorned the walls of my grandparents' house in London."

"Your grandparents knew," he pointed at the picture, "that that was your mother but they were sworn never to tell you." This was still too much to handle and he got up and walked out of the study, but Henry stopped him.

"Do you know what your mum died of?" he said. "She died of a broken heart, the son she loved more than anything, including me, didn't love her."

"What do you mean, including you?"

Henry turned and walked back into the study. He found a book on the wall and turned it. A secret door opened behind the desk and Henry grabbed a torch and Eliote followed. Half way down, he stopped at a slot in the wall.

"Pull the brick out and tell me what you see."

Simon did so and saw a grille, through which he could see his old room.

Then Henry walked further down the derelict passageway. Simon put the brick back into its groove and followed. He guessed where this passageway would come out and he was right; it was the annex where Henry lived.

"How long were you lovers?" Eliote asked.

Henry ignored his question and walked into a part of the priory Simon had never been to. It was similar in fashion to the rest of the house, but less ornate. Henry explained that this part of the house was the oldest part, and contained the priory lodges that once housed the monks.

Eliote followed Henry into a small comfortable sitting room with a small lit wood-burning stove in the fireplace surround. When he approached the window, he saw his mother's old room, which was how Henry had known he had been in there. Simon looked over at his friend. "You didn't answer my question."

Henry placed some more wood on the stove and then sat down in an old chair; he looked like he was a storyteller about to tell children some fantastic story.

"We weren't lovers as such, Master Simon," he paused, "we just loved each other's company."

Simon saw a pot of tea on the side and went and got himself some, then he grabbed a chair from the large kitchen table and came and sat down opposite. "How did your friendship start?" he asked the question as if interviewing a suspect.

Henry closed his eyes and remembered.

"It was a long time ago; I think I was an under-butler at the great Howden Hall. Your mother was about fourteen, and we spent all our spare time together, but as we got older we realized we were falling in love."

Eliote butted in. "So you were lovers?"

Henry gave him an evil stare and continued. "Your grandfather didn't like how things were going between his daughter, Lady Ann, and me an under-butler, so I was sent miles away and she was betrothed to your father." He stopped to pour himself and Simon another cup of tea. "Then your father married your mother, but on their wedding night your grandfather died. She went to her room where you father who was a drunk, spiteful, horrid, evil man, raped her." He drank some of the tea and Simon could see the hatred in his eyes. "After that, they never slept in the same room again. A month later, following some correspondence between Lady Ann and my new lord, I was asked to come back as Lady Ann's private secretary and butler. Eight months later you were born."

"So what you are telling me is that I am the consequence of that rape. Was my father ever charged?" he asked, with his policeman's head on.

Henry shook his head. "When you were born, the family welcomed you as a union of the marriage between your mother and father, the rape was brushed under the carpet so only a few knew."

The skeletons in the cupboard were being aired; Simon couldn't believe it.

"I always loved my father, broke my heart when he left, I didn't know he was that cruel."

Henry smiled warmly and nodded. "He was a cruel man, hated me," he pointed to himself, "but your mother got strong and started to stand up to him, even defending me." He paused, remembering sad times. "And then she had to be strong." He drank some of the tea.

"Why?"

Henry looked at him. "Because of you; you became ill, double pneumonia, it was touch and go whether you would survive, it was that bad, that they even had a painting commissioned of you, to hang in the family archives at Howden manor," Henry looked at a photo of Simons mother on his mantle piece, "Your parents of course blamed each other and they split up, but keeping their hatred of each other secret, they stayed together for you."

Eliote had never known any of this, but he wanted more. "Go on," he ordered and drank some more tea.

"Your father had several mistresses brought to him by some of the secret passages, but your mother didn't have any lovers, as she was a lady and heiress to the Mardon estate."

"But what of the passageway we have just come down?" Henry sat up straight.

"We discovered that hidden passage one summer's day, when she asked me to hang up a painting of you. I banged in the nail and a large hole appeared. We investigated the hole and found a passageway, which you can see ended here."

"Why did Dad really go? Was it because of my mother or me?"

Henry shook his head. "After defying everyone, including private doctors, you," he pointed at Simon, "got better, he didn't need to be here anymore," Henry looked at him, "he left Simon because he didn't love your mother, he was just here for the money and when they separated, your grandfather paid him a hellava lot of money, to never return. I believe he lives in London somewhere, wouldn't tell anyone, not even your grandparents."

Simon stood up and approached the entrance to the annex.

"Henry?"

"Yes, Master Simon."

"What do you know about Lord Mardon?"

"He is a good man, comes over and has a cuppa with me every so often, a bit snobby but a good man, why?"

"He was shot dead last night outside his study."

Henry looked surprised at the news and then a sense of realization hit him hard. "But that would make you…"

Eliote nodded.

"My aunt told me: the heir to the estate."

CHELMESBURY POLICE STATION

Eliote had left Henry and had got dressed and was sitting in the observation/briefing room. It was now late in the evening, but he didn't want to go home and face even more truths than the ones he had already heard; truths about the mother he'd hated and the father he had worshipped, a father who had raped his mother and he had been the outcome of that rape. For the first time in his life, he actually felt sorry for his mother and that upset him the most, the worst part was, he could never ask for forgiveness.

Trying to banish these thoughts, he grabbed his files and started to prepare for the briefing, he had the pen-like device in his hand and was looking at the screen behind him; folders were being opened and examined.

This technology was fantastic to him, he had everything that had been inputted into the computer on the screen, several lab reports, statements from interviews and from witnesses, pictures of the victims, information on them, he also had up files of cases that had not been solved, and now he was going through them, finding wrinkles to be ironed out for the morning's briefing at eleven. He was about to take a sip of his mineral water, when Detective Sergeant Day walked in.

"Miranda," he said, "thank you for coming in on a Sunday evening."

"No problems, sir. My boyfriend is busy today anyway, so I would have been bored on my own at home. Besides, when I informed Frashier I was coming in he asked me if I would help him go through the shooting case at Aden Close. He's struggling a little, I'm sorry to say guv; he has no solid leads except the car."

Eliote smiled. "You respect him a lot, don't you?"

She nodded. "Yes I do gov. He saved my life a couple of years ago. We were on a drugs bust together, and in the raid he nearly took a bullet for me, so I've got his back at all times."

"I am glad to hear it, Sergeant, I just wish I could respect him," he said, looking at his reflection in the monitor. "Maybe it's me; maybe I am not the person I thought I was." He thought back to his conversation with Henry and Lady Morden.

Day saw him in a world of his own and brought him out of his thoughts by walking to the computer terminal.

"I'll just put all the information for tomorrow morning's meeting in the computer and then I'll go and find Frashier."

There was a knock at the door and Eliote looked up and said, "Come in." Frashier walked in, looking like he had not been home for a few nights.

Even though Day had already told him, he thought it polite to ask. "Ah, Inspector, how are things going with the shooting in Aden Close?"

Frashier sat down and sighed. "It's not going too good. We thought we had our man, but he has a solid alibi, so I'm back to square one."

"Something will come up, wait and see, just keep plodding along," Eliote said.

Frashier nodded reluctantly. "If it's all right by you, sir, can I steal Day from you?"

"Sure, I just need her help in setting up this piece of equipment and then she's all yours."

Frashier sort of smiled, and said, "Thanks." He stood up and was about to leave when Day nudged him and he stopped and looked back at Eliote. "Guv, I'd like to apologize in front of Sergeant Day as my witness, for the behaviour you witnessed. Richard and I don't usually drink on duty."

Eliote smiled at him. "Make sure it doesn't happen again and I won't put anything on your file."

"Thank you, sir," Frashier said through gritted teeth and after smiling at Day he said, "See you tomorrow, sir."

Eliote watched him turn and walk out of the office, but before he closed the door, he called out, "Inspector don't forget, briefing at eleven, all case updates."

Frashier turned and nodded. "Gov." He looked over at Day, "Miranda, see you in a while," and then he left.

That evening, whilst Simon Eliote was trying to settle in to a new life in Chelmesbury, another was out hunting for his next prey. That night he would succeed.

***

THE DEATHLY ANGEL

By

Kevin Bailey

CHAPTER SEVENTEEN

The town of Glayton, where Steve Marston's 'Books for You,' was located, was like most large towns, with two distinct sides to its character.

One was like Dr Jekyll, nice, quiet, pleasant, a picture-postcard town, where people described it as "a wonderful place to visit; the residents are friendly and helpful and the scenery is lovely, with the River Severn running alongside the hill the town is situated on".

Glayton's historic buildings included a medieval town hall, a museum and a university, whilst the ruins of a castle sat at the bottom of the hill, just up from the main railway station. The town centre was located at the top of the hill.

But quite similar to the story of Dr Jekyll, Glayton held a dark secret which blighted its brighter side, because after dark it became a notorious haven for crime, and this was one of the reasons for the upgrades to Chelmesbury's police station, to try and tackle the drunks, druggies, murderers, rapists and thieves who seemed to operate in this and other Shropshire towns.

Mandy's, one of the best nightclubs in town, was quiet for this time on a Sunday night, even though the dance floor was almost full, but people were out enjoying themselves and if you were after a great night you came here.

The nightclub was in the old sector of the town, away from any residential areas and shops. It was once the old Chelmesbury Victorian Theatre, but Mandy the owner had spent a lot of money and time turning it into a nightclub, with another large building attached, which was the bingo hall.

In one corner of the dance floor, two tall men stood admiring the women and drinking out of bottles; they were also thinking about their friend James.

Jamie, the taller of the two, looked seriously at his friend David and said, "I visited Paul in hospital yesterday. He told me about James and then gave me a warning saying I had to watch my back."

David took a swig from his bottle. "And are you?" he asked.

Jamie shook his head. "What, me scared of this killer? Never. Bring it on, I say." He finished his beer and ordered another from a barman who had his back to the two.

"We all knew James was a pussy," Jamie continued. "He was only made captain 'cause he was the best player out of us all. Mind you, I should have been captain, I was the oldest and brightest star, no one was better than me."

"Sure, Jamie," David said, chuckling.

Jamie drank some more and looked around the room at the local talent. "I think it's time we mingled, Dave," he said, then excused himself and headed for the gents.

Dave watched him go and then ordered two more drinks, but he was distracted by a blonde-haired girl who was smiling at him and failed to notice the barman slip away.

The barman walked into the gents and headed for the urinals, walking past Jamie who was relieving himself. "Hello, Jamie," he said, "how are you keeping?"

Jamie did up his flies and looked over at the barman, who was wearing a hoodie. "You?" he said with venom.

The barman just smiled and nodded. "Yep, it's little old me."

Jamie walked towards the stranger, who seemed to tense up. "What do you want?" he asked.

The hooded figure stood up straight. "Nothing," he said, catching his reflection in the mirror and smiling evilly. "I want absolutely nothing from you, Jamie, I just saw you, that's all."

Jamie smiled. "You're still the same as you were when I used to beat you up; you're still that weakling, who had no strength to stand up for himself. That is why we used to pick on you, 'cause you were weak."

The lad turned and he was calm, collected. "I probably was, but that was then my oldest so called friend, but this is now."

Jamie laughed. "You're taking me on? Ha, pathetic, you couldn't even hurt a fly. I can still remember when you were little."

The lad stood still, no emotion in his face, sending an icy chill down Jamie's spine when he replied, "Ah but you're forgetting one thing." He pointed at Jamie. "You are the weak one now."

Jamie froze. "How do you mean?"

"Well," his eyes circled the room, "you haven't got your friends with you now, have you?"

"No," Jamie replied.

"Are those gallant friends of yours going to come to your rescue? I think not!"

A couple of people had come in to relieve themselves, and departed without paying any attention to Jamie or the barman.

"The room is empty," Jamie said. "You also have no friends."

“Yes, but I don’t need friends like you did.” The barman continued softly, so that no one except Jamie would hear, “When I killed James I didn’t need anybody. He begged me to stop.”

“You were the one who killed James?” Jamie hissed.

The stranger nodded. “I warned Paul that I would wait, wait for that time when you were alone, to punish you for what you did to me.” He paused and with venom in his voice he added, “I do not forget easily.”

The realization hit Jamie like a punch to the gut and he looked at the hooded lad, hatred in his eyes, his fists clenched.

“You bastard, he was one of my best friends. I’ll kill you for that.” Jamie went to close in on the lad and now they really did face up to each other. Jamie still had his fists ready, the anger from what the barman had said built up inside him, and he wanted revenge.

He pointed at his attacker. “You want a piece of me shithead? Well, come and get it. You’ll find I won’t be a pushover like James, because I am a better match.”

But the lad stood still. “That is why we are different, Jamie. I will not attack you in a public place, but heed my warning; I will wait, no matter how long it takes.”

Jamie noticed that the lad was about to turn. “Come on, shithead, me and you right now.”

A smile appeared on the hooded lad’s face. “You’re sure you want to die in a toilet?”

Jamie laughed. “Ha, I won’t die, you will.”

The smile on the hooded lad’s face disappeared and his eyes burned red with vengeance and hatred, just as if someone had switched them on. “James and Wayne both begged not to be killed,” he said, “and you‘ll be the same.”

“I will never beg like that, not like you used to.” Jamie’s words had the desired effect and he knew this was the best time to strike. Stepping towards the lad, he went to hit him with all the strength he had, but the barman simply and calmly stepped back, blocking his attack. He grabbed Jamie around the throat, lifted him up and pushed him into one of the cubicles, kicking the door shut and locking it. He took out his hidden knife and plunged it straight into Jamie's heart; blood poured down his victim's chest and into the toilet pan.

As on the previous attacks, the barman was filled with anger and hatred, and he stabbed Jamie in the chest again and again; blood sprayed the walls as he took the knife out of his victim. Then, for his coup de grace, he slit Jamie's throat.

After flushing the toilet, the barman flicked a card and the photo on to his victim's lap. There were now three circles on the photo. Then he turned, closed the door behind him and locked it with a coin. Wiping sweat from his brow, he cleaned the knife and calmly walked out of the toilet, heading straight for the club exit.

A bouncer on the door greeted him. "Hello, Sam, you're going home early, I thought you were here till midnight."

The lad smiled and shook his head. "Nah, just quit, it was dead boring." Hiding his face from the CCTV camera, he was gone into the night.

Back at the bar Dave was still talking to the girl he'd met whilst waiting for Jamie. Even though he was having a laugh with her, every time someone came out of the toilet, he hoped to see Jamie so he could introduce her to him, but he never came out.

Something was wrong and he excused himself from the girl and with a worried feeling inside of him, which was getting worse, he headed towards the toilet.

He entered slowly, looking around at the empty room. He shouted for his friend, but something made him look at the floor.

That's when he saw water coming from under the closed door of one of the cubicles.

"Jamie, are you all right, bud?" he called, but was met by silence. He crouched down and peeped under the door, and saw his friend slumped on the toilet, blood gushing still from the cuts on his throat and chest.

He ran out screaming, all the clubbers turned and looked at him. The DJ switched off the music and a bouncer ran up to Dave.

"What's up, mate?"

"Call the police," he replied. "Someone has killed my friend."

The hooded figure sat on a bench and watched as chaos erupted inside and outside of the club. He smiled evilly and stood up, stretching out his arms. The now recognisable shadow of an angel appeared before him and his smile widened.

Hearing sirens in the distance, he knew it was time to disappear.

***

CHARLOTTE'S HOUSE

Charlotte awoke in the night with severe pain in her chest, back and face; she sat up feeling like she'd done ten rounds with a boxer.

After touching her back she got out of bed and walked into the bathroom, where she turned on the light above the mirror and looked deep into her own reflection.

Something about her face disturbed her; there was blood trickling from her nose, so she bent over and took some tissue, then looked back into the mirror, trying to dab at the blood.

Placing a tissue deep up her nose, still desperately trying to stop the bleeding, she tried to remember the last time she'd had a nosebleed, but couldn't.

She took away the tissue from up her nose, expecting the blood to have stopped, but it hadn't; if anything it had got worst. It now gushed from her nostril, as if she had sliced a vein. She tried more tissue but no matter what she did, the blood continued to flow.

She walked back into her bedroom, grabbed the phone and dialled the emergency number, but as she went to place the phone to the side of her face, she felt wetness and looking down at the phone, she saw an incredible sight. Blood was gushing from the receiver.

Panicking, she looked around the room and saw blood trickling from the bedclothes and a puddle appeared to be coming from under the bed. Once again, she ran into the bathroom and turned on the tap, but blood gushed into the sink. She turned and looked down at the toilet pan, where blood bubbled up through the water.

She tried to scream, but as her mouth opened, blood started gushing from it; she fell to the floor, collapsing in a heap.

Lifting her head, she watched the blood slowly approaching as if attracted to her, and then the fear took hold. She was frozen to the spot, the blood got closer and closer like some hunter circling its prey, and then she felt it engulf her body.

THE PRIORY

Henry was startled awake as the phone on his bedside table rang. He stretched to the other side of the bed and lifted the receiver.

"Good evening, the Old Priory," he said tiredly.

"Hi, sorry to bother you, this is Detective Sergeant Miranda Day from Chelmesbury CID. Is Chief Inspector Simon Eliote available?" Henry got up from his bed unclothed and looked out of the annex towards Simon's wing, there were no lights on and so he assumed he was asleep.

"I think he is asleep," he said. "Is it important?"

"Unfortunately, it is," Day replied.

Henry sighed. "I'll try and put you through." He pressed a button on the phone and heard it ring.

Simon picked up the phone.

"Yes."

"Sorry to bother you, Master Simon, but I have a DS Day on the line. She says it's important, shall I put it through?"

"Please, Henry, and remember that it's just Simon."

"Very good Simon." Eliote sighed, knowing full well that Henry would never comfortably be able to call him "just Simon".

Then the voice of Sergeant Day came on and he was brought back from his annoyance at Henry.

"Sorry to disturb you Gov, but we have another angel attack." She paused and Eliote could hear the turning of the pages in a notebook. "Name's Jamie Tweeting," she said. "He was the second on the right of the photo, again like the others violently stabbed to death."

Eliote got up and put on his dressing gown and then replied, "Hold the line for a minute please, Sergeant." He transferred the call through to his study, then opened the extra door in his room, went through and picked up the phone.

"Are you still there Sergeant?"

"Yes Guv."

He sat down at the desk and swivelled to look at the board, where he had placed a copy of the football team photo and he circled Jamie.

He then turned back and continued to speak. "Where are you?"

"I'm at Mandy's Nightclub, Sir."

Eliote rubbed his eyes. "Sorry, where's that?"

"It's in Glayton."

"How do I get there, Sergeant?"

Getting out a plan of the towns of Chelmesbury and Glayton and using a florescent pen, he started to draw lines on the map, as she explained.

After five minutes examining the map, he knew roughly where he was going.

"I could get someone to pick you up, sir."

Eliote frowned. “I’ll find it, Sergeant,” he said. “I’m on my way.”

***

Charlotte awoke and sat up from the bathroom floor. After getting up she looked at herself in the mirror. There was no blood, not even dried on, so it must have been a bad dream; the realization that she had been asleep on the floor didn‘t register to her. She freshened up and walked into her bedroom, got dressed and sat on the end of the bed, to brush her hair.

Her radio alarm clock came on and the newscaster’s voice echoed through the room.

“This is BBC Radio Shropshire News. We open the news with reports that the Deathly Angel has struck again, this time in Glayton. Police who have been investigating the previous murder in Lovers Lane are working alongside officers from Glayton Police station in searching the crime scene at a local Nightclub.”

Charlotte turned the radio off and headed for her green Mini.

THE DEATHLY ANGEL

By

Kevin Bailey

CHAPTER EIGHTEEN

Following Miranda's instructions to the letter, Simon was soon nearing Mandy's nightclub. He drove past, turned the Saab in through the car park entrance and parked his car next to two squad cars. As he headed for the front door, Day in some protective overalls was waiting for him with a plastic bag.

"Hi, guv," she said, handing him the bag. He put on the protective overalls that were inside and then smiled at Miranda.

"Let's see what we got, eh?"

"Okay, sir, this way." She led Eliote across the dance floor and towards the cordoned-off area, where she lifted the police tape and she and Eliote entered.

Doctor Strong was examining the cuts, and when he saw Eliote he remarked sarcastically to Penny, "Wonder if he'll send me home this time?"

Simon looked coldly at him. True, their first meeting had not gone too well, but Simon was a man who would let bygones be bygones, so he stretched out his hand. Strong took off a glove and decided to accept the handshake.

"We will talk more about things later, but at this present time your analysis, please?" Strong nodded and looked back into the cubical. "The victim is about the same age as James, twenty-seven. It looks like he was in perfect heath, but died from multiple stab wounds to the chest and then the throat." He pointed to show Eliote the wounds. "Of course, I will know more when I get the body back to the lab." He held two evidence bags. "All we have at the moment is our attacker's calling card and another photo for your records."

Eliote took hold of the bags and looked at their contents. The calling card read, "You've been killed by the Deathly Angel" and above the words were two grey wings. In the photo, three of the players had scribbles around them. He turned to Day. "So we do have another Angel attack, but there is something curious about the photo. We have only had two killings, yet this photo is suggesting three. Something is very wrong here."

Day looked over at the body in the cubicle. "So somewhere out there, another victim could be waiting to be found?" Eliote nodded.

"Chief Inspector," Strong said, "after I have investigated the crime scene can I have a word with you?"

"I'll look forward to it," said Eliote, who then turned to Day, leaving Strong to his thoughts and his job. "Our top priorities on this case are as follows. One, find out why there are three rings around these players, and two, find the others before our Angel here does." He paused. "How's the photo inquiry going, anyway?"

"Too slowly, guv," Day said apologetically. "People I've shown the picture to don't recognize anyone on it."

He looked at her in a fatherly way and smiled. "Keep on it," he told her.

"Aye, guv."

Eliote and Day walked away from the Gents toilets and headed back to the main dance floor.

Eliote saw groups of people sitting around at the corners of the large room; some sat on the floor waiting to be allowed to go home.

"Have all the clubbers made statements?" he asked.

The sergeant nodded and replied, "Yes, guv." She indicated a big-busted, brunette woman talking to some constables. "That lady over there is Miss Mandy Schnell, the owner of the club."

Eliote walked towards her and introduced himself. "Miss Schnell, I am Detective Chief Inspector Simon Eliote. I would like to ask you some questions if I may."

"Of course, Chief Inspector," she said warmly with a German accent.

Eliote glanced around the room and spotted some smartly dressed people sitting near the door, being interviewed by some plain-clothed officers. "What are the bouncers like here?" he asked.

She looked at the people by the door and replied, "They're a good lot. They're devastated that they never saw this coming; they all do their jobs properly."

"They may do, Miss Schnell, but tonight, someone walked into this club with a knife and stabbed another clubber to death, then miraculously left. Can you explain this?"

"I can't." She paused and lowered her head. "This is the first time in the twenty years I have been in this business that anything like this has ever happened in one of my clubs." Eliote looked at the doormen. "Who out of them is the head doorman at the club?"

"Ritchie," she called, and a tall man looked over. She beckoned him to her, and introduced him to Eliote. "This is Ritchie Dawes; he is head of Security at my club." The two men shook hands.

"Ritchie, this is Detective Chief Inspector Simon Eliote from Chelmesbury CID."

"Hello, Chief Inspector," he said with a deep cockney accent, and Eliote guessed that he would probably be able to pick him up and throw him out single-handedly without even perspiring.

"Ritchie, can you tell me if you check each person that comes in to the club?" Eliote asked.

He tensed up. "Everyone except the staff, I know them all."

Eliote looked at the camera on the wall. "Do those work?" he asked.

Ritchie nodded. "There's a control booth up on the third floor; all the cameras are wired to that one place."

"Can I see the recordings?" Eliote asked Mandy.

"Ya," Mandy replied and looked at Ritchie. "Take Chief Inspector Eliote up to the booth, please."

"OK, thank you for your time, Miss Schnell."

"Anything I can do to help, Chief Inspector." Eliote smiled and then Ritchie escorted him up the two flights of stairs to the third floor.

"This way, sir," Ritchie said and led him down a corridor to a door marked "Camera Room". He placed a key in the door, unlocked it and then they entered.

The room was about the same size as a large bedroom; it had magnolia coloured walls and every inch of space was filled with pieces of equipment. Computer monitors lined the walls and a large display of sound and lighting equipment lay on desks.

In the centre was a large screen that reminded Eliote of the observation/briefing room back at HQ. Below it was an array of DVD recorders, numbered by camera.

Ritchie went to the recorder marked "Door Camera" and pressed Rewind.

Eliote watched the screen and saw images of police cars. When Ritchie pressed Fast Rewind, the image sped backwards, right to the beginning, and he pressed Play.

They watched as people were searched and allowed in, including the deceased, all looking forward to the night's entertainment.

"Fast forward," Eliote commanded. Ritchie obeyed and the images sped up, then Eliote noticed a hooded man with his back to the camera; he seemed to be hiding his face. On normal play, they watched as the hooded man walked towards the bouncers, his face still away from the camera. Then Eliote spotted something shining in the hood; it looked like the butt of a metal penknife. "Freeze," he said and Eliote pointed at the hood. "There, look." Ritchie turned and angrily said, "Shit."

"It's OK, you weren't to know." Eliote walked to the DVD player and pressed Fast Forward, until the deceased and his mate Dave walked in and were searched.

Eliote paused the recording and asked Ritchie, "Why are those two being searched, yet the hooded figure wasn't even though he was wearing a hoodie?"

Ritchie shrugged his shoulders, took out his phone and dialled a number. "Hi, Steve, it's Ritch. Were you on the door at…" he paused looking at the monitor, "at about eight-ish?" He listened to the reply. "You were. OK, can you come up to the camera room please?" He placed the phone back into his pocket and then waited.

A few seconds later a tall, bald-headed, skinny man in a long leather jacket with a black tie walked into the room and Ritchie introduced him to Eliote.

"This is Steve Halifax, assistant head doorman." The two men shook hands and Simon repeated his question to Steve.

"He wasn't checked 'cause he is Samuel Dalton, bit of a quiet lad, was one of the bar staff."

"Was?" Eliote prompted.

"Yeah, he quit just before the alarm was raised."

Eliote pondered this new information; at least he had a name for the attacker.

After thanking Steve, he turned back towards the monitor and pressed Fast Forward. Two hours later on the counter, he spotted the hooded man once more and he pressed play.

The hooded man walked under the camera and there again was the knife, but it wasn't as shiny as it was before, then after speaking to the doorman, he casually walked into the street and then into the darkness.

"I want all the tapes of the evening," Eliote said. Ritchie nodded and placed a CD into the recorder and recorded all the images and then handed them to Eliote.

Ritchie and Steve escorted Eliote back to the others and he approached a female DC who was taking down witness statements. He handed her the CD and said, "Constable Felts, take this back to the station, then you and DC Bent can go through it, see if you can spot our hooded Avenger, see if you can get a better image of him, anything."

"Right guv." She walked off and Eliote went to find DS Day who was walking back to the toilet area. Miranda turned and smiled at her superior.

"Guv, Miss Schnell has said that the two lads often come in on Friday and Saturday nights, they don't cause trouble and usually leave quietly before the club closes."

"When we are finished here, I want you to ask Miss Schnell for the personnel files on a Samuel Dalton," Eliote said.

"A few others have mentioned that name, guv. Could he be the killer?"

Eliote nodded. "It would seem so, but something isn't right and I can't put my finger on it. I want this Sam's address. What of the deceased's friend?"

Miranda looked down at her notepad. "Dave Freeman was so shocked at his friend's murder that the paramedics had to take him to hospital."

Eliote cursed under his breath. “Okay, Sergeant, you go and find the files and we’ll reconvene at the station and then go find this Samuel Dalton.”

“I may need a lift, guv,” Day said apologetically. “DC Felts took my car.”

Eliote nodded and handed her his keys, watching Strong approach from the corner of his eye. “Go and get the car ready, I’ll be with you as soon as this is over.” He looked towards Strong and Day nodded and left.

“Chief Inspector,” Strong called, “can I have that word now please?”

“Doctor, if this is to do with you and Frashier smelling of alcohol, then don’t worry; I have put the incident behind us.”

“I couldn’t care less if you were bringing us to the attention of Brightly or the Chief Constable,” Strong said coldly. “I wanted to talk to you about something my daughter told me, yesterday.”

Eliote raised his eyes. “Go on, Doctor.” He didn’t see what this had to do with him, but thought he would humour the doctor.

“Well, she is a pathologist at Hereford and was on duty a couple of days ago when Tenbury Wells police station called asking her to investigate a killing at a local factory. When she got there she discovered this.” He pulled out an evidence bag and handed it to Eliote.

It was the same calling card of the Deathly Angel, but this photo had only two circles around the players.

“Why did you not tell me about this sooner, Doctor?” Eliote fumed.

“I have been busy, since you sent me and Frashier home; I have not had the time.”

“You could have made time, damn you. This was a vital piece of evidence. If it wasn‘t for the fact that you are our chief pathologist, then I would have you arrested for wasting police time.” Everyone in the club looked over at the two men and could see Eliote red faced with anger. “What is it with this CID department? Since I have come here, I have had to put up with two of my team fighting me at all times, you and Frashier. Well, I’ve had enough, this is my team and if you don’t like it, go, I won’t stop either of you.”

“Fine, Chief Inspector,” Strong said through gritted teeth.

“I will no longer tolerate your attitude, Doctor,” Eliote said as the two men came face to face.

“And I don’t like yours either, Chief Inspector. I have been here for a long time, I have seen heads come and go, but you are a dying breed. You come here having a go at us for not being proper about our job, but so what if I had a drink? With the job I do, I need it.” Eliote stopped him.

“I do not condemn you for that, Doctor, I may on occasion have joined you, but when someone dies in mysterious circumstances I need my chief pathologist’s judgment not to be clouded by alcohol.”

“None of your predecessors ever thought my judgment would be clouded by anything. I had a drink with my daughter and she asked me to pass on this information to you, and this is how I am treated, with contempt.”

“I haven’t got time for this,” Eliote said, walking away. But Strong wasn’t about to be hushed up.

“You will make time, Chief Inspector, I am a valuable part of CID, I am a great help to you, but I can also be a bastard.”

Eliote stopped in his tracks, turned and glared at Strong. “Really?” he said. “Well, let me tell you something, Doctor. I too can make peoples’ lives hell. I am the head of this department, not you and most defiantly not DI Frashier, and like it or not, I am here to stay. Oh,” he paused and pointed at Strong, “I say whether you are a help or a bastard, as you put it, so we shall leave it at that.” Eliote turned and headed for the door and the awaiting Sergeant Day.

Day started the engine and placed the car in reverse.

“Well,” Eliote said, “because of the doctor keeping things from me, we now have another thing to do: find all the info on this Samuel Dalton. But first we’ll have to take a trip to Tenbury Wells’s police station, as it seems they have discovered our missing footballer.”

As they drove, Eliote said, “I seem to be upsetting the bandwagon here.”

Day smiled and said, “All the officers at the station are feeling a bit under pressure what with the relocation and a new head. You can’t blame them too much; Frashier and Strong are good workers if you’d give them a chance.”

Eliote looked out of the window and then back at Day. “Maybe I will,” he said. “Wish they were as happy as you.” She blushed and continued driving.

At Tenbury police station they parked and headed for the main reception. Eliote took out his warrant card and showed it to the duty officer, introducing himself and DS Day.

A voice from his past hailed him.

“Simon Eliote, it’s about bloody time we bumped into each other.”

***

THE DEATHLY ANGEL

By
Kevin Bailey

CHAPTER NINETEEN

Frashier sat in the front room of his spacious apartment, which was just off Chelmesbury High Street.

There was hardly any furniture in the room apart from a white leather sofa, a bookcase full of DVDs and a wall-mounted TV.

Frashier sat on the floor with his bare back to the sofa and in front of him on the wooden floor were all the files relating to the shooting in Aden Close.

The television was on and the video from the garage was on repeat, but Frashier wasn't looking at it, his scruffy notes on the film were in front of him on an A4 Pad.

"What am I missing from this case?" he said out loud. "Something…" He looked again but whatever it was, he couldn't see it.

He grabbed a can of cola and took a long drink, almost finishing it in one. After grabbing a pen he started to write again on the pad.

> *-Main suspect: Steve Marston; has an alibi but still I feel that he is connected, somehow-.*

"But how?" he looked up and saw the car on the screen drive away and then a thought came into his head. *What a brilliant idea.*

He got up and went to the pine desk in his back bedroom, where he sat down in the swivel chair, turned on his computer and waited for it to start.

Once it was ready, he scanned a picture of Steve Marston's car then went and grabbed the DVD out of the machine in the lounge and brought that back to the computer. Using one of the many programs on his computer, he superimposed the image he had created on to the film which forensics had copied for him. Using the mouse he made it fit perfectly, then he printed out the image.

Back in the lounge, he placed the image into a new folder and then wrote a note in his pad:

-Arrange meeting with Steve Marston, 11 o'clock.-

He smiled knowing that at eleven he was supposed to be at the briefing.

After he had retrieved the files scattered all over the floor and placed them in his briefcase, he grabbed his phone and dialled a number.

"Hello."

"Pickington, it's Frashier, can you pick me up at ten in the morning? I want to go and speak to Steve Marston again."

"But guv, the sleepy voice answered, 'DCI Eliote wants us all to attend a briefing at eleven o'clock."

"So?" he said bluntly. "I am investigating a murder; it does not stop when Simon Eliote wants a briefing."

"OK, I'll pick you up at ten, but any problems you deal with it."

Frashier smiled. "You know me, I will." He placed the phone back into its holder and turning on the telly, sat down to relax.

***

Detective Inspector Dick Robertson shook hands with Eliote, who looked over at Day and said, "Sergeant Day, I would like to introduce you to a rather large and annoying thorn in my side."

Robertson laughed almost wickedly. "More like a knife," he said. "So tell me, is this call business or pleasure?"

"Unfortunately, this time it's business," Eliote said.

Robertson escorted the two officers into an interview room and they all sat down.

"So what can I do for you, old friend?" he asked.

Day opened a folder that she was carrying, and said, "I understand you are investigating the gruesome murder of Wayne Warwick who, excuse the pun, came to a sticky end?"

The detective nodded. "Yeah, but how did you know?"

Eliote said, "Your pathologist on the case is the daughter of our chief pathologist, who became intrigued when she showed him this." He took out of his pocket a plastic evidence bag, containing the photo.

"Bloody hell it's the football team."

Eliote nodded and pointed to the faces that had been circled. "James Gaston, killed violently in Lovers Lane, Jamie Tweeting, killed in a night club in Glayton, and now your victim Wayne Warwick." He placed the photo back into his inside pocket. "We think that all three were killed by the same perpetrator."

"Sounds like he's a sick twisted son of a bitch," Robertson said. "This murder has brought a factory which employs many people here in Tenbury to a standstill. I have the Chief Constable calling me every morning with questions from the owner of the place, asking when he will be able to start production again."

"After finding out that our cases are possibly linked," Eliote said, "I asked the Chief Constable and he has agreed that I take charge. You of course will be the liaison between my team and yours during the investigation."

"So the two musketeers are back to fight the cardinal once again," Robertson said with a smile. "Well at least I ain't gonna have the Chief Constable ringing me and breathing down my neck."

"There is that, old friend," Eliote said, then looked seriously at him. "I have arranged a briefing at eleven o'clock at Chelmesbury Police Station; I would very much like it if you and several of your officers could attend."

Robertson nodded. "Of course, we will be there."

"Good. Now that's settled, I would like to inspect the factory."

Robertson stood up and the three officers headed out to Simon's Saab. Robertson commented on how Eliote had come up in the world since they had worked together. When they got to the car, they were greeted by Doctor Strong and a group of forensics from Chelmesbury. Eliote introduced the doctor to DI Robertson and then they headed for Yerroks Foods.

Police had shut off a part of the factory and the road from Clee Hill to Tenbury was shut; officers were diverting traffic on other roads, causing traffic chaos.

When the Saab neared the factory, Robertson showed his warrant card and they were escorted through the barricade and told to park near a large fridge. After getting out and putting on some protective clothes, they were taken to the scene of the crime.

Flick was waiting for them and she smiled when she saw her father. "Doctor Strong," she said formally, "it is a pleasure, please come this way." The red-haired pathologist beckoned all the officers to the main crime scene.

The area had been taped off, including all windows and any internal doors. Forensics officers were examining every inch of pipe-work and floors, and metal boards had been placed on the floor to stop contamination of the crime scene.

Strong's team were split up and assigned to work with Flick's team. Eliote was taken up the steps onto the plant and shown where the body was found.

"When we turned up here," Flick said, "the toffee was still in there. Wayne's body had been mangled and smashed by the large paddles." She handed Eliote a photo of the scene, which he studied and handed back.

"How much of the body has been recovered so far?" he asked.

She beckoned him into a side room just off the factory floor, where on one of the tables, a white sheet had been placed over several plastic containers which had the body parts inside. She lifted the sheet and Eliote saw the state of the body.

It was mostly just bone and muscles, and he saw what was left of the right hand. The tips of the fingers had gone, so had the fingernails.

"Do you think he was dead before he went into the vat?" he asked.

She shook her head. "My opinion is that he was unconscious when he was put in there, but boy would he have felt it, the shock would have killed him."

Eliote nodded towards some Forensic officers who were working in front of the huge vats. "Is that where the attack took place?" he asked.

"Yes, but to attack the victim with so much violence, lift the body off the floor, carry him up those stairs and throw him in there," she pointed to the vat, "would have taken a hell of a lot of strength, even for a strong man."

"So what you're saying this man could be a sort of superman?"

She shook her head. "No, but he must be physically and mentally fit."

Eliote waited while the doctor placed the sheet back over the containers and then the two of them walked back onto the factory floor. "I mean," she paused and pointed to the steps, "I have been walking up and down those steps all morning and it has tired me out, but to do it carrying the body, well, it would have killed me."

They walked up to Strong who was helping one of his daughter's team and watched him as he extracted a finger from a sieve and matched it to the left hand of the victim.

"Has anyone informed the family?" Eliote asked.

Robertson shook his head. "I was just going when you walked into the station."

"Okay, I'll need the family's address."

"Here," Robertson said, handing it to him. "It's on the other side of town."

"Take charge here till I get back," Eliote told Day. She nodded and went back to work, then he walked with Robertson to his Saab. After the two officers had removed their protective clothing, Eliote said, "We'll leave his family till tomorrow; first I need to speak to the person who found the body."

"But, Simon, surely we should go to the family first?" Robertson said.

"Dick, don't you think it's a little weird? The crime happened days ago, yet the family have not even reported him missing."

"I never looked at it like that," Robertson said, frowning.

"Another day isn't going to matter," Eliote said, and Robertson directed him to a bungalow on the east of the town.

When they arrived at the address, they found Burt was way too intoxicated to talk to them, so Eliote decided to try and locate this

Samuel Dalton. He phoned Sergeant Day and after getting the address, he and Robertson headed for Chelmesbury.

Eliote asked Dick to stay in the car while he approached the mid-terrace house and rang the doorbell. There was silence in the house and he looked in through the window. It was relatively tidy, no mess.

A tall man in smart casual clothes approached him and asked, "Can I help you?"

Eliote turned and took out his warrant card. "I am Detective Chief Inspector Simon Eliote from Chelmesbury CID. I am looking for a Samuel Dalton."

The man smiled and raised his arms and outstretched his hands. "Well, you found him, I am Sam Dalton. What can I do for you?"

Eliote put away his card and said, "You can come with me to Chelmesbury police station to help us with our enquirers."

"Why, what have I done?"

"Your name has come up several times in connection with the murder of James Gaston, Wayne Warwick and Jamie Tweeting."

"I don't even know who these people are..."

Eliote escorted him to the Saab and placed him in the back. Sam was still pleading his innocence when Dick got in beside him. Eliote closed the door and drove the Saab back to the station.

***

Next morning Frashier was picked up by Pickington and the two officers headed for Steve Marston's house. When they arrived, Frashier went to the door and rang the bell. Somewhere in the house he heard a dog bark and footsteps approaching.

Mrs Marston opened the door in just a towel.

"Oh, it's you again," she said with disgust. "What do you want now?"

"Mrs Marston, is Steve in?" Frashier asked.

"Yes, he's in his room, why do you ask?"

"Because, Mrs Marston," Frashier answered bluntly, "we want to speak to him again."

"Haven't you done enough speaking, Inspector? It's about time you found the real killer and leave my boy alone."

Frashier pulled out the fake photo and showed it to her. "Do you recognize the car in the photo, Mrs Marston?"

"Yes," she said almost sarcastically, "its Steve's and you already know that."

Frashier replaced the photo and continued, "Mrs Marston, that image was taken off a CCTV recording the night Teresa Bennett was killed."

Pickington turned away in disgust at his superior officer, while Mrs Marston looked shocked.

"Teresa Bennett was a…" Her sentence was cut short by a loud angry voice.

"*Mum*, don't you dare say anything nasty about Teresa." They all looked to see Steve wearing a hoodie and jeans sitting on the top step of the stairs. Tears were trickling down his cheek and he was looking seriously angry at his mother, whilst he spoke to Frashier. "You wanted to speak to me again Inspector?"

Frashier nodded and answered, "Some new evidence has come to our attention Steve, which we would like to ask you about." As he said this he felt his phone vibrating. The call was from Miranda Day's desk number. He returned it to his pocket. "Sorry about that. Look, Steve, is there somewhere we can go to talk?"

Steve told his mother to get out of the way and then he escorted Frashier and Pickington in to the house.

THE INTERVIEW OF SAMUEL DALTON

Back at the station Sergeant Day replaced the phone and saw Eliote approach her carrying several files.

"Ready?" he asked.

She nodded and grabbed some of the files on her desk, then the two of them walked towards Interview Room Two. They entered to find Sam Dalton sitting at the table, along with his solicitor, an attractive brunette.

"Recording interview of Samuel Dalton, time nine-forty. Present are DCI Eliote and DS Day," Day announced, looking at Sam's solicitor. "Also in attendance is…"

The solicitor said her name. "Cara Askew."

Eliote smiled warmly at her then opened his file and began. "Sam," he said, "where were you between eight and eleven o'clock last night?"

Sam thought about it and replied, "Was at home. I was watching a DVD, American Pie I think."

"Alone?"

"Yeah, the missus was out at bingo."

Day took out several photos of Mandy's Nightclub and placed them in front of Sam and Cara. "Have you ever been here?" she asked.

Sam looked at the photos and then at her. "Yeah, when I was in my twenties, we all went there. It was the cool place to be, it was a place for sex, drugs and dance, everything went on there."

Eliote took out the photo of the football team and showed it to Sam. "Do you know anyone in that photo?"

Sam pointed at Wayne. "Yeah, I used to date his sister, Mary; he was a good lad, I think he has a wife and a couple of sprogs." He paused, looking at the circles around each person. "Are these victims of that killer that's been in the papers?"

Eliote nodded and then as he showed Sam the pathology photos of the three victims, he said their names. "Jamie Tweeting, James Gaston and…" When he put down the last picture, Sam threw up all over the desk and files. The smell of vomit stung

Simon's nose and he too felt sick. He looked over at Cara who he noticed had been quietly watching him, listening as the interview had progressed.

"I think we should take a small break, don't you, Chief Inspector?" she said.

Eliote nodded. "I have a meeting in an hour's time, so I suggest we have a two-hour break."

Day arranged for Sam and his solicitor to be escorted to a waiting room, with instructions that he freshen up and that housekeeping come and clean Interview Room Two.

The waiting room area was equipped with comfortable seating, a sink and toilets, and had a space set aside for solicitor interviews.

Day headed to the smokers' room and after lighting up, grabbed her mobile out of her handbag and rang Frashier to find out whether he was going to be at the meeting. His phone rang for ages, then went straight to answer phone.

"Damn you," she said trying again, but there was still no reply.

After finishing her cigarette, she stumped it out in an ashtray and angrily headed for her desk.

One of the officers from Tenbury CID looked over at her and asked, "Are you OK, Sergeant?"

Day shook her head. "I hope Will, I mean DI Frashier gets here soon, he's already been in trouble with the governor for drinking on duty, now he's going to be late for a meeting."

"I hope DCI Eliote isn't as bad as DI Robertson," the other officer said. "If one of us were late to a meeting, he would have bollocked us up one side and down the other."

"He isn't that bad, but I pray that Frashier isn't doing it to piss him off."

"Why do you say that?"

Day looked up at the clock. “Shit, its quarter to – never mind Frashier, if we don’t get a move on we also will be late.” The two officers got up and Day escorted her new colleague to the observation/briefing room.

***

Simon left the interview room, got cleaned up a little in his office and then he headed for the observation/briefing room; when he entered he approached the lectern and started sorting out information onto the lectern’s computer system.

At roughly ten to eleven, DI Robertson entered the room and approached him. After a few pleasantries were over including Robertson saying that Eliote was “a lucky git for having this up-to-date CID unit”, the two friends watched as the room filled up with officers from Chelmesbury, Glayton and Tenbury CID units.

Eliote looked up at Day and her associate as they entered the room; she gulped when he beckoned her over.

“DS Day, have you seen DI Frashier or DC Pickington this morning?”

“No, Guv.”

“OK, they’ve probably overslept.” Eliote watched as the two officers found a couple of chairs and then looked at the assembled crowd. “Right then, before we start I would like to welcome to our team DI Robertson and several of his team from Tenbury Wells, who are going to be helping us with our enquiries till further notice.” He looked over at Robertson. “Detective Inspector.”

The DI approached the screen and pointed the pen device at some new photos. “These images are of a third victim, ‘Wayne Warwick.’” He pressed the button on the pen, the images showing what was left of the body. There were a few gasps from the room. “The victim was murdered four days ago in a fruit processing plant in Tenbury Wells; his body was then thrown into a vat of hot toffee.” Some faces reflected a natural disgust at the mangled remains in the photos and Eliote watched as one officer removed a sweet from his mouth and placed it into its wrapper.

He sort of smiled and then said, "Thank you, Inspector." Addressing the room, he continued, "I believe the victim was murdered by the same killer as James Gaston and Jamie Tweeting." He pointed at a picture of Samuel Dalton. "Helping us with our enquiries is this man, Samuel Dalton."

The officers in the room started to talk amongst themselves and then one officer from Tenbury station asked, "Is this a suspect, Guv?"

"He is someone I will need to talk to again as I have a feeling he knows more than he is letting on, but a killer?" He shook his head. "No, I don't think so. When I showed the picture of Wayne Warwick to Sam, he threw up violently all over the interview room. Tell me why a killer who has brutally murdered three people would throw up seeing these photos. It makes no sense." He took the picture down from the screen. "I have a few more questions for Sam and I have arranged for the head of security and the head doorman to come and identify whether or not Sam was the man coming or going from the club."

"So, Guv, where does that leave our investigation?" Day asked.

"It leaves us back at the beginning, I am afraid, Sergeant, well, apart from one small thing." He pointed at Sam's picture. "The killer must have known Sam, but how does he know him and does Sam know him? This is what we need to find out. Otherwise, like I said, square one, so back to basics, people."

Day and the rest of Chelmesbury CID looked deflated, Eliote could see this and looked back at the board and examined it again, hoping to see something he had missed. He shook his head, there was nothing, so he turned and looked back at his team of officers. "OK, people, so why do we think all these are victims of the same killer?"

"The photo of the football team, Guv," Day said.

"Correct, DS Day, all three friends were circled on the photo, and all three victims were found with the same photo, placed there by the killer, but the question is: which local football team is pictured here?"

A female officer was looking at the photo, her eyes fixated on the football strip.

DI Robertson saw her looking and coughed. "DS Lewis, is something wrong?"

"I think I recognize which team that strip represents," she said.

"OK, DS Lewis," Eliote said, prompting her for more information.

"It looks like they played for the old Glayton High School's football team."

"You are sure of that, DS Lewis?" Robertson asked. "Why haven't you told us this before?"

"Well, sir, I was on holiday when the crime was committed,"

"You are positive, DS Lewis?" Eliote asked again.

She nodded. "I should know, Guv. I used to go to that school before they knocked most of it down and replaced it with those hideous new buildings. They renamed it Chelmesbury Academy, and now most if not all of the kids in Chelmesbury and Glayton go there. I'm not surprised no one recognized the team."

Eliote smiled at her. "Thank you, DS Lewis." He wrote down what she had said. "You and DC Smith get on to the school and see if they kept any of the old documents or if any teachers remember the team." They both nodded and left.

Eliote continued, "Right, these three lads used to live in and around the Glayton, Chelmesbury and I guess the Tenbury Wells area, so I want loads of door-to-door enquires in and around the scenes of the crimes, I want vehicles stopped and the drivers questioned, someone in this town or Glayton knows who might have wanted these lads dead." He continued with further instructions for another ten minutes, and then paused as DS

Lewis came back into the room carrying a piece of paper. "Yes, DS Lewis?"

"Guv, I've been in touch with the school. Some records have been kept, and they say we should just pop in and ask."

He nodded and walked towards the door. "Right then, DI Robertson, can you work with DS Day?" The two officers nodded and Eliote continued, "I want you two to organize the door-to-door, use whoever you want. I don't want anything not checked, understood?"

"Aye, Guv," they said together and then Eliote grabbed his coat and addressed the whole team. "To work then people."

As the room emptied, he stopped DS Lewis from leaving. "You'll be coming with me," he said, looking over at Robertson, "if that's all right with you." His friend nodded and Lewis grabbed her coat.

They headed for Eliote's Saab, Eliote got in the passenger side and DS Lewis drove.

"Where to, Guv?" she asked.

Eliote fastened his seat belt. "Chelmesbury Academy please, Sergeant."

She nodded and started the car.

***

THE DEATHLY ANGEL

By
Kevin Bailey

CHAPTER TWENTY

STEVE MARSTON'S HOUSE

William Frashier and DC Pickington sat on a corner sofa looking at a shocked Steve, who was just staring at the image of his car.

"This has to be a mistake, I mean..." He paused still flabbergasted at the image. "This is my car and yet it can't be," he said, stuttering. "I d-don't drive it that much, it's too expensive, b-but how...?"

Frashier looked at the shocked Steve. "As I told your mother, that picture was taken from a CCTV image that has been magnified and digitally enhanced, so tell me why your car was seen driving away from that factory the night Teresa Bennett was killed?"

"I can't," he said shaking his head. "My car is in the garage, where it always is." He got up and headed for the sideboard and grabbed his keys. "This is where my keys are always kept, see?" He blew away the dust. "As you can see, I ain't used it for ages, there is dust on them."

"Have you a spare set?" Frashier asked.

"No, I lost those years ago when I went to a beach in France with my family."

Frashier sat back on the sofa and drank his tea; he was enjoying watching Steve squirm.

"So if you lost your spare keys and the others are covered in dust, why does this photo show your car driving away from the scene of the crime?"

"I don't know," Steve said abruptly.

Pickington got up. "Guv, I think it's time we left, he doesn't know."

Frashier also stood, snatched the photo out of Steve's hand, and then the two officers left.

Outside, Frashier turned and looked coldly at Pickington. "Why the fucking hell did you stop the interview?" he said angrily. "We were getting somewhere."

"No, we weren't, guv. Anyone could see he knew nothing; all you were doing was getting him upset. And that photo, why?"

Frashier replaced the photo back into the file. "I wanted him to think that was his car."

"But you know Steve has a solid alibi for the night they were killed, and we haven't even found the gun used to kill them."

"Your right," Frashier said, walking up to Pickington and looking him deep in the eye, "but you ever do that to me again and you will be walking the beat, do I make myself clear?"

Pickington nodded. "Yes, guv, crystal," he said with venom.

"Right, now get me to the station; I am going to see Brightly, I want a search warrant for the bookstore."

CHELMESBURY ACADEMY SCHOOL

When the new Chelmesbury Academy trust took over the Glayton and Chelmesbury high school, they decided to knock down all the decrepit parts.

The newer parts of the old high school were revamped and extended, then new state-of-the-art wings were built adjoining these old buildings; anyone who had gone to the old high school wouldn't recognize the place.

Detective Sergeant Gail Lewis parked the Saab in the visitors' car park and she and Eliote headed for the main reception area.

Children of all ages passed them, one almost knocking Eliote flying. After apologizing the fair-haired lad scuttled off to his classroom.

The two detectives walked into the main reception area, a large white room with seats and a glass window, which could be slid open to talk to the receptionist. DS Lewis approached the window and was greeted by a middle-aged woman.

Lewis took out her warrant card and introduced herself and Eliote. "We're here investigating the murders of three of the old school's previous students," she said.

"Yes, DS Lewis, I was the one who took the call, can you tell me of any of the activities they may have been in?"

"We think they were in the school football team."

"Ah, you'll want Mike Wexler then, he is our head of sport, and he coaches the local school football team." The receptionist stood up from her desk and pulled out a big black book. Opening the pages, she handed them a pen. "I'm sorry, but can I get you to sign in, please – security, you understand?" The two officers nodded. "While you're doing that, I will get Mike."

Eliote and Lewis signed their names in the book and waited.

Sometime later, a tall skinny man came bouncing down the corridor towards them; he was wearing a tracksuit and his hair was wavy.

"You wanted to know something about the football team?" he said.

Eliote nodded. "Something like that, Mr Wexler. Do you recognize anyone here?" He handed Mike the photo.

Mike concentrated on the photo and then said, "Well, it is our away colours, green and red, but the faces… I can't name them."

"The players would be about twenty-seven years of age now," Eliote said.

"Twenty-seven? Well, that answers the question, you see I only came here four years ago, just after they knocked down the old school and built this monstrosity."

Eliote sighed. "Is there anyone here who may be able to help us with our enquirers?"

Mike thought for a few seconds and then smiled. "Oh, I am so stupid! I was in the staff room the other day when Anthony Depson came in. We had a little banter going on between us, and he said that his last football team would have given mine a run for their money. I did some research and it seems that Mr Depson, before he had a terrible accident one morning on his way to school, used to be a PE teacher and coached the school's football team."

Eliote cursed under his breath. The way this meeting was going another two people could be dead. "Where can I find this Anthony Depson?" he asked.

Mike looked down the corridor. "He is our head of history at present until he retires next year."

Sensing that Eliote was getting annoyed at Mr Wexler, Lewis said, "It is important we see him urgently, Mr Wexler."

Mike asked the receptionist, "Is Tony teaching at this time?"

The receptionist nodded. "Yes, a group of year eights in room C15."

"OK, this way." Mike led Eliote and Lewis out of reception and along a corridor. Then he turned out of the corridor and across a courtyard; they went through a double door, up some stairs, down another longer corridor and then they arrived at a door marked C15, which Mike knocked on.

From inside the room, Eliote and Lewis heard the voice of an elderly man say, "Come in."

Mike opened the door. "Tony, I have the police here, and they need to speak with you."

The short, white-haired skinny man looked out of the door at the two officers with his small grey eyes, and smiled at the two. Remembering him, Lewis smiled back.

"Right, you horrible lot," Anthony told the class, behave for a few minutes." They all laughed. Eliote could see that the kids loved their teacher, and he wished he'd been taught by him. He remembered his teachers were horrible, sick and twisted, they didn't care about the students, all they cared about was the money that they made for the kids coming to stay at their school. It was a part of Simon's life he didn't like to recall.

Anthony's voice took him out of his thoughts. "World War Two was an adventure for some that they longed for, but for so many of the soldiers who left England, they would never return, So," he paused and looked at his own notes, "to read some of the soldiers' own diaries have a look at pages forty to seventy in the textbook - that should keep you going. Mr Wexler over there will be keeping an eye on you, too, so no monkey business, okay?"

Mr Depson beckoned Eliote and Lewis towards a small office at the end of the building, and said to Lewis, "Gail isn't it?"

She nodded, blushing. "Yes, Mr Depson. You taught me nearly ten years ago."

"Thought so, I never forget a face; so you became a police officer. I always thought you wanted to be a nurse."

"I did, sir, but I was young and my mum was a sister at the local hospital." She changed the subject quickly. "You haven't changed much, Mr Depson."

"Just got old," he said as they reached his office. "Come in please."

They entered and sat down.

"Mr Depson, I am Detective Chief Inspector Simon Eliote."

"Simon Eliote from up at the priory," Depson said. Eliote reluctantly nodded. "I think I went to school with your mum and your dad. He was a great guy and taught me a lot."

"Really," Eliote said sarcastically and he continued with the introductions, not bothered about the information Depson had imparted. "As you know, this is Detective Sergeant Gail Lewis, and we are investigating the deaths of…"

Depson butted in. "James Gaston and Jamie Tweeting."

Eliote continued, "And Wayne Warwick." This seemed to shock Depson and he sat down.

"Poor buggers, I heard about the murders on the news," he said.

Eliote handed him the photo. "This was left on all the victims."

Depson looked at it and smiled. "These guys were the best football team this school has ever had, they took us to the finals of the Inter County Cup in the year that photo was taken and beat the opposition a whopping ten-nil; they were great."

Lewis was writing down everything that was being said. "You don't happen to remember the players' names, do you, sir?" she asked.

He nodded and looking at the photo replied, "Terry Good, the three deceased, of course, the twins Edward and Sidney Smith and Mike Davies."

"What were they like as kids, Mr Depson?" Eliote asked.

"They weren't bad kids really, Chief Inspector, but like all kids they knew what they wanted and what they wanted was to be in that football team. But of course there were others who could have been better than them."

"How do you mean, Mr Depson?"

"They were bullies, Chief Inspector; they would beat up anyone else who got in their way. There was one lad, I think he had only been at school a few days before he was rushed to hospital with a burst kidney; he swore that he had fallen from a tree, but the doctors told me and the lad's parents that a burst kidney could only have happened from being hit quite hard several times."

"So that would have been a motive."

Depson shook his head. "Unfortunately that cannot be, you see he came back later and became friends with Mike and James, a lad by the name of David Freeman."

Eliote remembered the witness statement from Dave.

"He became a reserve," Depson continued, "and played in several games, always as a sub about ten to fifteen minutes from the end of the match."

"Anyone else you can think of, sir?" Lewis asked.

"Oh I'm sure I could give you another forty lads."

Eliote looked at Lewis and she got up. "Thank you for your time, Mr Depson."

Depson stopped them. "Wait, please, there was another lad." He scratched his head. "I can't quite remember his name; he was always quite a loner, sat on his own, always did his homework, always got to the lesson on time and was never late. He wanted to join the football team and then one day he never showed up." He thought for a moment. "As I recall, there was a phone call from the lad's home saying he wasn't coming back."

"Can you remember anything about him, Mr Depson?" Eliote asked. The teacher shook his head. "It is important."

"Sorry, I can't. Faces I remember, names are hardest and I am afraid that most of our own records were lost before the building work and I really can't remember his name. No, I'm sorry but I can't remember."

"That's okay," Eliote said and handed Depson a card. "If you do remember anything please phone me, the number's on the card."

They left the teacher to return to his class, jumped into the Saab and headed back towards the station. Eliote sat in the passenger seat and looked out of the window at the countryside, not paying much attention to the picturesque views, but deep in thought. Images spiralled as the case went round in his head.

"At least we have a breakthrough; the names of the players should help to jog a few memories," Lewis said, bringing him out of his thoughts.

"When we get back to the station, I'll have Records do a search of these names, see what comes up. I'll need you to go and inform Dick and Day of these names; that may help them with their door-to-door inquiries." She nodded and then he looked ahead at the dull road, returning to his thoughts.

The burning question in his mind was who was this lad? he had thrown away the possibility of Sam being this 'Deathly Angel', but something deep in his subconscious told him that the missing piece that would solve the case was the killer's connection to the three deceased.

***

Watching the Saab pull away from the school was a hooded figure. He had climbed high up into one of the trees that lined the boundary with a pair of binoculars and had watched the meeting unfold between the police and Mr Depson.

Looking down at the footpath below the tree, he now started to panic; this was the first time since he had started this campaign of terror that he had felt like this.

He wondered if Depson had told these officers his identity, but then he remembered seeing Depson in the street and the man whom he had admired didn't even remember him.

As he climbed down from the tree his conscious mind was wondering whether his plan of using Sam's identity had worked.

Then as he walked back around the boundary he knew what must be done. The next attack must take place soon and this time they would not see it coming. He smiled once more, and seeing the coast was clear, he disappeared down a slightly overgrown dark footpath.

THE DEATHLY ANGEL

By
Kevin Bailey

CHAPTER TWENTY-ONE

When Frashier and Pickington got back to the station, Frashier went to find Brightly whilst Pickington headed back to his desk. When he got there he sat down and looked at a photo of his family. Day, who was sitting behind him, saw him looking annoyed and asked, "What's up, Phil?"

He looked over at her. "Oh it is nothing, Miranda."

"Doesn't look like nothing to me. Don't forget that I'm your superior."

Pickington sighed and glanced around the room then replied softly, "OK, it's Frashier."

"What's he done now?"

"He's pushing it, obsessed with getting Steve Marston to confess to the killings in Aden Close."

"And just how is he going to do that? Marston has a strong alibi for the night they were murdered."

Pickington nodded in agreement. "I know and I tried to tell him, but you know Frashier."

She shrugged her shoulders. "That I do. So how is he going to force this confession?" Pickington approached her desk and bent down to whisper to her. "He's faking evidence."

"What?" she exclaimed.

"Ssh," he said placing a finger to his lips. "He faked an image from the CCTV to show that it was Steve's car leaving the factory." He opened the file, pulled out the picture and handed it to her.

She looked at it and then cursed under her breath, angry with her mentor. Frashier had instilled in her a sense of doing everything by the book, but this was not by the book. She looked over at his office, which was in darkness. Keeping her voice down so that only Pickington could hear her, she said, "He's a bloody fool. He's already in the Guv's bad books." She placed the photo in to her skirt pocket. "This is between me and you, understood?" she ordered and he nodded.

"Yes, ma-am."

Just then Eliote opened his office door and shouted, "DS Day, will you come in here for a minute please?"

Pickington stood up and headed for the canteen. Day watched him go and then headed for Simon's office.

"You wanted me, Guv?" He handed her a brown file and she opened it. "But, sir, this is the Howden Manor case."

Eliote nodded. "Yes, it is and I need you to deal with it as I am investigating the 'Deathly Angel' killings. I believe Frashier is dealing with the shooting in Aden Close, so that leaves just you."

"What of the Chief Constable ordering you to sort out the case, sir?"

Eliote looked sternly at her, like a father would look at a daughter when she had crossed the line. "I have every respect for the Chief Constable, Sergeant, but I am head of this department and if I order you to sort out this case, then it is up to me, not him."

Day nodded. "OK, Guv."

"Besides It will give you a bit of practice for when you are head of your own CID department and the way you are working at the present, I don't think it will be long before that assignment comes knocking." He smiled warmly at her.

"Thank you, sir."

Eliote went to the door and closed it, then turned and again looked at her. "There is another reason I am asking you to investigate this case, Miranda, but it is of a delicate nature."

"Guv?"

He beckoned her to sit in the chair. "I have a connection to the family," he said, "which the Chief Constable is not aware of."

"So you are related to the Mardons?"

"It is a distant connection," he lied, "and I don't want to discuss it. Also, I'd appreciate it if you didn't discuss this with anyone, Sergeant. Do I make myself clear?"

"OK, sir, if that's what you want."

He returned to his desk. "It is."

"I'll get up there and do my best, Guv."

He winked at her. "I know you will," She smiled and left his office.

After returning to her desk and grabbing her coat, scarf and handbag, she turned off her computer and headed out of CID towards her silver Vauxhall Insignia and set off for Howdon Manor.

When she approached the turning for the manor, she stopped the car at the bottom of the drive and got out. She headed towards a row of houses and started knocking at the doors, but no one was in. As she approached the last house she noticed on the ground some tyre tracks, which she remembered from the folder that Eliote had given her.

She returned to her car, took out her mobile phone and dialled Pathology. It rang for several seconds and then Strong answered.

"Sergeant Day, what can I do for you?"

"I'm near Howden Manor, looking at some tyre tracks. If I send you some photos, could you see if they are similar to the ones found up at the manor?"

"No problem, send them through."

She hung up, took some shots and sent them to Strong, then went back to the last house and rang the bell, hoping this place would be more fruitful than the others.

Her luck was in. She heard footsteps approach the door and a creaky old man's voice ask, "Who is it?"

"Hi, I'm DS Miranda Day, Chelmesbury CID, and I'm investigating the shooting of Lord Mardon. Can I speak to you please, sir?"

The door opened an inch or two on a chain, so Day took out her warrant card and showed it to the elderly man.

"Wait a moment," he said, then closed the door and removed the chain. "I can't be too careful these days, Sergeant."

"You are so right, sir," Day said entering. She was beckoned into a front room decorated with red carpets, red curtains and red and white striped wallpaper; on the walls were dozen of family photographs.

"Tea, Sergeant?" Day nodded and the man left. She stood up and looked at the photos.

One showed a younger version of the elderly man in a police officer's uniform being handed a piece of paper by a younger version of Lord Mardon.

"That was me being given a special commendation for bravery."

Day turned and looked at the man. "How long were you in the force?"

"Oh," he paused remembering, "about forty years, give or take," he said, and walked back into the kitchen as the kettle boiled. "Rose to the rank of inspector at the local branch, many years before the new renovation work."

The man returned carrying a tray of tea. Day took the tray and placed it on a coffee table and then the man poured the tea into two cups and handed one to Day.

"Nice, thank you," she said taking a sip of the hot tea, "Mr..."

"Wellington, George Wellington." He sipped his own tea. "How can I help you?"

"George, did you see or hear anything suspicious on the night Lord Mardon was killed?"

George nodded. "At about midnight I heard a car outside, so I peered out of my bedroom window and saw one of them four by fours parked. I've seen it on several occasions, it belongs to the house, I think."

"Can you tell me what colour it was?" Day asked.

"Not just that but the description of the lady who drove it; the vehicle was yellow and the driver had blonde hair. When I go up to the house to see his lordship, it's often parked at the front, alongside the game keeper's red Vauxhall Nova."

Day stopped him in his tracks and pulled out the fake photo. "Was this the car?"

George nodded. "That's the car, I believe it belongs to the manager of Books for You; his dad is the gamekeeper here."

Day had the nails for two coffins in her hands; had George just helped her solve two cases? "Thank you for the tea, sir, and the information."

"Don't mention it, anything I can do for a fellow police officer."

Outside, Miranda dialled the number for Inspector Frashier, who answered after several rings.

"Yes Miranda?"

"Sir, I've got something on the red Vauxhall Nova. It's used by Steve Marston's dad."

"Cheers, Miranda."

This was the piece of the jigsaw he'd been waiting for, and a weight lifted off his shoulders as he hung up.

Steve sat staring at the television but was not really watching it. He took a large swig from the glass of Irish whiskey in his hand and then topped it up from the bottle in his other hand. Tears trickled down his face, the anger boiling beyond anything he had felt before. Something was eating away at his soul.

His mother unlocked the door and entered. Steve placed the bottle and glass on the coffee table in front of him, stood up and approached her, evil in his eyes.

"Steve, what's wrong?" she asked worried at the state of her son.

"Does Dad borrow my car when I'm at work?" She looked at the ground, not wanting to answer him. "*Mum*!" he snapped.

"Yes," she said looking at him coldly, "at night when you're with your new girlfriend, but it's usually back before you get home, polished and as good as new."

"How does he get my car? The keys are always there," he pointed to the sideboard; "accumulating dust."

She went upstairs and brought back another set of keys.

"But I lost those in France; they have the key to Teresa's house on them." She stepped towards him, but he pushed her back. "Get away from me, you bitch." She went to slap him, but he blocked her and pushed her on to the sofa. Then with glaring eyes, he said, "So what time did he bring back my car?" She was opening her mouth to say something, but he screamed, "WHAT TIME DID HE BRING BACK MY CAR!"

"About twelve, I heard the post box rattle. Why?"

"He killed them, Mum, the bastard killed them." He broke down and she tried to comfort him but again he pushed her away. "No, leave me alone, you are to stay well away from me."

"We should call the police," she managed, but Steve stopped her.

"No," he said with venom. "I will deal with this and then I will deal with you." He got up and headed for the back door.

"Where are you going?" she said, afraid, but he had already left, slamming the door, before she could stop him.

She ran back into the living room, grabbed the phone and dialled 999. When she heard the emergency services answer, she informed them to get in contact with the man leading the investigation into the Aden Close shooting at Chelmesbury CID.

***

Day rang the bell at the front entrance of the manor. After several seconds, she heard footsteps and a butler opened the door, followed by Mrs Mardon who greeted her with a stern-looking expression.

"Where is the Chief Inspector?" she demanded.

"I'm afraid he's away sorting out other cases," Day said, displaying her warrant card. "I am Detective Sergeant Miranda Day and from now on I am in charge of this investigation and I need to know who owns a yellow four by four?"

Mrs Mardon looked coldly at her. "I do not like your tone of voice, Sergeant," she said, then turned and walked towards the drawing room. Day followed close behind.

"I apologize, Mrs Mardon, but I need an answer to my question. It is crucial to our investigation."

"And why is that, Sergeant?"

"We have reason to believe it's connected to the murder of your husband. I want to speak to the driver."

Mrs Mardon looked in a large mirror at her reflection and sighed heavily. "My eldest daughter Elizabeth owns a yellow four by four." She walked to a sofa and sat down. Pausing to drink some tea, she looked up at Day. "Does that answer your question?"

But Day simply asked bluntly, "Where does she live?"

"At The Green, a house owned by the estate; she wanted to be independent, like all you young people today."

Day turned and exited the drawing room, not even saying thank you, and left the manor before Mrs Mardon said anything else.

Back at CID, she was on her way to Eliote's office, when on the way up she was met by Strong.

"Ah, Sergeant, just the person I wanted to see," he said as he opened a file he was carrying and pulled out the photos she had sent him. "I have transferred these photos on to a computer and superimposing them onto the photo of the cast we took from up at the house, I have a ninety-eight point eight per cent match."

Day smiled. "So they are one and the same?" He nodded and she patted him on the back. "Thanks, I'm heading for the Guv's office."

"Be careful he doesn't bite," Strong said with a laugh and walked off, Day watched him go and then headed towards the office.

"Guv," she began, "I may have a lead to the killer of Lord Mardon."

Eliote beckoned her in. "Go on, Sergeant."

"I have a witness who saw a yellow four by four acting suspiciously at the end of the drive the night his lordship was murdered."

"Well done, so what next, Sergeant?"

"If I can find this four by four, then I may find the killer."

"So have you any names, Sergeant?"

She nodded. "I've spoken to Lady Mardon to ask if she knew who the vehicle belonged to."

"And?" he asked, raising an eyebrow.

"Well, she wasn't very forthcoming at first, but eventually, after several probing questions, she informed me that the vehicle belongs to her daughter Elizabeth. She has given me her address."

Eliote smiled and then said, "Well, you had better get Pickington and drive over there. Take some uniformed officers to help, I'll get you a search warrant." He picked up the phone and dialled Brightly's number.

Day smiled and replied, "Right, Guv," then left him to his work.

THE DEATHLY ANGEL

By
Kevin Bailey

CHAPTER TWENTY-TWO

Frashier was with a group of officers searching the offices of 'Books for You,' when Hagley pulled up outside the shop in his grey Vauxhall Vectra and ran in, flashing his warrant card at the two officers guarding the entrance.

When he found Frashier, he said, "Sir, the station has just received a call from Mrs Marston; Steve has gone to confront his father about the murders."

"So?" Frashier said dismissively.

"According to the station, Mrs Marston says her son is drunk and that on the night of the murder, her ex-husband borrowed the car."

Now Frashier was angry and annoyed. "If she'd told us that sooner, this case could have been solved." He grabbed his coat that he had placed on Steve's desk. "Where does Mr Marston live?"

"According to Mrs Marston, he lives at seventeen Hastings Avenue."

"Let's go, Hagley," Frashier ordered, running to the Vectra and getting in. "To Hastings Avenue and don't spare the gas." Hagley nodded and turned on his flashing lights. He looked in the mirror and saw the two extra squad cars behind him and then drove away quickly.

Frashier's phone started to ring; it was Brightly with an update. "Right, ma'am," he said and gave the news to Hagley. "The armoured response unit is on its way to Hastings Avenue. It seems Mr Marston is a groundskeeper, and has a licence to own several guns, so we're taking precautions." He paused and listened to more information from his superior. "Apparently, Marston's an avid collector of American army issue weapons," he said, grabbing the door as Hagley overtook several cars. Frashier gave a van driver a filthy look and then turned back to Hagley and continued, "It seems certain that Marston has several rifles in his possession."

"He could have an arsenal of weapons, then," Hagley said.

"That sounds a pretty good bet," Frashier said, his mouth twisting into a scowl.

HASTINGS AVENUE

The Avenue was your typical council estate; each house was similar to its neighbour apart from where the occupants had changed the front gardens to meet their own particular tastes.

Number seventeen was no exception; the front garden had been turned into a drive and a battered old blue Ford Escort was parked on it, the front tyres gone.

Steve walked up the path towards the brown front door; he knocked and waited, the anger boiling up inside him, the alcohol not helping his temper.

The door was answered by a middle-aged man with a small moustache and a goatee; his short stature made Steve look like a giant.

Through blue eyes he smiled at his son. "Well, this is an unexpected pleasure, my boy," he said and moved out of the way. "Come in." Steve walked past his father and into the front room.

The room was full of memorabilia from America: flags, signposts, number plates and an American jukebox, which was against one of the walls.

But the best piece of memorabilia that Mr Marston had in his collection was on the centre wall; attached by clips was a genuine rifle used by the American army. Steve walked towards it and his dad smiled. "You always were attracted to that rifle even when you were little. Maybe when I am gone, it will belong to you."

"Dad," Steve said trying to hide his anger "is that the weapon you used to kill them both?"

"What!" he snapped. "Are you mad?"

"Is it, Dad?" Steve shouted his temper reaching boiling point. "And don't lie to me; I'm not that little boy anymore."

His father held up a hand to placate him, but Steve's temper exploded. "Answer me!" he snarled. "Mum just told me that you used my car the night Teresa was killed!"

James sat down on the chair with his head in his hands and then he looked up at his son, his eyes moist.

"Yes, it is."

"Why?" Steve said, distraught. "Tell me why!"

"I couldn't bear to see you get hurt again when she wanted you back… when no one else wanted her."

"It's my life, Dad," he shouted, wiping tears from his cheeks. "It's my life." Turning, he grabbed the rifle off the wall and aimed it at his father.

"What are you doing, Steve?" Steve grabbed a clip and placed it into its slot on the rifle. "Be careful, son, that gun is now loaded."

"I know," Steve said calmly and switched off the safety, then squeezed the trigger.

***

Hagley swerved the car into Hastings Avenue and as they approached the house, they were greeted by the armed response unit, who had set themselves up outside.

Frashier and Hagley were putting on some protection when two shots were heard. Frashier looked at the others and bellowed, "Go, go, go," and the armed response team broke down the front door and went into the house, the two CID officers following at a safe distance.

When they entered the front room, they found James's body on the floor and the rifle on top. Blood trickled from two wounds in the man's head.

"Sir," one of the officers said, "the back door is open."

"Where does that lead?" Frashier asked, pointing to an area behind the fence.

"I think it goes to an old feed mill, and the railway lines."

"Quick," Frashier ordered and they all ran to the fence at the bottom and jumped over.

They entered a yard containing agricultural equipment, a long-haired man in a green uniform was being ordered to move pallets around on a green forklift, by his boss, a small woman with tied up hair and wearing spectacles.

When she saw them jump the fence and head straight for the railway lines, she shouted to the group of officers "Hey, you're not allowed around here."

Hagley showed his badge and ran on. Frashier got to the tracks first and looked up the line at the station, where he saw the figure of Steve standing near the edge of the platform. Somewhere in the distance he heard the sound of a passenger train, which was making its way to Chelmesbury station.

"Steve!" Frashier shouted, knowing they had only seconds to persuade Steve not to jump.

"You're too late, Inspector!" Steve said despondently. "I have to do this; I have killed my father because he killed the woman I love."

A group of people had gathered to see what was going on, and Hagley tried to shoo them away.

"It's not too late, Steve, please," Frashier said. "I know you're hurting but we can sort this out, get you some help. You don't have to jump."

"I do!"

"Think of your mother, think of Emily." Frashier heard the man sob at the same time as he saw the train appear in the distance. It was now or never.

"I am thinking of them," Steve said, and took two steps forward.

"*No*!" Frashier yelled, but the lad had gone.

***

Day, Pickington and a group from Forensics arrived at the Green and got out of their cars. Day looked at the house.

It was Victorian in design, with two large bay windows and a porch in the middle. She noticed the yellow four-by-four parked outside the small garage built on to the side of the house.

Miranda walked up the drive, opened the porch door and rang the doorbell. She heard footsteps approach and a blonde-haired woman opened the door.

"Hello, can I help you?" she said softly.

"Hi, I am Detective Sergeant Miranda Day and this is Detective Constable Phillip Pickington from Chelmesbury CID." She showed her warrant card and asked, "Are you Elizabeth Mardon?"

"Yes, I am." The woman nodded.

"Then I am arresting you on suspicion of murdering Lord Godfrey Mardon." She cautioned her while Pickington slipped handcuffs around her wrists, and placed her in the back of a squad car.

Day watched her leave and then ordered a thorough search of the house, including the attic, cellar and any outhouses.

A short while later they discovered, tucked away in a shed under some old boxes, a white top that tested positive for gun residue. She smiled. "Got ya," she said as a Forensics officer placed the evidence in a bag and returned to his search.

CHELMESBURY TRAIN STATION

The train had come to an immediate, screeching stop, throwing several passengers out of their seats, but when Frashier jumped down beside Steve, he could tell that he was too late and Steve's life was rapidly slipping away. He grabbed his phone and called for an ambulance, knowing it was useless.

"Stay with me, Steve," he tried, "stay with me," but Death was about to claim another life.

"Inspector," Steve gasped, as blood dripped from his mouth, "tell Mum and Emily… that I'm… sorry and that… that I loved them," and with that final word he passed into unconsciousness. Frashier tried in vain to resuscitate him.

When the ambulance arrived the paramedic confirmed that he was dead, so Frashier stepped back onto the platform and approached Hagley, who was getting witness statements.

"Are Forensics still at the house?" he asked and Hagley nodded.

"It's all been taken care of, sir. Dr Strong arrived about two minutes ago and is there right now."

Frashier patted Hagley on the back. "Thanks," he said, "keep up the good work," and with that he walked down the platform to the station entrance and through the door to the car park. Once there, he sat on a bench and stared at the ground. Doctor Strong approached him twenty minutes later.

"We've cleaned up the mess in the house and an ambulance has taken away Mr Marston to hospital." Strong sat down beside him. "He has two officers with him and is under house arrest."

Frashier looked up at him. "Is Mr Marston not dead?"

Strong shook his head. "No, Will, he was shot, but the paramedics don't think its life threatening. Steve's mother has been notified about the death of her son and really is in shock blaming herself"

"Thank you, Doctor." He looked over at the station. "Do you know what, I've been a police officer for many years, had to deal with suicide almost every year, but this has shocked me." He put out his hand. "I had him in my grasp," he clenched his fist, "but he slipped through my fingers and in the end it was for nothing," Strong put his hand on Frashier's shoulder.

"Some people have to do it, William, no matter what. He was one of them."

"Your right, Richard," Frashier said. "I think I need a strong drink."

Strong nodded and the two friends headed for Strong's car.

***

Up at the Green, Day and her team had examined every orifice of the house and after they had gathered enough evidence on Elizabeth, they took the bags back to the Station for analysis.

***

SECOND INTERVIEW OF SAMUEL DALTON

Back at the station, oblivious to the conclusion of the other two investigations, DCI Eliote walked into interview room one. His thoughts and concerns were to bring to justice this "Deathly Angel", and nothing else.

He sat down in front of Cara and Sam and then looked directly at Sam.

"Sam, do you know who this man is?" He handed him the photo taken from the security camera at the club.

"No, should I?" Sam said sarcastically. Eliote replaced the photo in a file.

"You should do, because according to the doorman at Mandy's Nightclub, that is you."

Sam was shocked. "B-but I… This must be some mistake."

"It just seems funny that a man works for a nightclub for three weeks and uses your name. I find that odd, don't you?"

Sam nodded. "It's obviously just a coincidence; I mean there are several Daltons in the area, even a few Sam's."

Eliote looked coldly at him. "Is there something you're not telling me, Sam?" he asked, not noticing the look Cara was giving him. "If I find out you're keeping something from me, then I'll charge you with wasting police time."

"Excuse me," Cara interrupted. "My client has at present done nothing wrong, so how dare you treat him like this?"

"Miss Askew, your client is the only lead I have in the identification of a serial killer, one who has for the past three weeks used the name Sam Dalton. I think that is more than just a coincidence." He looked back at Sam. "So?"

"What?" Sam replied angrily.

"Come on, Sam, I have been reasonable with you. I know you didn't kill them but even you must be puzzled." Sam nodded. "OK," Eliote said putting up his hand, "let's change this then." He stood up and walked to the outer wall of the interview room. "Let me see, if I wanted to get someone's name, I'd either go on a social networking site or I'd be in a pub and go up to a stranger and say…"

"Hang on," Sam butted in, "you may have something. Yes, there was this bloke," he said remembering, "a couple of weeks ago, I didn't recognise him, but…"

"Go on," Eliote commanded.

“Well, I was in the supermarket down the road, when a bearded bloke stopped me and said we used to go to school together. There was something familiar about him, but I couldn’t put a name to the face.”

Eliote walked back to the table and took out the photo and handed it back to him. “Is it this man?”

Sam shook his head. “I don’t know but he did have a bushy beard.”

Eliote smiled. “That gives us something to go on.” He looked at Sam and Miss Askew, and said, “OK, you are free to go, but we may need to ask you some more questions.”

As he walked towards his office Eliote was met in the corridor by Day who was looking flustered and carrying several files.

“Guv,” she said, “I have Elizabeth Mardon in custody and I am just about to interview her.”

Eliote smiled warmly as a father would to a daughter. “Okay,” he said, “I’ll need the reports on my desk as soon as you’re finished.”

She nodded and headed for interview room two.

Outside the room she was met by Pickington and the two officers were about to enter, when they heard a sweet commanding voice echo down the corridor.

“Excuse me, Sergeant Day.” They turned to see an old flame of Pickington’s who smiled when he saw her.

“Barrister Bellows, it is always nice to see you,” he said.

The strict-looking woman smiled back at him. “Likewise, Detective,” she said coldly. “Could I please be allowed to have a minute or two with my client?”

Pickington looked at Day who nodded. “Of course,” he said, and the two detectives waited outside whilst the barrister entered.

When the door opened Elizabeth looked up at her, expecting to see the two detectives, instead she got a shock. The barrister sat down beside her.

"You do not have to say anything, Elizabeth. If you don't want to answer their questions just say 'no comment', okay?"

"Why are you here?" Elizabeth asked.

"Your mother had a run-in with Sergeant Day out there and thought it best if I kept an eye on the station. I was outside having a smoke, when I saw them bring you in."

Elizabeth was about to say something when the door opened and in came Pickington carrying a large evidence bag and Day who had a file under her arm. Pickington had an audio CD in his hand which he placed in a CD recorder in the wall.

Day took the folder from underneath her arm and placed it on the table and sat down, Pickington grabbed a remote control, aimed the control at the machine, pressed record and then sat down.

INTERVIEW OF ELIZABETH MARDON

"I hope my client's previous encounters with the law are not going to be brought up in this interview?" Kate Bellows said. "My client has paid the price for those crimes."

"We are not interested in past crimes, Barrister Bellows," Pickington said, "just the truth."

"Very well, then proceed."

"Miss Mardon," Day began, "where were you on Tuesday night at about twelve o'clock?"

"Well, that's simple: I was in bed… alone."

"Do you own the yellow four-by-four parked in your garage?"

"Of course, my dear papa bought it for me as a gift."

Day took two photos out of the folder and handed them to Elizabeth. "For the record, I am showing the defendant the pictures of the tread found on the road near Howdon Manor and also the treads from her car."

"So they look similar to my vehicle," she replied. "So bloody what? I travel that road every day and I see loads of four-by-fours."

"The tyre tracks look very similar, wouldn't you say, Barrister?" Day turned back to Elizabeth. "Can you explain then why your vehicle was seen by an eyewitness leaving the drive to Howden very quickly?"

She shrugged her shoulders and replied, "No comment."

Day pulled out of her pocket the murder weapon in a sealed bag and placed it on the table.

"I have placed the murder weapon used to kill Lord Godfrey Mardon in front of the accused." She paused to look at Elizabeth. "Do you recognize the weapon, Miss Mardon?"

She shrugged her shoulders once more and replied, "No comment." Day looked like she was going to explode

"Miss Mardon, if you are going to keep saying 'no comment' then we are going to be here all night. I've nothing better to do." She looked at Pickington, "You?" He shook his head. "So it's up to you."

"No comment."

Day was getting angry; Pickington could sense it. "Miss Mardon," he said, "I'll come straight to the point." The barrister was about to say something but Pickington interrupted her. "Sorry, Barrister, I do respect you but please let me finish."

"OK," she said, giving in.

Pickington smiled and continued, "Your fingerprints were found all over the revolver."

"And when we did a thorough examination of your house," Day added, "we found these hidden in your shed, plus several other clothes in the attic." She placed the large evidence bag full of clothes on the table. "Here we have gunshot residue matching the revolver in our possession." Day looked at

Elizabeth with a grin. "Now say 'no comment' Miss Mardon."

Elizabeth started to cry. "You think you're so smart, but you don't know anything. Everyone thought of my father as a nice man, a kind man, but he wasn't nice or kind. Why do you think I moved out? I wanted my freedom."

"You killed him, didn't you?" Pickington said.

She nodded. "Of course I killed him. He was a racist bastard, and he wouldn't let me marry my African fiancé – 'over my dead body,' he said."

"So you shot him with his old revolver," Day said.

"I sneaked in late, knowing full well the dogs wouldn't attack me, but I made them bark, knowing my father was a light sleeper, knowing he would probably come and investigate. It was risky, though; because my father had a loaded rifle in his office."

"So what happened next?"

"I hid and waited and it wasn't long before he came down the stairs." She paused. "Then I fired the weapon twice."

"So, what happened after you shot him?" Pickington asked her.

"I ran out of the house hearing my family stirring upstairs. Not thinking, I threw the gun into the hedge and drove off. When I got to the bottom of the drive, I stopped and realized about the gun and the fingerprints, but I had done it, now I was free."

"But someone saw you?" Day asked and she nodded.

"When I saw that old busybody ex-copper looking at me from a window; I shot off in a flurry of gravel."

"OK. Miss Mardon, I think we have all that we need."

A little later, a uniformed officer escorted her to the cells. When he had locked the door, he wrote on the whiteboard beside the cell:

-Elizabeth Mardon, cell 12 awaiting trial for murder, ref Pic/Day 12023-

Day grabbed the CD and walked out of the room, leaving Pickington alone with Kate.

"It was a pleasure to work with you, Miss Bellows," he said.

"You too, as always," she said, then grabbed her belongings and left. Pickington watched her go and then set off to find Day.

THE DEATHLY ANGEL

By
Kevin Bailey

CHAPTER TWENTY-THREE

Monmouth Street was situated just off Chelmesbury's high street. It used to be cobbled, but as the years went by the local council had paved it over with concrete.

At the bottom of the street a grey Ford Focus salon was parked and watching this car was the hooded man.

When he saw that the coast was clear, he took out a key and aimed it at the car; the lights flashed and he opened the door quietly and got in. He placed the key in the ignition and after several failed attempts, he managed to start the car and drove away.

As he drove, his thoughts were full of hatred and revenge. He didn't care that he had just murdered several human beings or was planning to kill more; he knew they deserved it and to that end, nothing was going to stop him, not even the police.

He drove for about three miles and then turned over a bridge and stopped in a lay-by. Phase one was in operation, phase two was about to start, but the hooded man knew that the next part was the most difficult; the other killings had been easy compared to this one.

Taking off his belt, he got out of the car and headed for the residence of Sam Dalton. He had seen him leave the station and knew that he hadn't been kept in overnight; also no one had come to arrest him, so they must have swallowed his and Sam's story.

He knocked on the door and when Sam opened it, he froze to the spot.

"Hello, Sam, long time."

Sam let out a grunt. "You!"

The lad pushed him into the house and closed the door behind him, then followed him into the sitting room; Sam picked up the phone and was dialling the emergency services number.

"I wouldn't do that if I was you," the hooded figure said calmly.

Sam looked confused. "Why, I will get the reward for your arrest?"

The hooded lad smiled. "Yes, but then they will want to know why you allowed me in." He paused, looking around the room. "They will see that I did not break in." Sam seemed to waver. "Also, several of your enemies and maybe your Michelle will receive a package, containing several incriminating pictures. Oh, what a scandal that will be."

Sam replaced the receiver and looked coldly at the lad. "You are a heartless bastard." The lad again smiled and sat down. "I wish I'd never met you."

"I bet you do. You should keep your trousers on and your dick away from others, especially men. I mean, what would Michelle say if she knew what I knew?"

Sam stood up straight and approached the lad. "You stay away from 'Chelle I'm warning you…"

The lad remained seated. "Who are you kidding, Sam? You ain't got the guts; even if you go around the town saying that you do, and anyway I helped you get that reputation, remember? I needed you then, now I am going to let you go, I will not bother you again, you have my word." The lad took out of his pocket a memory stick and threw it at Sam. "This belongs to you now; my bargaining chip is no more."

Sam caught the memory stick and hissed, "OK, now get out of my house."

The lad stood up and approached the door to the sitting room. "I hope you have a long and happy life with Michelle," he said. "Take care," and with a warm smile he left the sitting room and closed the door behind.

Sam heard the front door open and close. He took a deep breath and relaxed; his reputation was now intact, but how had he ever allowed the mighty Sam Dalton to be cornered by a pathetic loser? He picked up the phone again and dialled a number.

"Hey," his beloved 'Chelle answered.

"Hey, babes, I'm back from the station… Yeah, it was a mistake… The lousy copper who interviewed me had to apologize, seems some twat had stolen my identity. When I find out who it is, I'm gonna make them wish they hadn't… OK, I'll see you next week, when you are back from your business meetings… yeah I Loves ya, baby." He replaced the receiver and approached a locked cupboard to which only he had the key. He rummaged around in the contents of files and accumulated clutter until he found a large brown envelope addressed to him. Clutching the envelope, he sat down in front of the open fire and stared into the flames.

A little later, he ripped open the envelope and removed the photos inside. He was disgusted that these had been taken; he thought no one had seen him and his lover. The first five images showed him down a darkened alley, performing a sexual act on a man. The next few caught the same act, but with their roles reversed. The final pictures showed the man buggering him and it looked as though they were both enjoying it.

"Great pictures," he said out loud and felt himself get aroused, "it's such a shame no-one will ever see them." One by one, he ripped up the photos and threw them onto the fire. When they had finished burning, he took hold of the memory stick, placed it into his laptop and looked at the images.

The first few were the same as the others he had seen, but then they changed to show a man beating the hell out of another in a factory. The man was wearing a hoody, and the anger he displayed was shocking.

Sam withdrew the memory stick quickly from the laptop and threw it onto the fire, watching as the plastic casing melted slowly and then caught fire.

When he was happy that all was destroyed he let the flames bear away his thoughts and ignite his anger; he wanted revenge on the person who had taken these photos.

'Your time is ending, I ain't afraid of you as you ain't got anything on me now.'

Looking around the room, he noticed that one of the photos had slipped out of the envelope and was below the coffee table. He bent down and picked it up.

It showed him having sex with this strange man, and he felt aroused even more than before, remembering the encounter. Grabbing his groin, he decided to enjoy the moment.

He stood up and headed for the bathroom, still holding the picture, but as soon as he opened the sitting room door, he got a shock as the hooded lad stood there wielding a large bronze ornament.

"Not afraid of me, eh, Sam?" the attacker said with venom and repeated Sam's early words "When I find the person I'll make them wish they hadn't," he remarked walking towards him, "I'd like to see you try," Sam was scared.

"Please no, I'm like you remember, please don't hurt me," he begged.

"You're nothing like me, Sam. You had friends to protect you, I had no one."

"You had me."

The stranger seemed to laugh at this statement and then turned, but before Sam could attack, he turned back quickly and smacked him across the head with the ornament.

Sam fell backwards, hitting his head on the small coffee table before he slumped to the floor. The lad crouched down beside his victim.

"Why are you doing this?" Sam said. "We had a deal." But he received no answer.

The hooded stranger took out the large butcher's knife and with one thrust stabbed Sam in the heart. Blood poured from his mouth and his last words to the lad were, "See you in hell."

He watched him die, then smiled and said, "I'm already in hell." The hooded lad cleaned himself up and wiped the ornament for prints; he took hold of the knife and placed it back inside a ready-made holster. Then, after burning the final picture, which was beside the body, he calmly walked out of the door.

He got in the Focus and drove away from the murder scene and headed for his home. Five miles further on, he turned into a private signposted road; after unlocking a padlocked gate he drove through and locked up behind him, then continued down a large overgrown track to some derelict buildings.

He turned into a yard and parked the car in front of a brick building that used to be a slaughterhouse, and then he pulled the hood over his head and walked home.

It took him another hour, always checking and rechecking that he was not being followed, until he emerged into a lane. Catching a glimpse of the Angel, he smiled and crept around the back of one of the houses. As he entered he heard an elderly man shout from the front room.

"Is that you Mathew?"

"Yes, Granddad, it's me," he said and entered the front room; the man looked up at him from one of the chairs.

"Take that hood off and go to bed. You've been having a few late nights recently and your mum wants you to be awake and able to pick up your brother the day after tomorrow and bring him home safely."

The lad took off his hood to reveal a disfigured face; his nose was bent and out of place, and scars surrounded his eyes; another large circular scar at his hairline showed where an operation had taken place, clumps of hair now growing around it.

"Good night, Granddad," Mathew said, and kissed him on the top of his head and went to his bedroom. He shut the door behind him, relocking it, and then walked to his desk, where a photograph sat of the seven lads that made up part of the football team. He stuck the photo on his computer's scanner and copied it, then printed out the picture and placed it in front of himself. Taking out a red pen from a drawer, he circled the people that he had killed.

"Three down," he said, then he circled another two players. "You're next."

He opened another drawer on his desk and pulled out a sheet of paper and an A5 book. Flicking through the pages, he found what he wanted. He scanned his eyes over the written list, the location of all seven players, their actions, their jobs and even their girlfriends; three had a line struck straight through.

He read down the list and came to the names of two brothers, Edward and Sidney Smith, and knew that they would usually be having drinks at the Fox pub around ten and would get a taxi home about twelve, more than a little inebriated.

A plan formed in his mind. He took out a small black book from the same drawer and wrote down his intentions and then he turned off the lights in his room and fell asleep.

CHELMESBURY CID

Eliote had got in again early, after a sleepless night. He went into the canteen, which was quiet, and grabbed a cup of coffee and some breakfast.

He was about to fork up some egg and bacon, when he saw the desk sergeant coming towards him.

"Sorry to disturb you, sir, but there is a phone call from an Anthony Depson for you." Eliote followed the sergeant out of the canteen and towards the front desk.

"Hello, Mr Depson, what's up?"

"I don't know if it is anything," the teacher replied, "but I was at home going through some old photos of the team and other bits of my history, when something occurred to me. That boy that never came back to school was one of the team's brothers; like I said before, I couldn't tell you which one it was, but I do remember that he had to have an operation afterwards."

"OK," Eliote said, "I'll look into it, and once again, thank you, sir, for your information, especially at this time of the morning."

"Don't mention it, I'm usually up this early most days, boils down to my army days as a sergeant major. Anyway, I hope you get this attacker before he kills again."

"I hope so too," Eliote said and hung up.

He walked back to the canteen to find his plate had been tidied away. After cursing out loud, which made several of the canteen staff look over at him, he walked out and headed back up to CID. He was approaching his office when Sergeant Day walked around a corner, nearly bumping into him.

"I'm sorry, guv, I was in another world," she said.

Eliote raised his hand. "No damage done. I was going to call you anyway, Sergeant. I have just had Anthony Depson on the phone, and I want you to check out something he has just said to me. Find out anything you can about a lad who was the brother of one of these players."

"Our leads tell us that only three of the players had brothers," Day interrupted him, "and we know that two of the seven are twins, which just leave's Mike; he has a brother, Mathew."

"Good, I want you to check out this brother." She nodded. "Find out why he left school and whether he had an operation; get DS Lewis to help you. According to what she said to Anthony Depson when we interviewed him, her mother was a nurse, so she may have contacts."

"OK, guv," Day replied and headed towards her computer terminal while he headed towards his office.

CHELMESBURY'S TESCO STORE

Charlotte Steel was pushing her trolley down the frozen veg aisle, when she came to an abrupt halt, a stabbing pain in her head, one she had not experienced for many years. Back then, though, it had not been this agonising; now it felt like someone was stabbing her in the head with a hot dagger.

She saw people moving around her in slow motion, but they didn't seem to see or hear her. Then a voice echoed around her head.

"Lotte, Loopy Lotte, come out and play."

She looked around the aisle to see who had spoken, but she realized that the voice was coming from that part of her mind she called, the "Black Hole".

The voice continued and she realised it was her own voice.

She closed her eyes and saw herself walking over a concrete floor to a hole. She was scared and looked in and saw that she was at the top of a large tornado; the voice seemed to be coming from the bottom.

"Come in and play. You haven't joined me for a while, come on." Charlotte walked to the edge, but she felt something break and she slipped in.

She did not feel scared as she fell, and opened her eyes to look around at the swirling tornado. It seemed to her to be blood that was swirling and as she went further in, she suddenly felt that she herself was spinning, not the tornado. Suddenly, as she was spinning round and round, the voice, which had continued to say the same thing over and over again, took on another sinister aspect and changed from her voice to an angry male voice.
"Oh, they have found me, but I am too quick for them. Tell them, Lotte; tell them to catch me if they dare." Then there was laughter. "You have the key, use it."
"How do I use it?" she screamed out, but she was never answered and fell to the floor in pain. Then, as suddenly as it had begun, the pain stopped.

She opened her eyes to see several shoppers and a middle-aged member of staff looking concerned at her.

"You okay, love? You passed out there." Charlotte nodded, but the staff member asked again, "Are you okay?"

"How long was I out?" she asked, looking at her watch.

"Only for a couple of seconds, love, that's all; looked like you were having a seizure or something."

"I get hot," she lied, "and pass out."

The staff member looked around. "But you're in the frozen vegetable aisle, love," she said.

Charlotte got up and after thanking her, headed out of the store, leaving the trolley of goods still in the aisle.

She had to see Simon Eliote now.

***

In another part of the town, Mathew parked the stolen grey Focus and watched the two identical twins walking into the Fox public house. He could not miss them as they both wore very similar clothes and hairstyles; they looked like an older version of Jedward.

As he watched them, a red taxi pulled up near the pub and waited. People got in and it disappeared, then ten minutes later it returned and parked up.

Mathew saw the driver sit and eat a sandwich and the plan in his head changed, but he still knew that this one was going to be a lot harder than the last murders. If he could pull this one off, he could then do the final one, the one he had been building to, the final scene.

In his rear view mirror, he saw a police car come around a corner and slow down as it approached. Mathew started the car and drove away; in the mirror he saw the police car follow him, so he stayed calm and drove normally.

He turned left and looked in the mirror again; the squad car turned as well, so now he knew they were chasing him, but he had to stay calm at all costs.

The castle came into view over the market square and he pulled up in front of a charity shop. The police car pulled in behind and put on its flashing lights.

Everyone in the square stopped what they were doing and looked over at the two cars and watched as one of the officers got out and approached him.

Mathew wound down the window and said, "Hi, can I help you, Officer?"

"Is this your car, sir?" the cop asked.

"No, it belongs to some family friends. I borrow it from time to time. Is there a problem?"

The officer nodded. "Yes, sir, it was reported stolen by a…" Mathew butted in.

"…By Mr George Sinclair by any chance?" Mathew asked. The officer nodded. "He does that all the time. He has been very ill, so he asked my granddad if I wanted to borrow it, to keep it going."

The officer grabbed his microphone. "Sierra Oscar from 187," he said.

"Go ahead, 187."

"Have found car reported stolen yesterday, driver says that he borrows it from a George Sinclair, can you verify information?"

At that precise moment a red taxi pulled up several feet away, Mathew swore in his mind, his plan had not foreseen this.

As he waited the officer kept his eye fixed on Mathew, so he knew he just needed to relax and stay focused.

"187 from Sierra Oscar."

"Go ahead."

The voice echoed around the square. "We have been in touch with Mr Sinclair and he says the only person who borrows the car is…"

Mathew spoke over the voice. "Mathew Davies," he said, pointing at himself.

The officer didn't look very happy. "Okay, thank you, Sierra Oscar, we will go and have a word with Mr Sinclair about wasting police time." He returned his microphone to his tunic and looked over at Mathew. "Where are you going, sir?"

Mathew felt a little relieved. If the officer had known who Mathew was, then he knew that he would have been arrested. "I borrowed the car yesterday to go shopping," he said, "but after having a few drinks, I decided not to drive home, thought I would have a ride around town, looking at the local talent, not that I could pull any of them." Mathew took off the hood, and the officer looked physically sick. He replaced the hood, and said, "Please don't blame George, he never knows when I borrow it or when I bring it back."

"Better get home, sir," the cop said, and then got into the squad car.

Mathew turned and headed back to the Fox; he was relieved to see the police car turn off and he was free. When he reached the pub he saw the taxi wasn't there; he cursed the officers for holding him up and looked at the time.

"Eleven o'clock. *Bollocks*."

He was just about to leave, when he heard an engine and saw the taxi reappear. He breathed a sigh of relief.

He got out of the Focus and headed for an off-licence and after paying for a bottle of vodka, headed for the taxi. He knocked on the window and the driver opened it.

"Are you free?" Mathew asked. The driver nodded and Mathew got in.

"Where to, mate?"

Mathew looked at his watch again. "The castle, please, as fast as you can." The taxi driver turned the cab around and drove away.

As they approached the castle Mathew directed him to a quiet spot and got out. He paid the driver and pretended to look down at the taxi's wheel.

"Hey, mate, do you realize that your tyre is flat?"

The driver got out muttering, "I bet it's those bloody nails." He looked down at the tyres and said to Mathew, "There's no bloody puncture, what are you on?" Mathew lifted his head and the driver could see the evil in his eyes.

"I ain't on anything, my friend, just need your car." The driver was about to protest when Mathew pulled out the bottle of vodka and smashed it down onto his head. The liquid exploded everywhere. The driver collapsed to the ground and with the same fury he had shown in his other attacks, Mathew repeatedly kicked him so many times in the head that he was rendered unconscious.

He smiled after seeing what he had done to the taxi driver and dragged him into the back of the taxi and shut the door. When he got in the driving seat, he turned back and stole all the driver details and wallet, threw them into a plastic bag and hid them in the glove compartment. Then, after replacing them with fake ones, he drove round to the hospital. He ran into reception shouting that he had just found a man lying on the ground, smelling of alcohol. Two orderlies came out pushing a gurney and with a doctor and nurse at his side, the driver was taken into casualty.

Mathew jumped back into the driver's seat and returned to the Fox Inn, parking up some way away. He got out and walked to the Focus. Using the key he had been given, he grabbed all his stuff from the car and locked the doors, jumped back into the red taxi and drove to the front of the pub and waited.

Luckily for him, he didn't have to wait long.

THE FOX INN

Mathew watched a crowd of people emerge from the inn and then spotted his prey. The twins emerged and looked around for their taxi. When they spotted the red vehicle, they walked towards it.

"Taxi for Smith?" one of them asked. Mathew nodded and the two lads got in.

"You're not Charlie," the other said.

Mathew looked in the mirror at Sidney. "He was rushed into hospital, some twat beat him up."

Sidney hiccupped and then smiled. "I hope he'll be all right. You've heard about this Deathly Angel?"

Mathew nodded. "Yeah I heard about him." He started the taxi. "So where am I going to mate?"

"201 Dead Man's Close, please," Sidney said.

Mathew nodded and drove away, the twins slumping in the back seat and soon dozing off. A grin appeared on his face and he continued to drive.

A mile down the road, he came to a signpost marked Wedsford, and turned in the direction of the village, which was approximately five miles further on. A mile later he doubled back into Chelmesbury, coming round the back roads, streets and housing estates of the Shropshire town and headed for his destination, the old Dead Man's Quarry.

He drove the red taxi up to the top of the quarry and stopped; one of the twins opened his eyes and looked around as Mathew opened his door.

"Are we home?"

Mathew shook his head. "Just stopping for a slash," he said, and the twin smiled and went back to sleep. Mathew walked to the boot, took out a duffel bag and placed it on the passenger seat, then placed another bag from the boot on to the side of the water edge and returned to the cab. After locking all the doors, he turned and gently tied the two sleeping passengers to the seat and head rests.

When he felt ready for the next step, he grabbed a diver's mask from inside the bag, placed the strap over his head and rummaged for a diving regulator and turned on an air supply. He felt the oxygen sweep over his chin.

Once all his checks were complete, he put on his own seatbelt and taking several deep breaths of fresh air, he placed the mask over his eyes and breathed through the regulator, then he revved the engine, placed it in gear and holding onto the steering wheel tightly, he drove the car over the cliff and into the dark misty waters.

As it hit the water, the taxi shook, waking the sleeping twins. They looked around, dazed and confused as the freezing water came in from all angles. The man in the front seat was looking at them from under his hood and mask.

"Help us," they shouted to him, but he shook his head looking at his watch. Mathew took off the regulator, pulled out a laminated copy of the photo and pointed at it.

"Sidney, you asked whether I had heard of the Deathly Angel. Well," he paused and stretched out his arms, "I am he." A look of terror filled the twins' eyes. "And now like your friends, you are going to die," he said.

Then he replaced the regulator and watched as the frozen water engulfed the whole of the taxi and the car touched the bottom.

Mathew who was almost glued to the chair was immensely enjoying the scene that followed; the two lads who were using every ounce of oxygen left in their system were fighting against their bonds, almost panicking.

Somewhere deep down inside of Mathew, a part of him that was the bullied child was dying slowly too and now a stronger man was born ready to fulfil everything he had set out to do and that would mean taking on his treacherous brother.

When he next looked up at the pair they were no longer moving, except from the flow of water, now as he made sure they had gone, he felt even happier, 'a little bit longer,' he thought before he unlocked the taxi and quickly swam to the surface.

He emerged into the air and took a couple of very deep breaths; the water was bitterly cold and it felt like it was biting him, as if wanting not only the two in the taxi but him too.

Using the last bit of energy in his reserves, he swam across to the bank and climbed out carefully; he took several more deep breaths and sat on the edge of the bank.

He closed his eyes, shaking, the cold getting to him. If he stayed here any longer, the cold would claim him too and his goals would die with him, so he stood up and headed for the other bag.

Opening it he found a large bath towel and placed it around his body to dry himself and keep warm.

He closed his eyes again and saw the victims, all five of them, then he saw Sam's face and heard his remark, "See you in hell". The words stopped him shaking and when he opened his eyes he could see the blue light from the taxi; bubbles were coming up to the surface, the last bits of air escaping from the car.

He looked around and saw the street lights of the housing estates not far away, the area named after this quarry. Using this new energy he had somehow gained from thinking about the victims, he placed the towel back inside the bag and started to run.

He got halfway to the housing estate and threw the bag over a hedge, and then continued to run to the houses. Several minutes later he was there.

People in the street ignored him and went about their business. Strange, Mathew thought, as he was in wet clothes. He stopped to take his bearings and then headed down a side road to a street with an old red phone box situated on a corner.

The phone box smelt like someone had urinated in it, but he didn't care as he lifted the receiver with his hand covered in his left sleeve, and covering his mouth with his right sleeve, he dialled 999 and got through to the emergency service.

"Police, I am near Dead Man's Quarry and I have just seen some stupid young lads driving a nicked red taxi," he said in a panicked voice

"OK, calm down, sir; let's start at the beginning. What's your name?"

Mathew smiled and lied, "Sam Dalton."

"Anything else you can tell us, Sam?" the controller asked.

Mathew tried to sound convincing. "Yes, they were doing handbrake turns and I saw them skid straight off the cliff face and into the water."

The controller asked Mathew to stay on the line and then transferred the call to Chelmesbury police station.

Mathew explained again and then after hanging up, he laughed and laughed, and he didn't stop all the way back to his house.

Now the biggest task of all was about to begin.

THE DEATHLY ANGEL

By
Kevin Bailey

CHAPTER TWENTY-FOUR

CHELMESBURY POLICE STATION

Charlotte drove the green Mini into the station, parked up in a visitor's space and got out and headed for the station.

"I need to speak to Detective Chief Inspector Simon Eliote," she told the receptionist.

"I am afraid the Inspector is busy. Can anyone else help?" the woman replied.

"No, I want Simon Eliote, no one else," Charlotte told her curtly.

The receptionist spoke into a phone and finally looked up at Charlotte. "Take a seat. The DCI will be down in a moment," she said.

Charlotte sat and waited.

***

Up in the operations room the call by Mathew was being dealt with by the staff on duty.

"One four seven from Sierra Oscar receive, over."

There was a pause and then a voice came through the speaker. “Go ahead.”

“Respond to caller stating car in dead man’s quarry, rescue helicopter and divers have been alerted and are on their way, check out please.”

“We are on our way Sierra Oscar, one four seven out.”

The two officers sat in a lay-by and after taking the call, the driver started the engine, fired up the sirens and lights, and headed towards the quarry.

When they arrived, a police helicopter was circling the lake, its searchlight pointed straight at the water.

They parked the squad car and cordoned off the area, then walked down to the water’s edge and to a mini-bus, where several divers were preparing to enter the water.

After the divers had checked their apparatus, they looked over at the deep murky depths and using the helicopter searchlight, they dived into the freezing cold waters.

The two officers watched with the head diver, who was waiting for the others to re-appear and report their findings.

“It must be freezing down there,” one of the officers said.

The head diver looked at his thermometer and gave the reading. “It’s about minus five on the surface.”

The officer shuddered and said, “Ruddy Nora.” When he looked down into the deep water again, he saw a light approaching the surface.

“Get ready, he’s coming back,” the head diver said, and put out his hand as his colleague surfaced.

He took off his regulator and said, “We’ve found the red taxi sitting on the bottom, and in the back are two bodies. And it was no accident, they were both tied in.”

One of the constables went to his car and contacted the station.

"You had better get forensics and our friends in CID down here; we have two dead bodies for them."

Just then there was a shout and the other officer ran towards him with a plastic bag.

"Look at this," he said, and showed him the contents, the photo and the card.

"My God," he spoke back to the controller, "You'd better tell our CID friends, it's the angel and he's struck again."

***

Back at the station, Simon met with Charlotte in an interview room. "What can I do for you?" he asked.

"The Angel knows you have discovered his identity," Charlotte replied calmly, her expression blank.

"How is that possible?"

"I don't know, but I know he does." She turned and looked at the wall. "He is speeding up his actions," she added. When Simon headed for the door, she stopped him. "I know you don't believe me, so I'll show you something," she said. "In a moment, someone will walk in with a message for you…" She walked to her handbag, took out a pen and piece of paper, wrote something down and handed the piece of paper to him. "Read it," she said.

Eliote read the words that Charlotte had written and as he finished, a knock came at the door and DS Day walked in. She gave a small smile to Charlotte then turned to Eliote and said, "Guv, two bodies have been found in a red taxi in Dead Man's Quarry. It's the angel," Eliote was flabbergasted and looked down again at the piece of paper, then over at Charlotte. The words she had written down were precisely the ones that DS Day had just spoken.

"How did you do that?" he asked.

She smiled. "It's my gift. Your sergeant didn't believe me, but do you?"

Eliote handed the piece of paper to Day and then back at her.

"I always believed you Charlotte," he looked at Day, "Right then Sergeant, let's get to dead man's quarry and," he looked in Charlotte's direction, "we will be having a guest joining us from now on," Charlotte smiled warmly; Day just gave a weak smile, then the three of them headed to Simon's Saab and Day drove away.

DEAD MAN'S QUARRY

Simon, Miranda and Charlotte arrived at the quarry and they walked to a white tent that had been put up next to the dark misty waters.

"Morning, Strong," Day said as she saw the doctor. He looked up at them and smiled.

"Morning, you three," he said, glancing coldly at Charlotte. "What's she doing here, Sergeant?"

"She is here because I want her here, OK?" Eliote said.

The doctor grunted and then continued with his work.

Simon pulled on latex gloves as he walked to the car. He opened the door and looked in. "What do you think happened here, Doctor?"

Before the doctor could answer, Charlotte closed her eyes and answered for him.

"He drove them into the water and using diving equipment, he watched them die; and he got so much pleasure from it too." When she said this everyone except Strong and Eliote turned and looked at her.

"She's joking, right?" Day said almost laughing.

The doctor shook his head and said, "No, we have found diving apparatus," he pointed at a table, "with enough air to survive for at least ten minutes. This killer did indeed watch them go, then swam to the surface."

"You can't have known that, Miss Steel," Day said, "unless you are an accomplice." Charlotte wasn't paying any attention to her and was just staring around the place. "This quarry has meaning to the killer," she said. "Something happened here." She closed her eyes and concentrated. "His father died here, suicide… my God…"

"You believe this woman, Guv?" Day said.

"Dead Man's Quarry is named after a man who committed suicide," Strong said.

"That could just be a coincidence, Doctor," Day persisted.

Eliote nodded. "It could be, Sergeant, so I want it checked."

She gave in and walked back to the car.

"I think we had better catch this bastard before he kills the last two," Eliote said.

"He will only kill one of the two," Charlotte announced.

Eliote looked over at her and was about to say something, when Day re-appeared. "Anything?" he asked her.

She shook her head. "Not yet, Guv, but the team are working hard to get the information."

Eliote walked towards the bodies and looked at the sheets. His phone rang. It was Brightly.

"Simon, when you get to the station, I'll want a report on all cases so I can tell the chief constable what the situation is."

"I'll do it as soon as I can, ma'am, but I'm a little tied up at the moment. The Deathly Angel has struck again." As he placed the phone back into his pocket, Day approached him.

"Guv, Strong has examined the car and it seems it had fake number plates." Day took out her notebook. "I've just had records do a check on the registration number, seems the plates were stolen yesterday morning and the car itself is a stolen taxi, the driver of which was attacked by a hooded lad."

"Good work, Day," Eliote said. "Have you got anything on the brother?"

"Nothing, but the quarry was indeed named after a local called Neil Davies who committed suicide twelve years ago; no reason or note to say why."

Eliote looked over at Charlotte who was talking to some officers. "She was right," he said.

"I'd better go and apologise," Day said and walked off.

"Is there anything else to report, Doctor?" Eliote asked.

Strong shook his head and replied, "No, I will have my full report on your desk by tomorrow night." Eliote smiled and then walked away.

Strong watched him join Charlotte and Day and the three headed for Simon's Saab. As they drove away, he said to Penny, his assistant, "He never stays long at the crime scene, does he?"

"He stays long enough," Penny said.

"I think he doesn't like the blood, it probably makes him squirm."

Penny laughed. "You're sick, Doctor."

He smiled and then continued with his work.

***

When they arrived back at the station, Eliote asked Day to take Charlotte for a tea in the canteen, then he headed for Brightly's office. Ten minutes later folders were across her desk and she was looking at them as Eliote gave his report.

"The shooting in Aden Close was committed by a revengeful father, who was trying to protect his son," he remarked. "The father is recovering in hospital and has been charged with the murders. When he is fit enough, he will stand trial."

Brightly looked at the notes he had written. "I see you have commendations for Inspector Frashier and his team on this case." Eliote nodded. "How is it going with you two?" she asked.

"It's a slow progress, but I am confident that eventually things will improve."

"Ok moving on," she opened another file, "what of the Mardon shooting? This one the Chief Constable is concerned about."

"You can let the Chief Constable know that this was committed by Elizabeth Mardon.".

She seemed surprised "The deceased's daughter?"

He nodded and continued with his report. "Another vengeful shooting; as you can see from the report that she accused her father of being a racist," Brightly read the report.

"I see you have commendations for DS Day and DC Pickington?"

"Yes Ma-am, I think all the team have worked well on these cases, they all deserve commendations."

They discussed some minor cases, Eliote gave her the notes he'd collected and she agreed everything was proceeding nicely. "Right what about this Deathly Angel affair?'

Eliote sat forward on his chair. "We think we may have a prime suspect, one of the footballers in the photo," he pointed to the picture, "had a brother. Something about him is making me concerned, and considering the brutality of his kills so far, if he is the killer, what, if any, are his intentions for his brother?" He paused. "I may need a search warrant."

"I'll get one prepared. Listen," Brightly continued, her tone concerned, "I understand you took Charlotte Steel to the scene of the crime."

Eliote nodded. "I thought she could be useful to the team."

"CID is your department, Chief Inspector, but please be careful as I don't want the press hounding us, asking why we are using a psychic instead of detectives, I would rather they helped us not hinder us."

"I understand, ma'am, but we want to get Joe Public working with us. I think that scheme is working, don't you?"

Brightly sighed heavily. “Yes, that may be so, but keep her away from Frashier.”

THE DEATHLY ANGEL

By
Kevin Bailey

CHAPTER TWENTY-FIVE

Saturday morning was a fine day in Chelmesbury, and the town echoed with the sound of children playing.

But it was quiet at the Academy school, apart from the occasional car that would whizz past the main gate. The only other movement was that of a dark figure scurrying across the huge playing field, towards the school buildings.

He climbed the tall steel gates on the perimeter and jumped down, surveying the surroundings and trying to picture the plan of the school from memory. As he was looking around, the sound of a door opening caused him to dart behind a wall.

When he looked cautiously over it, he saw one of the school's caretakers was pulling some chairs from a classroom and heading towards another door. The intruder watched as the caretaker took out a set of keys and unlocked the door. He smiled at this bit of good luck, because he had intended to go in through a window, but this was better. If the caretaker was in, then he would have switched off the cameras and the security alarms.

The intruder got up slowly and, checking he could not be seen, ran to the open door. In the corridor beyond, he heard movement from up ahead and crept forward, checking each room he passed to make sure it was empty.

When he arrived at the last room, he peered in through the small window in the door and saw the caretaker placing the chairs in to a storage cupboard. This was the intruder's chance to snatch the keys. He removed a large spanner from his rucksack, wrapped a cloth around it and eased open the door.

He approached the caretaker and brought the spanner crashing down on the back of his neck. The man hit the ground with a thud. He dragged his inert body into the storage cupboard and using the stolen keys, locked the door and then locked up the classroom behind him.

Now he was free to go anywhere, he took out a small map he had drawn from memory, and after studying it, he headed off down the corridor. Turning a corner, he saw a large door and some stairs going up to the second floor. Praying there was no one else around; he darted past the door and up the stairs as quickly as he could.

On the other side of the door at the top of the stairs was a long landing, doors going off it in all directions. He approached the door he wanted, C15, and looked through the small window to make sure the coast was clear, then opened the door with the stolen keys. Crouching, he slipped into the room, closing the door behind him and locking it.

After a couple of minutes alone in the room, the intruder bundled some stuff into his rucksack and unlocked the door. Now he had to escape, but that was easy. He made his way carefully to a door marked Library, entered and walked to the windows, which gave a panoramic view of the school and grounds. He opened a window and climbed through, lowering himself onto the hard white roof of an adjoining building.

After taking a moment to get his bearings, he set off across the roof towards the school's entrance gate.

At one point, he heard a door open below and he paused lying flat on his chest. When he peered over the top he saw a bald-headed man - apparently a second caretaker - come out of one of the craft rooms and walk across towards the science block.

The intruder watched until the bald-headed caretaker had entered the building, then when the coast was clear, he got up and headed for the end of the rooftop and lowered himself to the ground. His mission accomplished, he ran to the entrance gate, climbed it and disappeared into the darkness.

Opening his eyes, the caretaker who had been hit by the spanner, surveyed his surroundings 'where was he?' he thought 'and how had he got in here?' he tried to sit up, but his head hurt, he felt nauseous and felt like his body was heavy.

Rubbing the back of his neck he managed to slowly sit up, he could make out the light coming from around the two doors, placing his hands in front of him, he stumbled forwards heading for the light.

But as he neared the doors, he tripped over the stack of chairs and collided with the doors, which burst open on impact and he collapsed against a table, banging the front of his face on the edge.

Outside in the corridor, the bald headed Caretaker heard the commotion and stopped in his tracks, he shouted out.

"John?" knowing that the sound had come from one of the science class rooms, he quickly started towards the rooms and as he passed the doors he looked in, the first few rooms where empty, quiet, like a ghost town.

Then he looked into the last classroom at the end of the corridor, at first he saw nothing and as he was about to leave the door, something made him look back into the room and he spotted the doors to the storage cupboard open.

Grabbing his large bunch of keys, he fumbled trying to find the right key; eventually he did and unlocked the door.

He heard the faint sound of someone crying out and rushed to the noise, that is when he found John heaped on the floor, blood was gushing from an open wound on his head and from his nose, he fumbled in his other front pocket for his mobile and took it out, he dialled the emergency services.

***

“Sergeant Day, is DCI Eliote still here?” the receptionist called out as Miranda passed by.

“No, he’s gone home, why?”

The receptionist handed the phone over and Miranda took the call.

“DS Day.” She listened for a while and then answered, “Okay, I’ll come and check it out, Constable.” She handed the phone back to the receptionist, grabbed her coat and bag and headed for her car, just as Pickington pulled into the car park.

“Phil, can you get me to the Chelmesbury Academy,” she said.

Pickington sighed heavily. “But, Miranda, I’m not on call tonight, got a romantic evening planned with the wife.” Day gave him a look which he knew meant business, so he sighed again. “OK then,” he groaned, “as long as it doesn’t take long.” She smiled and got in beside him. He turned the car around and headed for the school.

They arrived at the school gates and were greeted by squad cars and an ambulance; two police officers lifted the tape when Day showed him her warrant card and Pickington drove into the school and parked behind a squad car.

DC Smith was already there and greeted them as they approached. “DS Day, DC Pickington, please, this way.” The two officers followed her into the inner sanctum of the school.

“So, report, DC Smith,” Day ordered.

“One of the caretakers, John Wade, was hit over the head by an unknown assailant. Uniform and the head caretaker, Alex Bozeman, have searched the school, but found nothing amiss.”

"Odd," Pickington said to Day, who nodded and continued to follow Smith down the corridor.

She led them to the staff room, where John Wade sat on a sofa being attended to by two paramedics. DS Day introduced herself and asked him what he could remember.

Wincing as he nodded a greeting, he explained, "I was taking a load of chairs from one of the old Craft, Design and Technology classrooms to the science room storeroom. As I entered the classroom, I felt a sharp pain on the back of my head; the next thing I knew, I woke up and I'm in darkness."

Day nodded and as she was about to say something, Pickington's phone went off, he went red in the face and turned and walked out of the room, Day turned back and looked at John. "Is there anything else, sir?"

"No, I'm sorry."

Day smiled warmly at him then turned and walked with DC Smith out of the room. Pickington was in one of the classrooms having an almighty argument with whoever was on the phone. Day guessed it was Mrs Pickington. He hung up abruptly and headed for Day.

"Sorry about that, ma'am, it was the wife," he said.

Day smiled. "I guessed that," she said, noticing how angry he was, "You go and sort out your wife; DC Smith here can give me a lift back to the station." With a grateful grin, Pickington darted off, and said, "Okay, back to business. Let's get some teams and check out every classroom, every outbuilding. John Wade disturbed somebody and I want to know what they were doing here!"

Miranda wrote in her report to Eliote that they spent the entire weekend searching the school, but found nothing to be missing or out of place, so the search was stopped.

***

Early Monday morning, Simon walked into the CID unit. Day wasn't at her desk, and he was about to walk away, when he spotted a crumpled-up picture in her waste bin. He reached down and examined it. It was the fake picture that Frashier had created.

When Day walked into the room and saw what Eliote was holding, her mind searched for an excuse she could give him.

"It was created to see if the car was similar in design to Steve Marston's," she lied. "When we discovered it was, it was thrown away," Eliote didn't believe her.

"Whose idea was this, Sergeant?" he said angrily, "DI Frashiers," she didn't reply "Where is he?" he demanded.

Day shrugged her shoulders and said, "Haven't seen him this morning, Guv."

Eliote almost ripped his office door off its hinges and headed towards Frashier's office, but it was empty. He spotted Pickington at his desk, going through the files from the weekend.

"DS Pickington, have you seen Frashier this morning?"

"No, I haven't Guv, sorry. He did ring in sick at the weekend, so he's probably still off."

Eliote returned to the red-faced DS Day and told her, "I want to see you in my office right away."

When she entered, she sat down and Eliote slammed the door, making her jump.

"Detective Sergeant Day," he said, "I know you are only protecting DI Frashier, but if I find out that he used this image in any interview with the late Steve Marston, then both you and he will be dismissed from the force. Do I make myself clear?" he snapped

"Yes, Guv," she said sheepishly.

"Good, now get out of my sight, and close the door behind you."

She did as was instructed and left the office.

Eliote stood up and looked out of the window, the anger boiling up inside of him. He knew it was about time that he confronted Frashier and made his feelings known, but was disturbed by the phone ringing on his desk. It was Strong.

"Chief Inspector, I am at the phone box where the call to the police was made about the taxi in the quarry. I think you'd better get here."

He wrote down the directions, replaced the receiver and walked out to his car.

Day watched him go and then grabbed her mobile and rang Frashier.

"Listen," she snapped at him, when he answered, "Eliote has discovered the photo-shopped image you created, and now he's put one and one together and come up with two."

"How did you know about the forgery?" he asked.

"Pickington told me. Eliote isn't happy, and he's threatened us with dismissal if he finds anything dodgy has been going on."

"He won't do that, Miranda," Frashier answered. "He hasn't got the balls. I'll deal with it."

"You'd better," she said with venom and then hung up on him.

***

Eliote went and picked up Charlotte and the two travelled to the phone box and found Strong dusting it for prints. He turned and smiled at Eliote and beckoned him over.

"This is what I called you here for," he said and pointed at some graffiti on the wall of the phone box. Eliote read the writing.

To the guilty,
Revenge is bitter sweet,
DA

"DA?" Eliote said. "Could that be 'DA,' as in 'Deathly Angel'?"

Strong nodded. "We also found blood on the floor, which has been sent to the lab for analysis."

"Have photos taken of the writing," Eliote said.

Eliote and Charlotte took a walk and saw a road signposted Dark Lane. He looked back at the phone box and Strong.

"Doctor," he shouted, "is this the other end to Lovers Lane?"

The doctor approached him and said, "Yes and no. You see, Dark Lane and Lovers Lane are actually two lanes." He pointed at a stone figure in the distance. "Do you see the statue of the angel?" Eliote nodded. "That is the old churchyard, belonging to the ruins of the church of St Matthew. The church itself was destroyed in a fire several years ago and the lanes that used to end at the church were joined; now the townsfolk often refer to it simply as Lovers Lane."

"Where is Dead Man's Quarry from here?"

Strong pointed to another road, just up from them.

"It's about two miles in that direction. The man who set fire to the church jumped off into the quarry and that is where it gets its name from."

Eliote's mind was in overdrive as he ran back to the phone box and looked at a map displaying both the towns of Chelmesbury and Glayton, which was on an information board next to the phone box.

He pointed at Dark/Lovers Lane, Dead Man's Quarry, Mandies Nightclub and Monmouth Street; all but the factories were linked by this phone box.

"Strong, bring your bag and come with me," he said, and then looked over at Charlotte. "You too, we are going to investigate that old churchyard. Something tells me we're near where the killer lives."

Nearby, buried deep in the undergrowth, Mathew watched the police at work. They were getting way too close. He realized that he had made a terrible mistake, which could now backfire on him. He looked over at his home. The police would surely go and investigate. He now knew that the photo was a mistake, especially as his grandmother had informed him that only the families had received the photo.

He watched Strong, Charlotte and Eliote disappear down Dark Lane and then crept into the underground stream and headed for home.

Strong opened the gate and he, Charlotte and Simon entered the rundown churchyard. The grass needed cutting and so did the hedges; chunks of masonry from the ruined church littered the place, graffiti plastered on them.

"Where do you suggest we go first, Chief Inspector?"

Eliote knew that there was one place he needed to go. He pointed at the angel.

"That way, Doctor," he said, and the three of them made their way through the overgrown churchyard to a clearing, where the stone angel pointed to the town centre.

Strong examined the statue, but Eliote wasn't interested in the angel. He examined the ground and he found what he was looking for: the earth had been disturbed.

"Strong," he said, and the doctor looked over at the detective who was pointing to the ground. He put on some protective gloves and using a trowel, he started to dig away at the surface, Eliote watched.

He hadn't gone far when he came across a long object covered in a dirty tea towel; the doctor slowly and carefully unravelled the object.

“My God,” Strong said, “I think this is the murder weapon, same striations on the blade and also there appears to be blood present.”

“There’s something else in there,” Eliote said, looking at the hole. Strong placed the knife into an evidence bag and then returned to the hole and exhumed the other item. It too was in a tea towel, but it was much smaller than the first item.

Again Strong carefully unravelled the object; it was the photo of the football team, but all the players had circles around them, and this photo had another member, a young teacher, whom Eliote recognized immediately as Mr Depson. He also had a circle around him.

“I think Mr Depson has been lying to me,” Eliote said. Just then in the distance he heard a bell ringing. “What’s that, Doctor?”

Strong stood up and looked over to where the ringing was coming from. “The Chelmesbury Academy,” he said. “It must be there fire alarm sounding.”

Eliote walked to the edge of the churchyard and peered over the hedge. There was the school in all its glory.

Children and teachers were lined up in rows and several other teachers were in front bellowing orders.

Something deep in Charlotte’s mind hurt: an image of the angel and of real pain. She tried to push the pain from her head; she was in a graveyard after all, and surely she must be feeling the pain from the relatives who had buried their beloved family in the graveyard.

But the thought would not go away.

“Chief Inspector, I’m afraid I’m going to have to go from this place,” she said as she started to drift in and out of consciousness, her body feeling weak and dizzy. “I’m getting strange feelings,” she said, sounding drunk. She heard Strong say something and both he and Simon ran to her, but they were too late and she passed out.

She opened her mind and was immediately surrounded by several dark figures, all ready to pounce, their hands made into fists, ready to punch.
"Please don't hurt me, I just wanted to be part of your team," she heard herself say, but this voice was young, scared.
She could sense from the figures' anger and menace that they knew what they must do and she could feel no remorse from the group and then they attacked.

THE DEATHLY ANGEL

By
Kevin Bailey

CHAPTER TWENTY-SIX

She opened her eyes to see Simon regarding her with concern. When she sat up she could feel pain, but there were no bruises.

"Charlotte, are you all right?" Strong asked.

"Yes, I'm fine."

"You don't look fine to me," Strong said. "You looked like you were having an epileptic fit."

With help from Simon, she stood up and then looked at the angel. "This means something to him, Chief Inspector; he uses its energy, its image, to focus his mind," she said then paused to touch it. "This is his Deathly Angel."

"I think you need to go home and rest," Eliote said. "Doctor, can you get Pickington to organize some officers to corner off this churchyard and then you and some of your team can do a thorough examination of the place."

"What about Frashier and Day?" Strong asked.

"No, Pickington can do it," Simon said bluntly. "I need someone I can trust."

Strong nodded and Eliote escorted Charlotte out of the churchyard to his Saab.

Strong watched him go, then took out his mobile and phoned Pickington and informed him of Simon's order. Pickington sighed heavily and hung up.

Strong stood looking at the church, but his thoughts weren't about the case; instead, he was wondering why Eliote had asked Pickington to organize the search. When he got back to the station, he would ask Day what the hell was going on.

***

Eliote dropped Charlotte off at home and then he himself went home to rest. Henry brought him in some dinner and as he sat back in his chair, he was disturbed by a phone call from Day.

She started by apologising for her actions. She had heard that Eliote had told Strong he no longer trusted her and this upset her.

"Miranda," he said calmly, "I forgot that you said you would do anything for Frashier, I admire that loyalty, but as I give people second chances, then I will not mention it again. Now, what can I do for you?"

"Well, sir, I was out last night with some friends from my college days and we got talking about school. Two of them went to Shrewsbury, but that doesn't concern the case, the other two, well, now that's a different story."

"Yes, go on," he said impatiently.

"One of them mentioned that they used to go to the old high school and when I showed them the photo, they remembered the footballers as the greatest team in the county."

"That would match what Depson said about the team being the best."

"It would, sir. My friend said that most people of the time would think the same."

Eliote drank some tea and then asked, "What about the other friend?" He heard Day turning pages.

"Well, she agreed, but later on, she took me to one side and said they were bullies. Like Depson said, anyone got in their way and they were disposed of."

"Interesting. So could this killer be after revenge?"

"It would seem so, sir." She paused and Eliote could sense that Day had worked hard for this information, to get back in his good books.

"Did she know of anyone who, as you put it, 'got in the way'?"

Day breathed in and out a couple of times as if calming herself down. "Yes, Guv. She said there had been a big incident which had been hushed up concerning these boys and another boy."

"Did she give you a name?"

"Sorry, Guv, she couldn't remember his name but said this boy was beaten nearly to death, but when the police interviewed some of the other pupils, they were too afraid to say anything and the boys were let off to win the final ten-nil, like Depson said."

So, Eliote thought, Depson was lying to me. As a teacher he would have known about anything serious against a child. He wondered what he should do next.

"OK, Miranda, I'll meet you in my office in an hour."

When he arrived at his office, Miranda Day was waiting all humble for him.

"OK, DS Day, report," he said.

She opened her notebook and read out the information she had gathered.

"DS Lewis has just got off the phone with a friend down at the hospital; she remembers a patient by the name of Mathew Davies, who came in to casualty with severe damage to his face, chest and legs. A brain scan revealed a blood clot, the emergency operation to clear it worked but due to the location of the clot, it has left the lad with severe mutilation due to scarring."

"That would explain the hood, and revenge as a motive," Eliote said. "Good work, Day."

"That's not all, Guv. I got on to the hospital myself and I have an address: Mathew Davies, number two, the Old Church Hall, St Mathews Road, Chelmesbury."

Eliote remembered the map on the board next to the phone box. The address was in walking distance of all the crimes. "Get a group of Forensics and officers together to meet me out the front," he ordered. "I think we have our Deathly Angel." He picked up the phone. "I need that search warrant, ma'am."

"OK, I'll get it to you," Brightly replied

"Everything is ready, Guv," Day told him a few minutes later. "We're just waiting for your orders."

"Here are my orders," Eliote said with a grin, "let's go and catch this bastard before he kills again."

The two of them walked out to the awaiting officers, who were standing by a mini-bus.

"Right, listen up," Eliote commanded. "I want the place searched. If our suspect, Mathew Davies, isn't there, then I want to know where he is. I want clues, specimens, anything that can nail this Angel. So, I want you to work in teams, no stone unturned. Got it?" Heads nodded. "Right then people, it's off to work."

The officers boarded the mini-bus, Eliote and Day got into Eliote's Saab and with the Forensics team behind, they set off in a convoy, picking up Strong on the way

2 THE OLD CHURCH HALL.
ST MATHEWS ROAD.
CHELMESBURY,

Eliote, Day and the rest of the officers and Forensics arrived at the house; it was up a twisty road.

Their first impression as they lay eyes on the building was that it was a large Victorian manor house, with bay windows on the bottom floor. The entrance had pillars both sides and a triangular roof. The gardens were green and lush and the only unsightly thing was an old shed, which looked like it was falling down.

Eliote walked to the double door and rang the bell. Deep within the house, he heard footsteps and then the right-hand door opened and he was greeted by a middle-aged woman.

She had mousy coloured hair, brown eyes and was approximately five foot nine, wearing an apron above her jodhpurs and T-shirt.

"Mrs Davies?" Eliote asked.

"Yes, can I help you?" Eliote took out his wallet and showed her his card.

"I am Detective Chief Inspector Simon Eliote and this is my colleague Detective Sergeant Miranda Day, Chelmesbury CID. Is Mathew in the house?"

She shook her head. "No, he's gone to pick up his brother and his friend from the airport, but he should have been back ages ago. I'm just about to ring him."

"Which airport is your son heading for?" Eliote asked.

"Manchester. His brother is flying back home from Spain; he's just spent a year over there."

"What car is he driving?" Eliote said quickly.

"A yellow Range Rover, why?"

Eliote took her into the sitting room, where they were met by an elderly man.

"What's going on Belle?" he asked.

"Seems they're looking for Mathew, Dad. I don't know why."

"What's that boy done now?"

Day beckoned her to sit in a chair, whilst Eliote left the room; he went to the minibus and grabbed the radio.

"Sierra Oscar from One-one-two; are you receiving? Over." He heard a female voice echo through the car's speakers.

"Sierra Oscar receiving. Go ahead, Over."

"Put an alert out for the transport police to stop and apprehend the occupants of a yellow Range Rover with personalised registration." He read out the registration number and then returned the radio and walked back into the house.

"Mrs Davies, we are investigating the deaths of five young lads."

"But what has that got to do with Mathew?" the old man replied.

Eliote looked at him. "And you are, sir?"

"John James, Mathew's maternal grandfather."

"I'm sorry to have to inform you both that at present Mathew is our main suspect in these murders."

Unsteadily, Mrs Davies beckoned him to go to the kitchen. "Can you get my tablets?" she asked. "I think they're above the sink in the blue box."

Day ran into the kitchen and grabbed the box, then returned and handed it to Mrs Davies.

Eliote walked back to the mini-bus, where Charlotte and several of his team were waiting. "Right, listen up," he said to them all. "I want a full sweep, remember, so get to work." As the officers left and proceeded into the house, he looked over at Charlotte. "I need you in Mathew's room. Tell me if you feel anything." She nodded and set off while he returned to find Day.

As Eliote and Day were with Mr James and Mrs Davies, one of the Forensics team was going through Matthew's bedroom, when he made a startling discovery. Charlotte looked at the object and then shouted down to Eliote who came running up the stairs.

"What is it Charlotte?" She handed him the black book; Eliote opened it, and read the first paragraph.

I saw James and his friend walking from the pub, he had so much happiness in his face, laughing about a girl, he won't be smiling or laughing again, I stabbed him so many times, he has almost as many holes as a tea bag.

Stapled to the book was a picture of the first victim, which had been taken from the photo. The images in Charlotte's mind started again, and she felt dizzy.

Eliote noticed she'd grown pale. "You okay, Charlotte?" he said, but she didn't reply. Instead, she swooned and fell forward into his arms.

"Lotte, loopy Lotte." She heard the evil voice from within the "black hole", and laughter, which deafened her. She stepped to the edge of the swirling mists and heard her name being called again: "Lotte, loopy Lotte, come and play," but this time, instead of falling in, Charlotte gulped and then jumped into the whirlpool.

She felt like she was falling further and further into her own mind, the images in front that passed by were swirling like some faulty television screen, showing scenes from her past, the family and friends she had lost, past lovers.

A swirling bright light appeared from below, illuminating her, stopping the falling motion and then an image appeared next to her and held her hand.

Charlotte recognised the young man straight away.

"Hello, Lotte," he said, smiling.

"Father, am I dead?"

He shook his head and smiled warmly, holding her hand tightly. "Come with me," he said, and in a blinding flash of light Charlotte was standing on a school field; her father was gone.

The school was nothing like the Academy that now stood in its place, old dilapidated buildings, a mighty hall, several football pitches.

Suddenly she was aware that she wasn't alone.
"Father?" she said. But instead of the young man, it was a twelve-year-old boy. She tried to speak to the boy, but he was too absorbed watching some older boys approaching him. The twelve-year-old smiled at one of the boys, but they surrounded him, like a pack of dogs.
Charlotte could feel the hatred in the boys' minds and the fear in the twelve-year-old.
"What's going on?" the boy said to the group and Charlotte realized who the boys were; their adult pictures flashed as she looked at each one around the group.
Then James spoke.
"Mathew, you made a mistake trying to show up Dave to Depson, so you could play in the match on Saturday."
"But I want to play; I am good enough to play for you." James punched Mathew in the stomach; Charlotte felt the pain and the others just laughed, then she heard a voice and the group moved out of the way as a skinny teacher approached. Charlotte didn't recognise the man but saw the pride in his eyes at the group of lads, which changed to shock, when he saw Mathew.
"What's going on here then, lads?"
James whispered something into the teacher's ear and he looked at the group angrily. "I told you to do that outside the school." The lads all looked at the ground in shame.
"Were sorry, Mr Depson."
"I can't have you lot expelled, especially as it's the final on Saturday. I put a couple of grand on you to win. No, that won't do." He looked around the field and then towards a road at the bottom, Charlotte could see in the distance the

old stone angel pointing back at them as if a witness to this betrayal.
She turned back and looked at the young teacher, who was speaking still. "Take him out of the school boundary, what you do then is up to you." James nodded. Mr Depson looked at the young Mathew. "I don't want this lad ruining our chances, so make sure he doesn't come back. Well, go on and make it quick."

Charlotte felt her own hatred boil up, but the fear and pain from the lad was overwhelming her and she looked at the twelve-year-old Mathew with pity as he sat on the floor crying. Something made him look up at one of the lads, but the lad ignored him.
Now the realization hit her like the group would hit the young Mathew. His own brother had helped to turn him into the monster he was; the revenge he had shown his victims was nothing to the pain and suffering he would bestow onto his brother. The group was just a stone used to sharpen his anger and hatred.
As she watched the group drag Mathew kicking and screaming out of the grounds, she no longer felt pity for him; she felt pity for the group and that pity increased in strength as they gave Mathew a good hiding.

Mr Depson, who only had pride in his boys and the greed of winning the money on the game, watched them go and had no remorse for what he had asked the lads to do, he just stood and listened to the thuds from the punishment he had asked them to bestow on Mathew and kept a lookout.
Above the pain from Mathew was the betrayal of his brother. Charlotte could feel Mathew shouting out for him, but the feeling from his brother was sadness, betrayal and also something else was there and Charlotte hated this feeling. This brother was scared for his own neck.

She turned back with hatred and disgust for Mr Depson. If she had a gun he would be dead. Mathew wasn't the Deathly Angel, Depson was; Death in the disguise of a man in high authority, a man who created the ultimate betrayal and thus the creator of evil.

Suddenly from nowhere her young father appeared next to a shiny white door. She still felt upset and angered by this encounter and looked at her father.
"Why did you die, Dad, just when I needed you?"
The man shook his finger at her and then pointed at the door. "That is a question I will answer one day, but now it is time for you to go."
She stood up and walked up to the door and opened it. Beyond was a shining light and she walked towards it.

THE DEATHLY ANGEL

By Kevin Bailey

CHAPTER TWENTY-SEVEN

Simon was relieved when Charlotte opened her eyes.

"Are you okay?" he asked. "You gave us quite a shock."

"Yeah, I think so," she said sitting up and looking around. "How long was I out?"

Simon smiled and answered, "About ten minutes. Can you explain what happened?"

She shook her head and then she saw the book beside him and picked it up.

"Are you sure that's wise, Charlotte?" Simon said. "Last time you picked it up, you were literally out cold for an hour."

"Chief Inspector, do you want to find out more about why Mathew has killed this group?" He nodded. "Then read this," she said and handed him the book.

Eliote read the beginning and then looked at her in shock. "Mr Depson made them beat him up?"

She nodded. "Now read on."

He sat down on a chair and continued to read.

I have found my second bully, Wayne Warwick, working as a factory operative, but I was too late to kill him; someone else beat me to it. This copycat killer was one of Wayne's lovers and I witnessed his deed with hatred in my heart. He looked like me, but he had more vengeance than I have. I will be careful as I go after this one and do to him what I should have done to Wayne.

"Shit, I think Wayne was killed by someone else," Eliote said. "According to Mathews' journal, this killer made us think it was him, but whoever it was will wish they hadn't."

"Does the journal say who?" Strong asked, taking out another blood-covered notebook.

Eliote shook his head and continued reading.

I have found out where this copycat killer lives, but instead of killing him, I have used his name.

Eliote looked up from the book. "Strong, where's Day?" The doctor looked blankly at him.

"She's downstairs. Why?"

"She needs to go and arrest Sam Dalton; she'll need a warrant. Oh, and you'd better go with her."

Strong nodded and left, just as Robertson entered.

"Dick, how did the trip to Wayne's family go?"

"It was a strange interview. Michelle was glad he was dead, he'd been having an affair with a male mate and he had left her last Saturday. She didn't tell me who it was."

"Your case is simple, Dick. Wayne's killer was Sam Dalton, not the Deathly Angel."

"Sam Dalton?"

Eliote nodded. "Yes, he knew there was a serial killer on the loose. He had read the paper and knew that he wore a hood, so he copied The Deathly Angel and killed Wayne because he was his lover and Wayne had found someone else. But unbeknown to him, Dalton killed a man who was marked for death by our serial killer; I think Sam is in grave danger."

“What about the photo and the calling card?” Robertson asked.

Eliote raised his hand to silence him and went back to studying the journal.
“Ah, here it is,” he started to read out loud.

> *“After seeing the killer leave, I thought ‘why not,’ so I placed the photo and card next to the vat and left, but I think ‘the cook’ saw me.”*

“Well, that solves my case,” Robertson said, smiling. “I’ll get my team together and help DS Day arrest this Sam Dalton.”

“Okay, buddy, till the next time,” Eliote said, shaking hands with his friend.

“I hope you get this bastard, Simon,” Robertson said.

“I will,” he said confidently. “Now go and get Sam.”

Robertson headed off to find Day, leaving Eliote to read more of the journal.

***

They skidded to a stop outside Sam’s house and Robertson knocked on the door. There was no reply, but something made the hairs on the back of Day’s neck stand up and she turned to her colleague.

“Do you see that, Inspector?” she said, pointing to a small window next to the door, where hundreds of flies were buzzing around behind the net curtains. She turned and looked at the car, beckoning Strong, who grabbed his leather case and headed for the door.

When Day tried to gain entry, she found the door was locked. She grabbed a pair of gloves, used a brick to smash the small window and putting her hand behind the door she opened it.

The smell reached them immediately, an overpowering combination of rotting flesh, human waste, and stale blood.

Strong opened his bag, pulled out a box of face masks and handed one each to Day and Robertson, then the three entered the house.

What they saw was disgusting. The decaying body of Sam Dalton was laid out in the sitting room, coated in a gruesome layer of wriggling maggots. Beneath him was a pool of congealed blood, in which more maggots frolicked.

Strong stopped the detectives from entering any further into the room, stating health and safety and also contamination, then took out a protective suit, got dressed, placed a mask over his mouth and entered on his own.

Kneeling down beside the body, he performed a rapid but careful examination of the remains.

"What's your conclusion, Doctor?" Day called from the doorway.

"Killed the same way as Jamie Tweeting and James Gaston, I am certain of that," he said. "A slight indentation to the skull…" he looked around and spotted a small amount of flesh on the coffee table corner.

"Cause of death, Doctor?" Day asked him politely.

"I think it was the impact of his head falling against that coffee table," he took a few measurements. "I'll know more when I get the body back to the lab."

Day turned and headed back towards the car, took out her phone and called Eliote.

"Guv, Sam Dalton is dead," she told him.

***

Eliote was annoyed. The news from Day was not good. He thanked her and ended the call. He should have known that Sam was a killer; he had felt something wrong about him when they had first met, but Sam had played the innocent party well.

Strong's team were still examining every inch of the room. Eliote got out of their way, found a chair and then continued to read the journal.

Spurred on by the arrival of a new Detective Chief Inspector at Chelmesbury CID, I decided that the twins had to be the next on my agenda. If I could pull this off, then nothing would stop me.

So as a favour to my granddad, I have been giving karate and other self-defence classes to his old mate George Sinclair; this has worked out in my favour.

He stopped reading and looked around the room where he sat. Cobwebbed certificates hung on the wall, and when he walked towards them and examined them, he found they were for karate and jujitsu; Mathew was a black belt in both. Eliote returned to the journal.

I dropped George home one night and he invited me in for a drink, I met his dad and whilst there he said I could borrow his car anytime I liked as he didn't use it much. He gave me his spare key and I left.

But George Sinclair is a fool; after scouting around town for a perfect place to kill the twins, I was bringing his car back, when I was stopped by two policemen who thought I had stolen it.
I was relieved when they contacted George and he explained I was the only one who borrowed the car. They then allowed me to go and kill the twins and I almost laughed as I drove away.

THE DEATHLY ANGEL

By
Kevin Bailey

CHAPTER TWENTY-EIGHT

Simon Eliote froze to the spot. He couldn't believe how unlucky those two policemen who had stopped him were. If only they had realised who they had, then possibly the Deathly Angel case could have been wrapped up and four men would be alive.

Eliote beckoned Detective Constable Hagley over when he walked into the room. "Get on to the station," he instructed Hagley, "and see if anyone stopped a car belonging to George Sinclair."

Once the DC had left, Eliote continued reading the book.

Then I stole a taxi and picked them up. They were bullies, but they were helpless when they strapped themselves in and I drove off the cliff where my father killed himself after he found out about what my brother had helped do to me.

For that I can never forgive my brother or God, so that's why I called myself the Deathly Angel.

The Angels took the twins as I watched; the look of horror on their faces as the water took them was a sight for sore eyes. Now I must hurry, the police are closing in. I hope they don't get to the real betrayer, Mr Anthony Depson, before he finds my little present.

Eliote took out his phone and dialled the number for Frashier but only reached his voicemail. He cursed and hung up, then dialled Day's number. When she answered he was blunt with her.

"Miranda, I know you're busy with Robertson, but I need you to bring in Mr Depson for questioning." She was about to say something but he added, "And hurry – I want him brought in now!"

Eliote finished with the journal and called to one of the forensics officers, "Anything else to report?"

She nodded. "We've found another book. It looks like he kept a list of his equipment – an inventory, so to speak. Everything he owned is in this book, including diving apparatus."

Eliote thanked her but the woman wasn't finished.

"Also," she continued, "there's this..." She walked to a small bureau, opened a drawer and there between two adult magazines was a small penknife. There were traces of blood on the magazines.

Charlotte walked towards him, holding a picture of a group of children, looking smart in their new school uniform. She pointed to a skinny boy in the middle of the second row.

"Mathew?" Eliote said. He took the picture off her and examined the face and the faces around. "So he was well liked."

"Just been talking to Mathew's grandfather," Charlotte said. "He was a happy, popular teenager, but after the incident, he changed, didn't trust anyone."

"Can you blame him?" Eliote said, then as he looked at the picture in more detail, he noticed the young face of a schoolteacher. Simon could tell who it was, the skinny teacher who years later he had met: Mr Depson.

"Chief Inspector…" He heard his name shouted and returned to Mathew's room.

"What is it, Penny?"

She handed him two photos; one was the school photo he had just looked at, but this time Mr Depson's face had a circle marked around it. The next picture was the school football team; they were all there and Mathew had circled them as he had killed them.

Eliote handed the book back to one of the forensics team and then took the pictures off the wall and carried it down to the front room where he had left Mrs Davies and Mr James.

"Your colleague tells me that you think my Mathew is this Deathly Angel," Mrs Davies said, pointing at the cover of *The Chelmesbury Chronicle*, with its headline, DEATHLY ANGEL STRIKES AGAIN.

"Mrs Davies, this is going to come as a shock, but yes, we do believe he has tortured and killed five men in revenge for an attack that happened when he was twelve."

"What attack? He was knocked down by a hit and run driver. His brother found him and got him to hospital."

"I'm afraid your eldest son was part of it, Mrs Davies."

"This is some kind of joke. What proof have you got?" Mr James asked.

Eliote showed him the picture. "Do you recognise these people, Mr James?"

He looked at the photo and smiled. "Sure I do, this is a photo of my eldest grandson's football team. We are so proud of him; he's won lots of medals and trophies all over the world."

"Is that so?" Eliote said. "Well, look at this: Jamie Tweeting, dead," he pointed at another, "James Gaston, dead, Edward and Sidney Smith, both dead, murdered by your grandson, Mr James. And then there is Wayne Warwick." He pointed to another pupil. "Wayne's killer has been found murdered, as well."

"You're lying," Mrs Davies said, shaking her head. "He wouldn't do that, he wouldn't…" She started to cry.

Eliote approached her and crouched down on the floor. "Mrs Davies, he has, he even confesses it in this black book." He showed her the book but she just sat there shaking her head.

"I just don't believe it, he wouldn't, I brought him up to be proper."

Eliote stood up. "Have you tried phoning him, Mrs Davies?"

She nodded and replied, "It just keeps going to answer phone, Chief Inspector."

Eliote looked over at Mr James, then back at Mrs Davies. "If Mathew wanted to kill your eldest son, is there anywhere he could take him?" Mrs Davies shook her head.

"The old JMAK knacker's yard, over in Wedsford," Mr James said, "where his dad and I used to work. Mathew and his brother Mike used to hang out there; it's been unused for several years now."

"Could you show me on a map where it is?" Eliote asked.

Mr James stood up and grabbed an old set of keys. "I'll do better than show you on a map," he said. "I'll take you there."

***

Mike Davies felt cold. He opened his eyes into darkness and he couldn't see anything, except a distant light from a broken window above him. He thought he could detect a dark image moving in the blackness, but it could have been his mind playing tricks on him. What wasn't his imagination, however, was the sour smell of rotting meat.

He tried to stand but found he couldn't; chains were attached to his hands and feet. He felt around behind him and discovered the metal hooks. The realization of where he was brought a chill to his bones. He was in his grandfather's slaughterhouse.

He remembered being picked up by his brother and sitting in the back of his family's Range Rover, when he had fallen asleep.

Suddenly a thought came to him: if he was here, where was his friend Terry?

"Terry, are you there?" he called. "Terry, Terry…" He heard a groan in the darkness.

"Yeah," a voice answered, and Mike heard chains clattering. "Where are we?"

"I think we're at my grandfather's slaughterhouse. I used to come here as a kid with my brother Mathew."

Mike heard the chains rattle once again and then Terry asked, "How did we get here?"

"I think Mathew brought us here." Mike heard movement from somewhere in the dark. "Mathew, is that you?" but silence was his only answer.

"Why would your brother bring us here?" Terry asked.

"I don't know. Last time I came here, my father was still alive and I was explaining to him why I helped you lot destroy my brother's life."

"We destroyed your brother's life?" Terry asked, clearly confused.

"Yeah, remember the week before the final, there was that kid who told Depson about Dave."

"What, that little kid Depson told us to sort out? That was your brother? You never told me."

"I was scared you lot would beat me up if I tried to help him," Mike answered.

"We wouldn't have done anything, he was your brother, your own flesh and blood; our loyalty to family was always stronger than the group. He must really hate you."

A sad voice echoed down the building: "Oh, I do." And the darkness was filled with the unmistakeable sound of a knife being sharpened.

"Matt is that you?" Mike shouted out into the darkness. "What's going on?"

"It's payback time, my dear brother. You and Terry are the only ones left of your gang of bullies, the others are dead."

"No, you lie," he said almost stuttering. "You wouldn't hurt a thing, you were always weak."

Mathew continued sharpening a knife. "I was weak, but I got strong. I'd tell our mum, that I was going for a drive, but actually I was learning karate. Mum never put up my certificates downstairs, she'd only put up your awards, your certificates. Our mother loved you more than me."

"Mum loved us both and you know that. She cared for you after the operations, got you into another school, made sure you were always cared for."

"Don't you dare speak about my mum," Mathew spat at him. "You have no right. You ended being her son, the day you helped them beat me up."

Mathew had drawn near now, and Mike felt his pure rage when he hit him across the face. He banged his head against the wall, blood gushed from his nose and he slumped forward, the chains stopping him from falling to the floor.

"You see, Mike, I can never forgive you for what you did; you not only destroyed my life, you destroyed Dad's, and now your time is coming."

Mathew landed another blow and another, and Terry shouted, "Mike, are you all right? Mike!"

"Oh, isn't it lovely," Terry heard from the darkness, "you concerned about your friend. I would commend you for an award, if you weren't a bully."

Terry shouted out into the darkness, "I was never a bully, we wanted to be the best and sometimes being the best, you have to sacrifice things that are important to you."

The sound of knife-sharpening stopped and only silence filled the darkness.

"You're so right, Terry, one must sacrifice things for the cause," Mathew said, laughing cruelly.

***

Back at the old church hall, Eliote instructed Hagley to keep an eye on Mrs Davies, and once that was sorted, he and Mr James headed for the JMAK knacker's yard, blue lights flashing and siren blaring. He got on the radio and requested backup and an ambulance at the Wedsford location. "We may have casualties," he told them.

***

An electric shorting noise echoed around Terry and when a couple of lights came on, he saw that both his arms were tied by a chain to a large steel bar, which was attached in the middle to a winch.

The bar, chains and winch were used to pull dead animals from high-sided metal-backed lorries. He realized he was dangling from a great height and could feel his shoulders aching under the strain of his body.

How long till they buckled, he couldn't tell.

Once his eyes got used to the lights, he looked around him and then at his friend Mike, who was chained to some bars; blood was trickling from his nose onto the floor and he was slumped forward.

"Mike, are you okay?" he called, and when he looked up into the rafters, he could hear the squeaking of rats, running backwards and forward along the beams informing their friends that food could possibly be coming.

He felt a cold draft and watched as a hooded figure shut a sliding door and turned in his direction, the hood covering his face.

"Hey, let me down!" he demanded, but as the hooded figure approached, hairs rose on the back of his neck when the cold red eyes stared at him.

"Oh, you'd love that, wouldn't you, to be free to bully me again?"

"Mathew, I have no intention of bullying you."

"And I have no intention of letting you down. You see, I need you, Terry."

"What? Why do you need me?"

Mathew slapped his face gently a couple of times. "You'll find out."

***

Simon Eliote and Mathew's grandfather Mr James sped along the back roads, breaking every speed limit, the blue lights and sirens warning drivers and pedestrians to get out of the way.

"Why would Mathew take Mike and Terry to the old slaughterhouse?" Eliote asked.

"He's trained to butcher animals," Mr James said, and that was enough.

Eliote skidded around a corner and said, "My God, we'd better hurry. When was he trained?"

"When he left school, his appearance didn't get him many jobs, so I offered him a job at my slaughterhouse; he had been coming there since he was a young boy, anyway. When he accepted, he became a better slaughter-man than me or his dad; he was so skilled with a knife, could skin a cow without hardly cutting into the meat." He waved his hands around, pretending to hold a knife.

Eliote sped down the back lanes and finally emerged on the main road, where he signalled to go left.

"Why did he stop being a slaughter-man?" he asked Mr James.

"Well, after a while, something inside him started to change, it was eating away at him, so he gave up the slaughtering and would just sit up in his room for hours playing music. He'd go out in the Range-Rover after dark, not coming in till the early hours, and we suspected there was a woman but he never brought her home."

"According to his journals, your son committed suicide at Dead Man's Quarry." Mr James nodded and then looked out of the window and Simon could feel pain.

"Yes, he was so distraught when he found out about Mike and Mathew, the pain he felt sent him mad, he blamed God so burnt down the old church and then to spite Mike, he jumped into the quarry. He just couldn't live with the fact that his favourite and eldest son could help to hurt his young brother. It was an unbearable time for us all."

"So Mrs Davies doesn't know?" Eliote asked.

Mr James shook his head. "No." He paused and looked at Simon with sad eyes. "There was no woman, was there?"

Simon shook his head. "I don't think there was, Mr James, unless you accept the stone angel in the old St Mathew's graveyard as a woman."

Mr James sighed. "That old statue," he said and held on tight as Eliote swerved around a corner.

"Sorry about that," Eliote said. "You were saying about the statue."

"Yeah, even when he was a child, Mathew was always fascinated by that Angel. When he would go missing when he was a young boy, we would find him curled up in front of it."

Eliote saw lights in the distance and knew that time was running out. "I know this, Mr James, if we don't get to that slaughterhouse soon, those two lads will end up being buried there."

***

Mike looked up and saw Mathew with his father's knife behind his back talking to his friend Terry, who was looking at Mathew with fear in his eyes.

"Matt, you don't have to do this," he said.

Mathew stopped talking to Terry and turned and smiled at his brother.

"Ah, so you've re-joined us," he said and returned the knife into a plastic knife box that was attached to a belt around his waist. "Good, it's time to get on with the business at hand."

Mike could see his friend was gagged. "What business?" he demanded.

"The business of revenge my dear brother." Mathew walked away from Terry and approached Mike with a stool and sat down in front of him. He pulled back his hood to reveal the scars.

"Put it back on," Mike said, "you know it makes me sick." Mathew didn't do anything but stare at his brother

"But brother, this is what you helped to do to me." He pointed at his face. "I have to look at this face every morning when I get up and again when I go to bed," he said with venom, "so look at it." Mike looked away but Mathew grabbed his face and pulled it back. "LOOK AT IT," he screamed. Mike started to cry.

"You think I have no compassion, Matt, but I do, I felt your pain and suffering, I was at the hospital every night, hoping you would be all right, told the team I didn't want anything to do with them and I too left that school and joined another."

Matt looked coldly at him. "You want me to feel sorry for you? Ha, pathetic, you have freedom, I don't, you can travel the world, all I have is a prison cell."

Mike looked away once more. "What are you going to do with us?"

Matt stood up. "I am going to have fun. First I will sort you out and then I will sort out the animal that is tied to the bar up there."

"What? He isn't an animal, he is a human being."

Matt hit him again and when he lifted his head, Matt's eyes seemed to be red as he looked at him.

"He stopped being a human when he helped you all beat me up; I have no compassion for him, you or the others I have killed." He laughed, "Mike you should have seen their faces when I attacked," he gloated, "it was a picture."

"You're not my brother; you are a mad, twisted, evil, creature."

"You made me that way, brother," Mathew said with venom, and with the same furious rage he had shown to all his victims, he grabbed a rusty axe and using its blunt edge smashed it down onto both of Mike's lower legs. The sound of the impact was like a thousand eggs being stood on. The pain was unbearable to Mike and he screamed in agony.

"I hope one day you can forgive me, Matt."

Matt spat at him. "NEVER!"

"I am so sorry, Matt, I love you, always have and I always will." The pain was unbearable; he felt like he was going to die, but Matt slapped him.

"I haven't finished with you yet, brother, you ain't going to die, you are going to be a prisoner in that house, just like I was." He stood up and took out the sharp butcher's knife and approached Terry.

Mike screamed, "Don't do it, Matt," but he was too late. Matt plunged the knife into Terry's stomach and slowly started to cut it open, his intestines fell to the floor and the smell was unbearable.

"All I will say is it will be over quickly, my friend," Mathew said as he opened the cavity and cut out the heart. He then turned and walked with the still beating heart to Mike and sat back down on the stool.

Terry slumped on the bar, but Mathew was more interested in watching the muscles of the heart in his hand stop beating and then he looked at the scared soul that was his brother and remembered this was how he had felt when they had ruined his life.

"I leave you, Mike Davies, like you left me, with a broken heart," he said; there was no remorse in the voice, he was calm.

"What now?" Mike asked.

Mathew stood up. "The rats can finish Terry off," he said. "As for you, who knows," He placed the heart in front of Mike and walked to the sliding door and opened it, switching off the lights. The yard was dark once again, but it was not silent, Mike heard the clanging of chains and then the sliding door closed and then several seconds later he heard the banging shut of a gate and then he heard the scratching and squeaking noises of the rats as they got closer and closer.

He screamed out, "HELP!"

***

THE DEATHLY ANGEL

By
Kevin Bailey

CHAPTER TWENTY-NINE

Eliote was met by several squad cars and they headed for the abandoned slaughterhouse. After Mr James got out and opened the main gate, they drove into the yard and Eliote was about to order his officers to encircle the building when he heard a ghastly bloodcurdling scream.

Eliote and Mr James ran to the sliding door and after struggling, they managed to open it. Mr James turned on the light and they entered.

The image they saw made even Simon feel sick. Hundreds of rats were feeding off the remains of Terry Good; they were in his stomach area, his eyes were being eaten, and there was even a rat in his mouth, which had fallen open after the gag had been removed and the rat was feasting on his tongue.

But what made it even creepier was that a bulb had been rearranged to display the image of Terry and in particular his shadow, which had the form of an angel. In the middle of the shadow-angel was Mike, who was watching the encounter, sobbing uncontrollably.

"Mike," Mr James shouted, and Simon slammed a metal bar against some machinery, scattering the rats. This allowed them to approach Mike.

After lowering down the corpse of Terry Good, Eliote took off his long coat and placed it over the remains. Then he asked Mike, "Where's your brother?"

"The thing that was my brother left about five minutes ago," Mike said, looking forlornly at the coat covering the remains of his friend. "I didn't hear a car, so he must have gone up the old track, which is behind the back of the yard." Eliote ordered some officers to take a look.

Two paramedics entered the building and after Eliote and Mr James unfastened his chains, they injected Mike with some anaesthetic for the pain and took him and his grandfather to the ambulance.

Eliote watched them go and then saw Penny, Strong's assistant, approach the macabre scene with a large plastic box, which looked almost like a cool box. She walked up to the coat-covered body.

"I'm guessing this is the remains of Terry Good," she said enthusiastically.

Eliote nodded. "What's left of him, Penny and over there on that stool is the deceased's heart."

She walked over and placed the quarter-eaten heart into an evidence bag.

"Okay, Penny, I'll leave you to it," Eliote said, and walked out of the building as a white minibus entered the yard and several forensics officers got out and headed for Penny.

Eliote took refuge in his car, watching the hive of activity as Strong's team scoured the yard for clues to a killer he knew he must catch. As he debated his next course of action, a male voice echoed through his car's speakers.

"Guv, we're travelling towards Shrewsbury on the A49, and we have a yellow Range Rover in front travelling well over the speed limit. The registration and description matches the one you gave out before."

Eliote smiled and said, "Good, pull him up and get him back here."

"Right guv."

***

Just south of Shrewsbury on the A49, one of the main trunk roads through Shropshire, the officer sitting in the passenger seat of the unmarked Vauxhall Vectra looked over at the driver and gave him his instructions.

"You heard the guv, let's get him."

"Right," He changed down, accelerated and came right up behind the yellow Range Rover, turning on the lights and sirens.

In the vehicle Mathew looked in the mirror and smiled. He dropped it down a gear and sped up to one hundred and forty miles an hour.

"Unmark Zero three to Sierra Alpha," the control operator answered.

"Go ahead zero three."

"Vehicle travelling down A49 at one hundred and forty miles an hour, approximately 5 minutes from Chelmesbury at present speed, I require assistance," as he let go of the button, Eliote's voice came over the speaker.

"Unmark zero three from 112, I'm on my way."

Eliote was driving quicker than he had ever done; the road seemed to rush past him, while his thoughts were on the actions still to come.

He grabbed his radio. "All units move in for the kill."

Eliote looked in his mirror and five squad cars were following, in the distance he could see blue flashing lights, so knew that at any moment he would come face to face with the Range Rover, he turned on his sirens and blue lights, then using the other squad cars; he blocked the road and waited.

A couple of minutes later, when he saw the Range Rover approach, he shouted over to a constable and gave the order for the spike strip to be deployed.

The Range Rover swerved, its tires bursting on the spikes, and Mathew struggled to keep control. It swerved more acutely, went down an embankment and smashed into a tree.

Eliote and some of the other officers ran down the embankment and headed for the damaged vehicle. He opened the driver's door and pulled Mathew out, just as the vehicle exploded.

Minutes later, Mathew was arrested, placed in the back of a squad car and driven away.

***

At the same time Mr Depson walked proudly up the stairs towards his office, thinking about the next day's vital lessons. World War Two was the exam material for the year 11 exams, so he needed to make sure all the pupils would know everything.

He opened the door with his key, placed his coat and briefcase on his desk and then headed for his classroom. The door was open, but he knew that the police had been examining the classrooms, leaving some tidy but others, including his, less so. He cursed as his first lesson was only an hour away. He approached his desk and took out the key

He opened the drawer and everything flared white for a second before sinking into an impenetrable, permanent blackness. The entire school shook as a large explosion engulfed the classrooms.

***

As Miranda Day neared the academy, she saw huge flames in the distance; behind her she heard a siren and pulled over to let two fire engines hurtle past. She turned on her flashing lights and followed.

When she turned into the school, she saw the two fire engines on the grass in front of the main classroom area. The fire-fighters were rushing around the appliances getting the equipment to put out the huge fire, and a squad car was putting up tape around the entrance to the school. Day showed her warrant card to the officers and was told that a member of the public had rung the emergency services. She thanked them, then took out her mobile and rang Simon.

"Yes, Sergeant?" he answered.

"Guv, I'm at the Academy. Part of it is on fire."

"Okay, stay there and keep me informed of any discoveries," he told her but she suddenly screamed.

"What's up, Sergeant?" Eliote demanded.

"Oh my God," she said and explained that someone had come crashing out of an upstairs window. Fire-fighters ran to the body and doused the flames, but it was too late. Miranda walked over to the body only to discover that Depson was dead. She hoped this would be the last victim of the Deathly Angel.

CHELMESBURY POLICE STATION

When William Frashier walked calmly into the observation/briefing room, everyone ignored him, all that was except for a rather angry DCI

"A word in my office, please, Inspector," Eliote said curtly. Once the door was closed behind them, Eliote laid into him.

"Where the fucking hell have you been?" he hissed. "I know the suicide shook you up, but get over it. I had a large investigation going on and when I need my number two, he is nowhere to be found."

"Permission to speak openly, sir," Frashier said through gritted teeth. Eliote knew what was coming but nodded anyway. "I do not like you Sir, I don't like your methods and I want to leave this station."

"Okay, if you want to go then go." He pointed at the door. "I can't stop you, but remember this, Inspector: you will always find others like me and then what are you going to do, run away like a coward again?"

Frashier looked coldly at Simon. The word "coward" had clearly gotten to him, but Simon just ignored him and continued with his roasting. "I see great things for you. You use your initiative and I like that in an officer; like the photo, even though it was wrong I was impressed."

"Whatever," Frashier said.

"Inspector, go home and have a long think about your future and then come back and see me, when you decide what you want to do."

Frashier turned and walked out of the door, slamming it behind him as he left.

Eliote shook his head, thinking that one day Frashier would make a great Chief Inspector, all he had to do was baton down the hatches and work hard, just like he had done.

Just then there was a knock at the door and Charlotte walked in.

"Ah, just the person," he said as she sat down in front of him and smiled. "It's time to interview Mathew, want to sit in on it?" She nodded and they walked out of his office to the interview room, where they were met by Pickington.

"How's the wife?" Eliote asked warmly. Pickington sighed.

"She's okay, guv; a little pissed off that I'm working so many late nights, but we will get there."

"Right, so let's go and clip the wings of this Deathly Angel," Eliote said.

Pickington nodded and the three of them entered the interview room.

INTERVIEW OF MATHEW DAVIES

As they entered, Mathew looked at them with contempt, but Charlotte felt that he was at peace, as if a huge weight had been lifted off his shoulders. He had achieved his goal and now he didn't care what happened to him.

Pickington placed a CD in the machine and pressed record and then spoke clearly into the microphone.

"Interview of Mathew Davies, officers present Detective Constable Phillip Pickington and Detective Chief Inspector Simon Eliote, sitting in on the interview is Miss Charlotte Steel."

The solicitor in attendance said, "Can I ask why Miss Steel is present at this interview?"

"She is part of my team," Eliote told him. The solicitor gave Steel a stern look and then deliberated.

"Detective Chief Inspector, my client has decided to plead guilty to all of the crimes especially with all the hard evidence you have shown to me and him."

"Very well," Eliote said, "but I'd still like to ask your client a couple of questions."

"Of course, he is willing to answer all your questions."

"Mathew, why did you kill the five, but not your brother?"

Mathew pointed to his head and the large scar that was visible. "This is the reason, Chief Inspector." He took off his hood and Eliote, Pickington and Charlotte could see the horrible scars on Mathew's face. "They did this to me, they got on with their lives, met girls, settled down, had children, whilst I sat at home scared of going out. Then I made a pact with myself: I would punish these people… and so I made my plans."

"So you wanted revenge even on your own brother?" Pickington asked.

"My brother I hated most of all. He just stood there and helped them beat me up. I looked up to him but he wouldn't help; he was scared they would turn on him. He was so proud of that bloody team."

"So what were you going to do with your brother?" Eliote asked.

"I've done to him what I wanted to do; you see, I had no intention of killing him, but I've made him suffer. He must now rely on Mum the way I did, with no friends, nothing. My revenge is complete."

"And Mr Depson allowed the bullying?" Mathew nodded. "That's why you killed him too?"

"He was the instigator of these deaths, Chief Inspector." He smiled as he looked at the clock on the wall. "I'd say he should be quite crisp by now, he would have felt the pain."

"He felt the pain all right," Charlotte said. "I know this, but he had no remorse for what they did to you; to him, you were just an obstacle."

Mathew sniggered. "Well, I'm glad he felt the pain."

"Didn't you hear what she said, Mathew?" Eliote said. "He had no remorse."

"And I have none for him, he was a monster and I hope he rots in hell."

There was now only one lose end still to tidy up, Eliote looked over at Pickington and nodded, "We've found Sam's body," he said, the sergeant pulled out a picture from the file in front of him and showed it to Mathew, both men noted that he didn't even batter an eyelid at the picture but smiled evilly.

"I see he's in a right mess."

"So why did you kill him?" Eliote asked, Mathew replied calmly.

"You mean the poof?" Eliote didn't like the word 'poof,' but nodded. "Before the incident, I had always liked his wife Michelle, but Sam got there first, then when I'm doing my investigations into the football team, I see him down an alley with Wayne Warwick in what can only be described as a rather compromising position. I took a couple of pictures and sent them to him, so he was mine to do with what I wanted, the mighty Sam Dalton, ladies' man, hard case, but really a poof."

"And you followed them to the factory?" Pickington asked.

"I had followed Wayne on several nights, saw him meeting someone else, and I knew that Sam would go spare if I told him, so I did." He gave a quick smile. "I hoped that Sam would beat the crap out of him, but he did more, much more."

"He used your alter ego and killed him," Eliote added.

Mathew nodded. "He also killed his lover. I helped him dispose of the body, and someday you may find it, but not today." He sat back on the chair almost proud of what he had achieved. "That's one secret I will take to my grave."

"Well, I think we have enough to put him in front of a judge," Eliote told Pickington, who nodded and pressed a buzzer on the wall.

After they had taken Mathew away, Charlotte asked, "What do you reckon will happen to him, Chief Inspector?"

"Oh, he'll probably end up in some secure hospital for the rest of his life," Eliote said. Pickington nodded.

"Let's hope he never gets out." Eliote agreed and the three of them left the interview room and headed back to CID.

THE DEATHLY ANGEL

By
Kevin Bailey

CHAPTER THIRTY

Eliote addressed his entire team, including Charlotte, in the briefing room.

"I would like to say how proud I am to be working with a fine bunch of officers and human beings; this is a great station and hopefully I see myself being here for many years to come." There was a mighty cheer and Eliote beckoned them to stop with his hands. "I am sure that if he was here, Detective Inspector Frashier would…" a voice appeared from behind him, which made Simon and all the team turn and smile.

William Frashier looked around the circular room and after smiling at the team, he finished the conversation that Eliote had started

"I am also proud, well done," he paused "and I would also like to apologize to Miss Charlotte Steel, who I hope will work with us again," she smiled and William started to clap to her, then the rest of the team including Eliote started as well.

The clapping seemed to go on for a while until Eliote looked at the team and stopped them.

"Right after all your reports have been filled out and they're all on my desk," he looked over at Constable Pickington, "that includes yours too Pickington!" the officer went red in the face and the room filled with laughter, Eliote raised his hand and spoke over the laughter, "once this is done, you can all go home,"

As he listened to the cheers, Eliote felt at home for the first time in years. But when he looked at Charlotte she was staring coldly at him, sending a chill down his spine.

He ignored this feeling for a while and continued, "As long as nothing bad happens tonight, I want you all in bright and early in the morning," he became more serious, "there are more 'Deathly Angels' out there for us to catch, so goodnight people," the team then dispersed.

Charlotte was still staring at Eliote and as he approached, she turned and ran out of the room. He was taken aback by this and tried to chase after her, but after a few minutes he had lost her.

He asked Day to go and find her and see if she was OK. Meanwhile, he grabbed his coat and headed for his car. Strong caught him before he left.

"That was a noble thing you did to Frashier, Simon. He can be a dick sometimes but he's a good copper."

Eliote nodded. "He is, Doctor, I hope he will fulfil his dream."

"With you as his superior, I'm sure he will," Strong said and held out his hand. Simon took it and Strong smiled warmly, "A few of us are having a get-together down at the Horse and Hare, fancy coming?"

Eliote looked at his car. "I may pop in for a quick half later," he lied but Strong just smiled.

"If you're passing, please pop in."

Eliote nodded and Strong walked away, leaving him to throw his belongings into the boot of his car, fire up the motor and head home.

But as he was driving past the entrance to the Mardon estate, he stopped and looked up at the historic manor house. Thoughts came into his head.

If his grandfather had not given the title to his mother's cousin, Simon would now be sitting in that glorious manor, with some aristocratic wife, several children and a loving mother.

But would he be happy? He wondered, looking at the long lawns, the picturesque scenery and the quaint lakes. No, he wouldn't be happy, he decided. Being a policeman made him happy; it was all he had now.

He placed the car into gear and drove off up the long track to Howden Hall. When he arrived at the top, he found removal trucks were waiting to clear out Lady Mardon's belongings.

Pulling up alongside his aunt, he wound down the window and she approached him.

"Come to check whether we have gone?" she said bitterly. "Well, we haven't yet, but the place should be ready for you in a few days."

Eliote turned off the engine, got out and looked down at the lakes.

"I was sitting at the bottom of the drive, wondering whether this is the life for me, in this beautiful house, acting as lord of the manor."

"Well, nephew, you'll get your chance," his aunt said sarcastically and looked over at the removal men, beckoning them to begin.

"Wait," he said. "Auntie, I would never be happy as lord of the manor and quite frankly it would drive me to despair. I know what makes me happy." He looked at the Saab and then back at his aunt. "So the title and house belongs to you and your heirs. I will see a solicitor and draw up the right paperwork. This is your home and your children's, just as the Priory is now mine."

Apparently stunned into silence, she simply kissed him on the cheek and smiled at him.

"Thank you, Simon. You are welcome here anytime."

Eliote hugged her and headed back to the Saab. "Cheers," he said. "I may come round for Christmas."

She laughed and he drove off, back to the Priory.

A mile from home a green Mini came up behind and started to flash its lights. Simon pulled into a lay-by and the car followed and stopped behind him. Charlotte got out, still looking coldly at him.

"What's up? You ran out of the observation room so quickly, I was worried for you." Charlotte continued to stare at him. "I cannot say, Chief Inspector."

Eliote laughed. "Is it about my future?"

She shook her head and said bluntly, "When are you going to tell them about your gifts?" Eliote froze.

"How did you know I have gifts? It's something I try to hide."

"I sensed it earlier when we were in Mathew's house, but didn't know if you were aware of it or not."

Eliote got out of his car and approached her. "Yes, I'm aware of the gift," he said. "I sense pain and suffering, discovered it when I visited Auschwitz as a child. I passed out just inside the gate and because of it; I tend to not stay long at crime scenes."

She smiled. "Just be careful, Chief Inspector, especially with the other gift."

"Why, just because I can clear my mind and take on the persona of others, I have to be careful?"

She nodded. "If it is not done properly, you may never come back."

"I am always careful; Miss Steel," Eliote said bluntly, "and I don't fear the future." He turned and walked back to his car.

"You should," she shouted after him. He looked back at her. "I must warn you, Chief Inspector, don't trust those around you because one will betray you and that betrayal will lead to your death."

She jumped back into the Mini and drove away.

As he was taking in what she had just told him, a voice echoed over his speakers.

"There's been an incident in Grove Way. Doctor Strong is en-route."

Eliote sighed. "No peace for the wicked," he said out loud and then answered the call. "No problems, Sierra-Oscar, I'm on my way, 112 out."

He started his car and drove off.

THE END

BUT SIMON ELIOTE WILL RETURN

Printed in Great Britain
by Amazon